Blackbirds

A London Blitz novel

Melvyn Fickling

TBC
The Book Conspiracy

© Melvyn Fickling 2018

Melvyn Fickling has asserted his rights under the Copyright, Design and Patents Act, 1988, to be identified as the author of this work. First published digitally by The Book Conspiracy Limited in 2018. All rights reserved. No part of this publication may be reproduced, stored in a retrieval system, or transmitted in any form or by any means, electronic, mechanical, photocopying, recording, or otherwise, without the prior permission of both the copyright owner and the above publisher of this book.

Paperback ISBN: 978-1-9997484-5-6
E-book ASIN: B07KX715SL

Cover art © Peter Larry
Author photograph © Janice Alamanou
www.melvynfickling.com

Table of Contents

Part 1 – **Aurora**

Chapter 1	**8**
Chapter 2	**16**
Chapter 3	**24**
Chapter 4	**36**
Chapter 5	**47**
Chapter 6	**64**
Chapter 7	**74**

Part Two – **Meridiem**

Chapter 8	**84**
Chapter 9	**94**
Chapter 10	**103**
Chapter 11	**112**
Chapter 12	**129**
Chapter 13	**138**
Chapter 14	**151**

Part Three – **Vesperum**

Chapter 15	**160**
Chapter 16	**172**
Chapter 17	**181**
Chapter 18	**191**

Part Four – **Noctis**

Chapter 19	**202**
Chapter 20	**211**
Chapter 21	**215**
Chapter 22	**222**
Chapter 23	**228**

Glossary of Terms   231

Author's Notes   235

Sources   237

Dedicated to Jan Feeney with love

Night shall be thrice night over you,
And heaven an iron cope.
Do you have joy without a cause,
Yea, faith without a hope?

The Ballad of The White Horse
G.K. Chesterton (1911)

PART 1

AURORA

Chapter 1

Sunday, 6 October 1940

A teasing breeze cut through the wrought iron gates, agitating the early autumn leaf fall around Bryan Hale's shoes. The funeral attendees drifted away in groups and he maintained a respectful distance while they departed. Molly remained alone at the graveside. As Bryan approached, she looked up with red-rimmed eyes.

'Thank you for coming. It's a long trip for you.'

Bryan put his arm around Molly's shoulders, 'Andrew was my best friend,' he said, 'he was the best of men.'

Molly's chin dropped and she crumpled against his chest, sobbing gently.

Bryan clenched his jaw against his own emotion, holding her as much for his own comfort as her need for support. She took a deep breath and the sobbing subsided.

'Would you like to go for a walk, maybe get some tea?' Bryan asked.

Molly straightened herself, wiping the tears from her cheeks. 'I have to go and feed my baby,' she smiled through her tears, 'I have responsibilities, you know.'

'Of course,' Bryan took her hand and kissed it. 'I'll always be there.'

Molly squeezed his arm and turned for the gate.

She climbed into a car and Andrew's father closed the passenger door after her. He glanced over at Bryan, loss and empathy in his gaze. Bryan nodded once and looked away. The car coughed into life and moved down the lane. Bryan bowed his head and surrendered to his own quiet tears.

Someone nearby cleared their throat, awkward and self-conscious. Bryan raised his head, blinking the moisture from his eyes to focus on a man dressed in rough, mud-streaked clothes. A flat cap dangled from one hand, the other clasped a spade. The man glanced at the soil heaped on boards next to the oblong hole in the turf and raised an eyebrow.

'Yes, sorry,' Bryan muttered. He squared his shoulders to the grave and drew himself a touch straighter, but he did not salute. Andrew wasn't in the RAF anymore. Swivelling on his heel Bryan strode back through the arch.

The man jammed the cap onto his head and plunged his spade into the heavy, clodded earth. The rhythmic, boxy echo of soil striking oak receded as Bryan walked away from the cemetery gates along the road towards The Railway Hotel.

People slowed their pace as they passed him on the pavement, offering wan smiles of condolence. None of them knew who he was, but in the small town of Wells-On-Sea they had all known about Andrew, and Bryan's RAF uniform broadcast the obvious connection on this funeral day. Face after face looked into his eyes, searching for something to take away, something to talk about, something that might place them closer to events they had no hope of understanding.

Bryan's breathing constricted around the bubbling anger in his throat as he fought the urge to shout in their faces about the fear, the bullets and the fire, how much he hated and loved it at the same time, how better men, indeed the better man now inside that wooden box, had gone to an early grave to save them their lazy, gossiping hours of freedom. He struggled to bite his tongue and they mistook his anger for grief, gifting him the mantle of disguise he needed to make it back to the hotel porch.

The *clunk* of the closing door brought the manageress into the hall.

'Will you be dining with us tonight, Mr Hale?'

'No.' The word rang harsh, he cleared his throat and continued in a softer tone, 'I'm leaving today. I won't be staying another night.'

'Oh,' the woman dithered, thrown by the change. 'Would you like me to prepare your bill?'

Bryan started up the stairs, 'Yes, please.'

He fished the key from his pocket and pushed his way into the room. Scooping his shaving gear into a toilet bag, he glanced into the mirror and paused. A haggard edge pulled at his features, his tear reddened eyes added an aged weariness beyond his twenty-eight years. Behind it, he discerned a faint shadow of fear, the unspoken, uncertain count of days separating him from his own hole in the ground.

Bryan slung his duffel bag over his shoulder and descended to the hall. The manageress stood waiting, twiddling with a hand-written bill. Bryan took the bill and scanned the scrawled writing. The total included the room charge for the second night. He glanced up, but the woman had busied herself straightening a picture on the wall. Bryan folded a ten-shilling note into the bill and handed it back.

'Keep the change.'

Bryan pushed through the door, back into the crisp, early autumn day. The brisk breeze was bedecked with the salt and seaweed smells of a North

Sea fishing harbour. He wrinkled his nose against the onslaught, set his back to the water and walked down the hill towards the railway station.

Steam billowed above the station's slate roof. An engine had just arrived and would be ready to leave the terminus within the hour. He'd make it back to London in time to catch a bus to Kenley.

***

The train clonked and lolled as it slowed into its approach to Liverpool Street station. The unlit urban landscape echoed the darkness in the carriage, the city's life made anonymous under its thick curtain of blackout, its packed acres of buildings skulking behind a delusion of safety, hoping that a simple absence of light might deflect the German night raiders.

The carriage lurched over points, rousing Bryan from a fitful snooze. Squinting through the carriage window he could make out the looming silhouettes of tenements lining the track, here and there a leaking glimmer of light outlined an ill-fitting curtain. His eyes were drawn up to the black dome of the night sky and a spasm of anxiety crawled over his skin.

A conductor sidled through the carriage, 'No alerts yet tonight, ladies and gentlemen. Have a safe onward journey.' He passed to the next carriage and his litany drifted back, 'No alerts in London yet tonight...'

The train jolted to a halt and Bryan pulled his duffel bag from the overhead rack. He champed against the dryness in his mouth; he needed a drink. Shuffling off the train he skirted around the throng of travellers and strode towards the station entrance. Once outside he paused to make out his surroundings in the dark. Cars and buses trundled past and people tripped and stumbled on their way. Across the road a door opened, a brief slant of light escaped with the hubbub of voices and the clink of a bottle against glass. Moving with exaggerated care across the road, Bryan headed for the now-closed pub door. On the far pavement, he bumped into an older man who cursed under his breath as he disappeared into the gloom. Bryan scrabbled for the handle and pushed through the heavy curtain inside the door.

The immediate warmth in the smoke-filled room relieved the press of hovering menace suspended in the blank, black skies outside. Bryan lit a cigarette. Drawing deeply on the smoke, he moved to the bar.

'Pint of bitter, please.'

As he waited for his drink he glanced about. A few uniforms dotted the room, mostly soldiers. Other men wore civilian clothes, standing at the bar in drinking groups or sitting apart, at tables with their wives.

Bryan's eyes came to rest on a table directly across the room. Four people sat there. Two sailors in uniform accompanied two young women. One woman chatted with some animation to the sailor at her shoulder who leant forward, watching her lips as she talked and laughed. The other woman stared straight back at Bryan.

'One pint of bitter, sir.'

The barman set the dimpled mug down and Bryan turned to pay him. He waited for the barman to retrieve his change from the till, thanked him again and took a long draft of the ale. He could still feel the woman's eyes penetrating his back. Taking another long draw on his cigarette he surveyed the room again, avoiding a direct glance at the group's table. From the corner of his eye he caught the smile spreading across the woman's face as she continued to stare at him. He abandoned his ruse of nonchalance and returned her gaze.

The woman sat with her legs crossed. Her skirt and blouse looked smart, but not flashy, and her shoes had moderate heels. Her long dark hair was pinned high and a slight thrill fluttered in Bryan's stomach as he imagined it falling free. Her eyes shone deep chestnut, their shape emphasised with black liner. Her nose was straight and thin, and her lips celebrated in vibrant red lipstick. These features were infused with beguiling magic by the widening smile that beamed from her face.

Bryan glanced at the woman's female companion, a blonde with a slightly blocky figure. She continued to talk and gesture, her sailor raptly entangled in her words. The other matelot glanced from one woman to the other, laughing half-heartedly at the blonde girl's stories, sipping nervously at his beer.

Bryan's attention returned to the dark-haired woman. Her gaze remained unbowed for long moments, then she dropped her eyelids and came to a resolve. Standing, she walked across the bar towards Bryan, leaving her handbag and coat draped on her chair. The blonde stopped her flow of words and frowned. The nervous matelot's face dropped in confusion.

Bryan maintained eye contact as the woman stopped before him. She chewed her lower lip for a moment and squinted into his face.

'You have no idea who I am, do you?' she said.

'I'm afraid you have me at a disadvantage,' Bryan answered.

'Jenny Freeman,' she raised her chin to look him square in the face. 'I was in your year at school, Bryan.'

'Good Lord, yes,' Bryan's shoulders relaxed, 'the name does ring a bell.'

'I was quite skinny and very shy,' she smiled, 'and you were rather tall and quite loud. Anyway, now you're here, I have a use for you.'

'A use?'

'I need saving from the Navy,' she grimaced, inclining her head towards the sailors. 'My flatmate Alice got herself a date. He had a friend. I got talked into it, but...'

'Oh, I see, yes.' Bryan gulped down the rest of his beer and slung his duffel bag across his shoulder. 'I'll follow your lead.'

Bryan walked with Jenny back to the table, picked up her coat and held it for her to put on.

'I have to be away, everybody,' she held up a hand. 'This is Bryan, an old friend. He's offered to walk me to the tube station.'

'Gentleman,' Bryan nodded to each sailor in turn. 'Miss,' he raised his cap to Alice. Placing his hand on the small of Jenny's back, he guided her between the tables to the door.

Once outside they lurched to a halt, their sight momentarily disabled by the dazzle of the bright lights they'd just left.

Jenny tutted, 'I will never get used to groping about in the dark.' She gripped Bryan's arm. 'Can you see anything yet?'

People-sized shapes loomed around them as their eyes adjusted.

'It's starting to come together.' Bryan placed his hand over hers, 'Where are we heading?'

'Northern Line. Bank station is probably the easiest. This way.'

They set off along the pavement.

'Thank you for getting me out of that, it really wasn't any fun at all.'

'Your friend… Alice? Will she be alright?'

'I wouldn't worry about Alice.' She smiled up at Bryan, 'So, you're wearing RAF uniform. Which branch are you in?'

'Fighter Command,' Bryan said. 'Bluebird Squadron. Spitfires.'

'You're a fighter pilot?'

'Yes.'

'Crikey, what's it like?'

'Very fast and not a little dangerous.'

Jenny laughed, 'Sounds a bit like Alice.'

Bryan joined her laughter, 'And what do you do?'

'Ministry work. Archiving and records mostly. Can't say too much about it. They made me sign a bit of paper.'

They came to a crossroads and Jenny squinted into the darkness.

'Straight across here.' They hurried across the road and stepped up onto the curb. 'So, what brings you to London with your duffel bag?'

'I'm on the way back to my squadron at Kenley.'

'Have you been on leave?' Jenny asked. 'Visiting your girlfriend?'

'I was attending a funeral,' Bryan said, 'a friend from the squadron.'

Jenny stopped and looked into his face, 'I'm sorry, Bryan. I didn't mean to be so clumsy.'

'Think nothing of it,' Bryan said. 'And I don't have one.'

'Excuse me?'

'A girlfriend,' Bryan started walking again, 'I don't have a girlfriend.'

They continued together for a short distance before Bryan broke the awkward silence, 'Which means I can buy you a drink sometime if you'd like.'

Jenny said nothing for a few steps, her eyes fixed on the ground. Then she nodded, 'I think that might be nice.'

The pavement became more crowded and many of those that thronged about them carried suitcases and rolled blankets. Caught up in this implacable human flow they swept around a corner to the sandbagged Tube station, a dull glow emanated from its depths.

Jenny pulled Bryan to one side. 'Here.' She took a small notebook from her handbag and wrote down a number. She tore off the page and pressed it into his hand. 'This is my home number. I do a fair bit of overtime these days, so you'll have to trust to luck to find me there. Thanks again.'

She stood on tiptoes, planting a kiss on his cheek. As she turned to leave, a low wailing penetrated the middle distance, rising to peak at a flat, mournful moan. The shelterers quickened their rush for the stairs and Bryan gazed upwards as searchlights pricked and probed at the clouds. A policeman stood nearby, ushering the crowd off the pavement. Bryan tapped his shoulder.

'What's the best way to get to Victoria?'

'Down the steps, sir. Look for the Circle Line eastbound.'

Bryan smiled his thanks and started down the steps. Some way ahead he spotted Jenny amongst the crowd streaming through the open barriers, his eyes drawn to the sway in her walk. In a moment she vanished, swallowed into the throng flowing down the tunnel towards the Northern Line. Bryan slowed to read the signs overhead, jostled by the river of people moving around him. He found the eastbound tunnel and squeezed down the steps to the platform. He picked his way through the groups of shelterers, each marking their territory for the night with blankets.

Bryan found a clear spot midway down the platform and lit a cigarette. Minutes later the next train arrived and he stepped onto the near-empty carriage. Already flushed from exertion and his chance meeting with Jenny, the stuffy warmth in the tube carriage pricked sweat onto his eyebrows. He removed his overcoat, folded it carefully and sat down, tucking his duffel bag between his calves. A man opposite studied Bryan's uniform with a mixture of interest and disdain.

'You a pilot?' a slur dulled the man's voice.

Bryan nodded, 'Yes.'

'So why don't you get up there and fight the bastards?'

Murmurs of approval drifted down the carriage from a group of women. An elderly man made no noise, but peered over his glasses at Bryan, waiting for his answer.

Bryan looked around the group and back to his questioner.

'That's what I have been doing. Almost every bloody day.'

The man barked a laugh, 'What good is that if they're coming back every bloody night?'

The tunnel's darkness flashed to the bright lights of the next station, Aldgate. The man's eyes remained steady and hostile. Bryan stood up and stepped from the carriage. Better to wait a few minutes for the next train than to continue in an argument he had no interest in winning.

Prostrate Londoners filled most of the space around him, bedding down on the smooth, hard platform, trading comfort for safety. Bryan kept his back to the carriage while the train drew away. Directly in front of him a small girl in grimy clothes slept with only a thin woollen blanket between her and the warmth-sapping concrete. Three inches from her face a large gob of snot and spittle glistened in the lights.

Swallowing hard, Bryan fixed his attention on the white tiles that covered the curved tunnel wall and waited until a train whined in behind him. He boarded, avoiding eye contact as he sat down. The tube train whisked him away through the tunnel, alternating darkness and harsh illumination. The lights at each station revealed a different human tableau; people hunkered on the indurated platforms, grasping to them the things they treasured the most. Mothers clasped their children; the children clasped their dolls. Above ground, their homes, temporarily abandoned for the sake of subterranean safety, stood at ransom to the random interplay of gravity and high explosives, of switches thrown and buttons pressed thousands of feet above them in the cold, dark sky.

Victoria station rolled around. Bryan bundled off the train and up the stairs. The chill night air dried the sweat on his face. Shivering, he pulled on his overcoat while booming explosions reverberated from the station walls in a demonic rhythm set by a nearby anti-aircraft emplacement. In the distance, the soft crump of bomb-blasts drifted on the air. Bryan hefted his duffel bag and walked out to the lines of buses. A ticket collector strolled past.

'Excuse me,' Bryan caught him by the arm, 'I need to get to Kenley Airfield.'

The man pointed at a double-decker parked in the row.

'That one there,' he smiled at Bryan. 'You're a lucky man. It looks like you've caught the last bus.'

Chapter 2

Monday, 7 October 1940

'Flight Lieutenant Hale,' the man shook Bryan's shoulder. 'It's 6 o'clock, sir. Time to get up.'

Bryan parted his dry lips with a drier tongue, 'I pray that God may one day bless you, Hopkins.' He rolled over and reached for the mug of tea steaming on his bedside table, 'What's the weather like?'

'Good enough to expect a visit I'm afraid, sir.' Hopkins pulled Bryan's uniform from the wardrobe and brushed the lint and stray hairs from the jacket. 'Bluebird are on readiness from 11 o'clock. Your bath's ready.'

Bryan bathed and dressed in silence. In front of the mirror he combed his hair. He noted new lines scoring his forehead and his eye sockets harboured shadows. Maybe he needed more sleep?

Bryan walked to the mess, nodding acknowledgement to saluting airmen along the way. Sitting alone, he quickly despatched a breakfast of fried eggs and toast with another mug of hot, sweet tea. He signed the mess chit and stepped outside, sniffing the air with predatory interest. The milky autumnal sun struggled to get above the treetops, but he could already tell that Hopkins was right. The Germans would be over today.

He took a detour out onto the field past the dispersal pens. It was the longer route to his office, but he felt mildly disconnected, still unsettled by the previous day's events and drawn by his viscera to be close to the aircraft.

Bryan quickened his pace against the morning's chill and headed out towards his own Spitfire. The pungent ghost of aviation fuel laced the air, and on the other side of the field a ground crew fired up a Spitfire for engine tests: the rough cough of the starter battery giving way to the full roar of its Merlin engine. The sound helped Bryan settle back into his own skin.

He arrived at his plane to find his rigger working on the guns, checking and greasing the mechanisms from beneath the wing.

'Morning, Mortice,' Bryan stooped to peer under the wing, 'is she ready?'

'She won't be long,' the rigger smiled. 'Just making sure everything's in order. Y'see someone else took her up yesterday, sir. While you were away at the...' the rigger looked down, a frown crumpling his brow.

'The funeral?' Bryan finished the sentence. 'It all went well, Mortice. Andrew had a wonderful send off.'

'I'm glad, sir,' the rigger's face brightened, 'Mr Francis was a good 'un.'

Mortice went back to his work and Bryan sauntered away, lighting a cigarette. Thoughts of Andrew, sirens and Jenny tumbled around his head. He took a hard pull on his cigarette and fished in his trouser pocket. His fingertips found the slip of paper. He unfolded it and gazed at the number for long moments.

***

Bryan sat at his desk watching the smoke curling up from the cigarette balanced on the ashtray's edge. The door rattled to someone's knock.

'Come in,' Bryan said without raising his head. The door opened to admit Harold Stiles, Bluebird Squadron's adjutant. He carried an armful of paper files. Bryan looked up as the other man sat down.

'Ah, Madge,' he drawled, 'you've brought paperwork. How nice.' He wrinkled his brow, 'I'll be flying in an hour or so. Can't it wait? I'll do it if I come back, I promise.'

Stiles ignored the banter.

'Good morning, Bryan,' he laid the files on the desk, 'I trust all went smoothly.'

'Yes, it did. Until I got back to London.' Bryan grimaced across the desk, 'Some people think we're not working hard enough.'

'Which people?'

'People on a bloody tube train, Harry.' Bryan picked up his cigarette and stubbed it out with some force. 'I believe they're called the general public. They suggested I should be flying about in the bloody dark shooting down the bombers.'

'Well,' the adjutant leant forward, 'that's not possible in Spits; the exhaust flames mess up your night vision. But...' He paused.

'But what, Madge?'

'There's some hush-hush developments concerning a specialised night-fighter force. Onboard RDF, that sort of thing.'

'So?'

'So... they're asking for top-notch pilots to volunteer.'

Bryan's eyes narrowed as he regarded the older man, 'This RDF... it's going onboard what, exactly?'

'Mostly Blenheims...'

'Mostly...'

'They're planning to use Hampdens in the western sectors.' The adjutant chewed his lip as the silence settled like foreboding.

Bryan lit another cigarette.

'I am not,' he stabbed a finger at the other man, 'repeat not, going back to flying those decrepit old crates.' He pushed his chair away from the desk and stalked to the window, 'I have a Spitfire, and that's what I intend on keeping. Your boffins can get their cab drivers from somewhere else.'

The adjutant sighed, 'I just thought I'd mention it.' He flipped open the file of papers, 'We do have some serious paperwork to get through.'

Bryan ambled back to his desk.

'Why? What's the flap?

Stiles cleared his throat, 'I'm afraid they're taking Bluebird out of the front-line.'

'What?' Bryan exploded. 'Why? Where to?'

'They're rotating us to a quieter section. It's intended to give the lads a rest.'

'A rest?' Bryan slumped into his chair. 'The ones that did all the bloody hard work are dead,' Bryan's eyes bulged with outrage, 'they're getting plenty of rest.'

'I'm sorry, but it's come straight down from the top. There's nothing I can do. We move out in two weeks' time.'

Bryan dropped his head into his hands.

'Where to?'

'Scotland.'

***

Jenny stuck out her jaw at the mirror as she applied her lipstick. It was getting low and make-up had already become scarce in the shops. Hopefully all the women in London would run out on the same morning and they'd all be forced to go to work that day *au naturelle*. She smiled at the idea as she combed her fringe into place. She paused at the sound of a key in the flat door and her smiled broadened.

'Good morning, Alice,' she called. 'Will you be joining us at work today?'

Alice's disembodied voice carried down the hallway, 'Yes. But I need a bit of a swill first. Will you wait for me?'

The gush from the bath taps clattered onto the enamelled tub. Jenny walked down the hall and leant on the door frame watching her friend undress.

'And if that porter looks at me funny one more time I shall swing for him.' Alice squirmed in her underwear. 'Unhook me, Jen, there's a love.'

Jenny leant forward to spring the brassiere, 'Will you be seeing your sailor again?'

'No. They sail at lunchtime today.'

'They?' Jenny sat down on the toilet seat as Alice climbed into the steaming bath water, 'You didn't?'

'You and the porter can think what you like, I'm saying nothing.' Alice splashed some water onto her face and lathered the soap. 'Who was that you left with? Some sort of Brylcreem Boy?'

Jenny nodded, 'He's a Spitfire pilot.'

Alice's jaw dropped and she blinked through the soap bubbles. 'Nooooo...' she cooed, 'you lucky cat.'

'I knew him from school. It was pure chance he came into the pub. He'd just come back from leave.'

'And you're seeing him again, aren't you?' Alice's eyes bored across at Jenny.

'You know what I think about wartime relationships. How can anything last if it's built on shifting sands?'

Alice cocked her head, 'You *are* seeing him again.'

Jenny smiled 'I gave him our telephone number.'

'Ha-hargh,' Alice splashed the water with her hands, 'the Ice Queen thaws at last.'

Jenny stood and straightened her skirt.

'I'll admit it does all seem dangerously romantic. Now hurry up or we'll be late for work.'

***

The pilots of Bluebird Squadron emerged in small knots from the readiness hut, laughing and joking as they walked along the perimeter track. A man disengaged from a group here and there as they passed the dispersal pen containing his Spitfire. Ground crews bustled around readying the aircraft, tightening panels and connecting starter batteries.

Bryan emerged last and walked alone across the airfield in a straight line to his fighter. As he arrived, the rigger stepped back from his work.

'Good morning, sir. Anything special on today?'

Bryan shook his head as he vaulted onto the wing.

'Control has got an empty screen so they've decided we should go on a routine patrol.'

The rigger followed Bryan onto the wing and helped strap him into the cockpit.

'Let's hope you get lucky, sir.'

The rigger jumped down and Bryan went through his start-up procedure as engines burst into life around the airfield.

Bryan fired up his own engine, waved away the chocks and taxied out to the grass runway. He swung into the wind and waited for his section to form up, Pilot Officer Simmonds behind his starboard wing, Pilot Officer Agutter behind his port. When all was set, he waved an arm from his open cockpit and pushed the throttle open.

The Spitfires bounced across the grass. The tails lifted first and then the whole craft wobbled its way into flight. Bryan led his section into a circuit while the other three sections formed up and took off. Once the twelve fighters came into squadron formation, Bryan flipped on his radio transmitter.

'Bluebird Leader to Bluebird Squadron, climb to angels twenty-seven, vector zero-nine-five.'

The heading would take them deep into Kent, bisecting the route to London for any raiders crossing the Straits of Dover from the Pas de Calais.

As Bluebird levelled out at twenty-seven thousand feet, the radio crackled to life: 'Beehive Control to Bluebird Squadron. Observer Corps have called in a small raid travelling north-west. The enemy aircraft made landfall between Folkestone and Dymchurch.'

'Bluebird Leader to Beehive,' Bryan squinted into the haze on his starboard side, 'thank you. We'll keep a look out.'

They droned on in the grey sky, eyes scanning for any movement that might betray the whereabouts of the intruders. Small puffs of white smoke to the south-east broke the stalemate.

'Bluebird Leader here,' Bryan called his squadron, 'there's anti-aircraft fire over Ashford. Yellow section only, follow me, we'll take a look. The rest of you maintain course and altitude.'

Bryan banked away from the squadron and pushed his throttle fully open. Simmonds and Agutter followed suit.

Craning his neck to look first ahead of, and then behind his wings, Bryan searched the flat brown fields signs of movement, the flit of a shadow or the glint of a Perspex canopy. The barrage over Ashford ceased and the white smoke thinned and dissipated on the breeze like a throng of departing ghosts. Bryan banked left to come around and behind where he suspected the raiders to be if they were headed for London.

'There!' Bryan shouted his triumph, '11 o'clock below. About a dozen bandits. They look like 109s.' Bryan thumbed his safety catch to 'Fire', 'Follow me down. Tally-ho, Yellow Section, Tally-ho!'

The Spitfires eased into a dive, trading their height advantage for increased speed. Dipping below the altitude of their quarry, they pulled up into the raiders' blind spot, closing fast.

Bryan chose the pair at the back of the enemy formation, opening up on the closest with a long burst at one hundred yards. Something dropped away from the Messerschmitt and its pilot flipped into a steep dive. Bryan's speed threatened to careen him past the second German fighter. In desperation he kicked his Spitfire into a skid and hauled back on the throttle. He passed diagonally under the 109's tail and ended up in formation on the enemy's starboard side. Bryan looked across at the German pilot. His head was averted, searching for his wingman. Bryan dropped his flaps to brake his speed, fell back behind his opponent and loosed off a three second burst that ripped into the upper fuselage from wing root to wing root, throwing a cascade of shimmering Perspex shards into the slipstream. The Messerschmitt rolled over and flew inverted, straight and level for a long moment, then gradually curved into a dive towards the muddy fields below.

Bryan jinked furiously to check for danger on his tail, then pushed his throttle forward and dropped into a wide bank to the south. The German force was fleeing for the coast, harried by his two wingmen.

Mindful they were outnumbered, he flipped to transmit: 'Bluebird Leader to Yellow Section. Break off and reform. Repeat, break off now.'

Bryan continued the bank into a lazy orbit, waiting for his section to reach him. Glancing down, he spotted the burning wreckage of one of his kills. He cast around for the other. Six or seven small wisps of smoke rose in delicate spirals, like campfires scattered through the fields, but there was no sign of the second plane.

Bryan's radio crackled to life, 'Yellow Two approaching you now.'

Seconds later, 'Yellow Three in formation.'

'Alright, Yellow Section,' Bryan said, 'let's find the rest of the squadron and go home for lunch.'

***

Yellow section landed ahead of the others and Bryan led them across to the readiness hut where Fagan, the intelligence officer, waited to take combat reports. Bryan swung himself into the chair in front of Fagan's desk and lit a cigarette.

'Two 109s for me,' Bryan blew a stream of smoke towards Fagan, 'Agutter and Simmonds are claiming one each damaged.'

Fagan peered over his glasses at Bryan, 'Where did the engagement take place?'

'Five or six miles north-west of Ashford. Yellow section caught a squadron of 109s on a heading towards London,' Bryan's face split into a fierce grin, 'it was the perfect bounce.'

Fagan paused in his writing and looked up again, 'Go on.'

'Well,' Bryan tensed forward in his chair, 'we caught them cold from behind. I put a four second burst into the first and a chunk of his underside broke away. I hit the second one with a three second burst, most of that ended up in his cockpit.'

Fagan grunted, 'And what type of bombers were they escorting?'

Bryan shook his head, 'No bombers.'

Simmonds chimed in, 'They had extra fuel tanks,' he said, 'when we waded in, they dropped the tanks and made a run for it.'

Fagan leant back in his chair. 'The Observer Corps report one Messerschmitt crashed, with no parachute, in the area north of Ashford.' He nodded at Bryan, 'Your second attack, I suspect.' He flexed his fingers and frowned. 'They also reported a very scattered bombload hitting the same area. But you didn't see a bomber.' He looked from man to man, 'So, where does that leave us?'

Bryan blinked. 'Messerschmitt 109s with bombs?'

Fagan nodded. 'It would explain why they were heading towards London rather than promenading up and down the coast like they normally do.'

Bryan chewed his lip. 'They came in fast and low. Without the heads-up from the Ashford anti-aircraft batteries we would've missed them.'

'Mmm. It is a bit worrying.' Fagan picked up the telephone and waited for the operator. 'Get me the Sector Commander, will you?

Chapter 3

Tuesday, 8 October 1940

'They can't move us now, Madge,' Bryan hissed. 'The pilots I've got are settled, half of them are decent flyers and they do what I tell them without question.' He gesticulated at the fighter planes dispersed around the perimeter track, 'It's madness to move perfectly serviceable Spitfires to Scotland. There are no more fat bombers waddling along at ten thousand feet begging for the Hurricanes to shoot them down, at least not in daylight. The pheasant shoot is over, damn it.'

The two men walked through the cool morning air, dew from the rough grass beaded their polished shoes.

'Was it ever really a pheasant shoot?' the adjutant tutted, 'that's a bit of a stretch.'

'Say what you like, Harry, things have changed.' Bryan lit a cigarette and sucked hungrily at the smoke. 'Maybe what we saw yesterday was a trial run. But think about it,' Bryan stopped walking and faced the adjutant, 'when they're escorting bombers, the 109s fly slower, and to compensate for that, they fly higher. We knew when the bombers were coming, how many there would be and which direction they were heading. Practically every time we could get a pop at them before the escort fighters closed the gap.'

The adjutant nodded, 'Yes, I follow that.'

'Well,' Bryan continued, 'now they can slap 500lb bombs under one squadron of 109s and escort them with another squadron. They're faster,' Bryan warmed to his theme, 'and they come in at zero feet, too low for RDF. There'll be no warning until they're over the heads of the Observer Corps and it's too late to scramble any interceptors. That's a free-run straight through to London.'

'It's a terrible thing to say, but I'm not sure this number of bombs could be considered significant. Not when you weigh it against what they're doing at night.'

'It doesn't need to be significant.' Bryan flicked his spent cigarette away over his shoulder. 'The Observer Corps will call in the raid, the ARP will set off the sirens and London will head for the shelters.'

'Winston thinks London can take it,' the adjutant mused. 'They've been under the cosh for over a month now and they've behaved magnificently.'

'What choice do they have, Madge?' Bryan lit another cigarette. 'Who do we speak to about keeping Bluebird on the frontline?'

'There is no-one to talk to, Bryan. It's done. We'll all be in Scotland in two weeks.' He placed a hand on Bryan's shoulder, 'For Pete's sake accept the facts. You need the rest as much as anyone.'

Bryan shrugged the hand away. 'From tomorrow Bluebird is on standing patrol by sections,' he looked squarely into the adjutant's eyes, 'on rotation, three fighters patrolling the London corridor at any one time. Exactly like we did over Dunkirk.'

The adjutant shook his head, 'You can't do that without a General Order.'

Bryan's gaze didn't waver. 'We start tomorrow.'

'But... the rules.'

Bryan turned to walk away. 'The Germans have changed the rules, Harry.'

Wednesday, 9 October 1940

The leaden grey of pre-dawn nibbled at the black night sky as Bryan clumped through the door onto the wooden floor of the readiness hut. The assembled pilots dragged themselves to their feet, hushed conversations dying mid-sentence. Bryan waved them down and waited for the scraping of chairs to subside.

'Yesterday, Yellow Section engaged a Staffel of 109s. It turns out some of the bandits were carrying bombs. It's our assumption they were trying to sneak through to London for tip-and-run attacks.'

A murmur rippled around the pilots.

'Sector have been informed of our suspicion and I'm sure they'll be having a conversation with the Air Ministry, who will no doubt put a committee of experts on the case next week.

'In the meantime, we're going to run standing patrols. One section taking off every fifteen minutes. Patrol east-north-east to Rochester, south-west to Tonbridge and back to base. Refuel and re-arm as required and wait for your next turn. The flight times should mean we have two sections in the London corridor at any one time, flying in opposing directions.

'We'll be searching for groups of 109s, most likely in single or two Staffel strength heading for London, probably flying low. Some may be carrying bombs, some may be escorts. It's possible that control will call them as they cross the coast, but from there it will be hit and miss for the Observer Corps to track them. Any questions?'

The room remained silent.

'Right. I don't really have permission to do this, so please log these as training flights. Red section first, then Green, Yellow, then Blue. That's all.'

***

Bryan taxied out to the runway and waited while Simmonds and Agutter formed up behind him. He checked his watch and flipped his radio transmitter on.

'Bluebird Yellow Leader to Beehive Control. Yellow Section requesting permission to take off on training flight, over.'

'Beehive Control to Yellow Leader. This is the third training flight we've logged in less than an hour. What's going on?'

'Practising to be perfect, Beehive. Now, can we bloody well take off or not?' The static crackled in his ears for a moment.

'Beehive Control to Yellow Leader. You are clear to take off.'

'Shiny-arsed bastards,' Bryan muttered to himself as he waved his arm out of his open cockpit and throttled forward. The three Spitfires surged across the grass and lifted into the air.

Wheels clunked into wing bays and Brian switched to transmit, 'Yellow Leader to Yellow Section. Angels ten only, repeat angels ten. Yellow Two, scan port. I'll quarter the starboard. Yellow Three, watch our tails.'

'Roger that Yellow Leader,' Simmonds voice crackled back.

Then Agutter's; 'Yellow Three here. I'm weaving.'

Bryan set course for Rochester and the three Spitfires levelled out at ten thousand feet. Two pilots scanned the ground ahead and to the sides, the third wallowed back and forth in a series of banks, scanning the skies above and behind for danger. The minutes passed.

'Yellow Three to Yellow Leader,' Agutter's voice broke into Bryan's concentration, 'Three aircraft at 2 o'clock, heading south-west. Must be Green Section.'

Bryan craned his neck over his starboard wing, searching for the aircraft. He spotted them, picked out as tiny silhouettes against the backdrop of haze hanging over Maidstone. As he watched the aircraft's black outlines changed. Their wingtips lifted and the trio banked into a starboard dive.

'Yellow Leader here. They've seen something. Follow me, line astern.'

Struggling to keep the silhouettes in sight, Bryan hauled into a wide starboard bank to bring his section into a tail-chase with the other Spitfires, tearing north-west towards London.

'Christ, they're moving. Buster, Yellow Section, buster, buster.'

Throttles pushed through the gate and engines vibrating in protest, Bryan's section slowly gained ground.

'Bluebird Yellow Leader to Bluebird Green Section. We're approaching you from behind.'

Bryan's slightly higher altitude gave him a view over the chasing fighters to their quarry. Still far ahead of them, flashing low against the fields and roads he made out seventeen or eighteen squat, dark shapes. Half-a-dozen of them peeled up and back to meet their pursuers.

'Spread out Yellow Section. Here they come.'

The shapes resolved into yellow-nosed Messerschmitt 109s and the flash of gunfire sparkled on their wings and cowlings. Two hollow bangs clattered Bryan's port wingtip, like a man hitting paint tins with a lump hammer. Then the 109s flashed overhead.

Bryan held straight and level and glanced into his mirror. Simmonds clung in dogged formation behind his starboard wing. Agutter had vanished. Perhaps downed in the fire that had hit Bryan, or perhaps he'd wheeled with Green Section to engage the Germans. Bryan's eyes remained fixed straight ahead and he counted twelve 109s barrelling at full throttle towards London.

'These are the evil bastards with the bombs,' the thought struck him with an implacable certainty.

Below, the fields broke against the ragged shoreline of the conurbation, like a brown sea held at bay by the manmade megalith of urban sprawl. Rooftops streaked beneath as the chase dropped to two hundred feet. The faces of people on pavements upturned in shock at the flashing aircraft and their snarling engines, ripping so low across their sleepy streets.

The Germans fanned out, splitting into pairs. Bryan hung on to the closest and Simmonds stuck with him as they edged into range. A wide road opened out below. One of the 109s dipped and opened fire. Bryan gasped as lorries and cars swerved and crashed under the hail of cannon shells and bullets. Holes flecked across vehicles, dirt and stones kicked into the air. Bryan nudged his nose lower, dipped below the tail of the German fighter and squeezed out a burst of fire. Hits slashed into its tail and the 109 reared up from the impacts. Climbing with it, Bryan sunk another burst squarely into its wing roots. The Messerschmitt rolled into a lazy parabola, trailing white smoke in a languid spiral. The Thames dashed by beneath Bryan as he climbed and banked away from the combat. The German plane rolled at the top of its loop and dived into the river's murky waters, its bomb exploding on impact, sending a cascading fountain of grey spume into the air.

Screwing his head around, Bryan searched for the other intruder.

There!

With Simmonds on its tail, the other 109 jinked into a right bank, heading back across South London. Bryan turned to chase them.

A black shape fell from the 109. Wobbling through its languorous, curving descent, it crashed through the slates of a terraced house. The explosion sucked the roof downwards and blew the façade out across the road.

Bryan hunched his shoulders into the chase. Getting closer, he could see ribbons of gun smoke trailing from Simmonds' wings. The 109 stopped jinking, waggled its wings and lowered its undercarriage. Simmonds broke off his attack and the German dipped into a descent.

Bryan throttled back and looked on as the 109 went into a landing approach towards a large patch of green common land in amongst the network of streets and houses.

'Tut, tut, my friend,' he purred to himself, 'there's no surrender for you. Not today. Not after what you've just done.'

Bryan dropped his flaps and shadowed the Messerschmitt into its approach. As its wheels touched the grass he thumbed and held the firing button. A furious hail of ordnance bracketed the German plane, kicking up gouts of grass and soil around and beneath it, shredding panels and shattering the Perspex cockpit hood. The machine lurched on a punctured tyre and swerved violently, crashing into a tree and tipping its tail into the air like a broken bird. Bryan glanced down as he overflew the scene, noting the white figure eight painted on the enemy's fuselage.

'Yellow Leader to Yellow Two,' he raised his flaps and throttled forward, 'form up. We're going home.'

***

Bryan and his wingman curved in to land at Kenley. As they descended, the three Spitfires of Green Section approached from the south-east, one trailing white vapour from a damaged engine. The station fire tender and ambulance rolled across the grass to the far end of the landing strip in anticipation. Bryan touched down and taxied away to his dispersal pen, checking in his mirror that the damaged fighter landed safely behind him.

Ground crew met him at the blast pen and manhandled the Spitfire around on the concrete pad to face outwards, ready to scramble once ammunition and fuel was replenished. Brian pulled back the hood and the rigger vaulted onto the wing to help unfetter him from his straps and webbing.

'Any joy, sir?'

Bryan nodded, 'There'll be two extra sausages on the tea table back at Abbeville this evening.'

The rigger laughed and jumped down onto the grass, taking the parachute from Bryan as he climbed from the cockpit.

'Someone did throw something at me, though,' Bryan walked out to his port wingtip. Two small holes and a pronounced crease marred the surface of the wing a few inches outside the roundel painted on its top surface.

The rigger squinted at the damage, 'Machine gun bullets.' He ran his hand along the surface, 'Nothing too serious, I'll get them tidied up and patched.'

'I've a horrible feeling that Agutter might have collected rather more holes than I did,' Bryan lit a cigarette. 'Fix her up as quick as you can, Mortice, we'll be flying again soon.'

The rigger hurried away to get his toolbox. Bryan paused and gazed towards the damaged Spitfire at the end of the landing strip. Vapour curved up from its now silent engine and men stood on the wings each side of the cockpit. Bryan flicked away his cigarette and strode towards the machine.

Getting closer, he saw the cockpit hood was still shut. Close behind it on the starboard side something had torn a ragged hole in the upper fuselage.

A medical officer stood waiting next to an empty stretcher.

'What's happened?' Bryan asked without preamble.

The medic glanced at him, 'Looks like a cannon shell hit just behind his head. The canopy runners are bent out of shape. They can't shift it.'

'And the pilot?'

'The right side of his face is shredded, shrapnel from the explosion. Almost certainly concussed and very probably drifting into severe shock.' He shook his head, 'Bloody amazing that he got the thing down.'

An airman arrived at a steady run and handed crowbars up to the men on the wings. Bryan lit another cigarette as he watched the groundcrew jabbing and levering with the tools, 'He didn't really have any other choice, did he?'

The cockpit hood gave way with a crunching rend of metal and the men bent it back on its jammed runners, leaning against it to give the man inside room to move. Supported by helping hands, the pilot raised himself with the infinite care of the violently injured. He pulled his tattered leather helmet off his head and his right ear came with it. Someone pressed a field dressing onto his lacerated cheek before he slumped into the arms of his rescuers who lifted him carefully down to the grass.

Bryan walked towards the readiness hut. Behind him the ambulance sped across the airfield to the gates, bound for a hospital in Croydon, the fire engine bumped back to its station on the perimeter and the heavy tow truck emerged from the maintenance hangar, belching black smoke from its exhausts as it lumbered towards the broken Spitfire. A group of armourers busied themselves hauling belts of ammunition out of the machine's wings like the intestines of a slaughtered animal and Kenley settled back to the sedate rhythm of its warped normality.

Bryan stepped into the hut and strode to Fagan's desk. Fagan leant back in his chair, his hands clasped behind his head, like a maths professor puzzling with a knotty problem.

'Sit down, Hale.' He unclasped his hands and picked up his pen. Tapping the end rhythmically on his notepad, he continued, 'It appears you were right about the German fighter-bombers, and Beehive Control is' – he chewed the inside of his mouth as he sought for the right word – 'relieved that Bluebird happened to have two sections in the air on training flights.'

'Yes,' Bryan leant forward and crushed his cigarette out in Fagan's ashtray, 'bloody lucky, that.'

'Squadrons from Tangmere and Hornchurch are now running standing patrols.' Fagan looked at Bryan over his spectacles, 'So Bluebird can stand down for the moment.' He cleared his throat and pulled a piece of paper across the desk towards him, 'Simmonds has already given me his combat report.' He scanned the paper, 'I understand you downed a 109 yourself and' – this time the pause was more deliberate – 'shared in the destruction of another one?'

Bryan nodded, 'Sounds fair.'

'The observers at Woolwich Docks have confirmed seeing the first one crash into the river. The other one ended up bent around a tree on Dartford Heath, apparently while attempting a forced landing.'

Bryan nodded sagely while he lit a fresh cigarette.

'We've had complaints, Bryan.'

'Complaints?' Bryan blew a stream of smoke across the desk.

'It seems the German was attempting to surrender and you opened fire on him when he was defenceless.'

Bryan remained silent.

'It's been suggested that was unsportsmanlike behaviour.'

'Unsportsmanlike?' Bryan leant back in his chair and looked up to the ceiling, 'Exactly what kind of a game are we involved in here? Perhaps the civilians living in the street where he dropped his bomb could think of a name for the game.' Bryan grimaced in mock concentration, 'Perhaps the young pilot whose just left the station in an ambulance, wearing half his face as a necktie could think of a name for the game.' Bryan straightened, drilling his gaze directly at Fagan, 'Perhaps you can ask Agutter, *if* he ever comes back, to think up a name for the bloody game.'

Fagan squirmed under the weight of Bryan's suppressed fury, 'You can't rewrite the Geneva Convention to suit yourself, Hale. We should be proud of the things we have to do to win this war.'

Bryan stood up and turned to leave, 'I am.'

***

Bryan leant back from his paperwork and gazed absently through the window for long moments. The steadily darkening sky muffled the movements of the silhouetted ground crews, reducing the men to an army of wraiths throwing tarpaulins over engine cowlings and winding hoses onto petrol bowsers. He stood, walked to the window and shut out the scene with the heavy blackout curtains. He sighed and returned to the documents on his blotter. Switching on his desk lamp, he pulled it closer over the forms and letters he had to check and sign. The knock at the door came as a welcome interruption.

'Come in.'

The adjutant entered and closed the door softly behind him, 'Good evening, Bryan.'

'Is it, Madge?' Bryan gestured at the papers, 'All this bloody bumf simply to move a squadron four hundred miles north.'

'I have news on Agutter.' The adjutant sat down, 'The head-on attack shattered his windscreen and damaged his engine. He lost power and couldn't see where he was flying, so he decided the safest thing to do was bail out. The army should deliver him to us tomorrow.'

'And that other poor sod?' Bryan dithered, searching for a name, 'The one that took the cannon shell.'

'Browning,' the adjutant said. 'The boy's name is Browning. He'll survive, but he's badly disfigured.'

Bryan lit a cigarette, 'I'm sure his mother will still love him.'

The adjutant dropped his gaze and removed his cap, 'He had a fiancé, Bryan. They planned to marry this coming weekend. You signed the leave form yourself.'

A silence dangled between the two men, finally broken by the older man.

'Look, I know what you've been through this summer, and I've seen stronger men crack under less pressure. Most of those that don't crack are protecting themselves by pretending it's not really happening, that the whole thing is nothing more than jolly japes in the mess and drinking too much, with a bit of flying thrown in every now and then. It was exactly the same in the RFC during the last war.

'But you, Bryan. I've never seen anyone take it so' – the adjutant searched for a different word and failed – 'seriously.'

Bryan looked into the older man's face and his focus relaxed, 'Thanks for the news about Agutter. It will be good to have him back on Yellow Section.' With that, Bryan returned to his work.

The adjutant sat for a moment in silence, then stood and replaced his cap, 'Speaking as a friend, I think once we get to Scotland you should look for a companion. Let somebody draw out your softer side, while it's still there to be found.'

The adjutant left and Bryan continued to scribble signatures on stock lists and maintenance reports. Getting to the end of the pile, he placed his pen in its holder and the documents in the out tray. Leaning back in his chair, his eyes drifted over to the hazed black Bakelite telephone and its corroding chrome dial glinting in the lamplight.

***

The tube train rattled into Balham station and the packed legion of office workers shuffled and jostled to face the doors. Amongst them, Jenny and Alice stepped from the carriage and picked their way through the early shelterers to the stairs. At the top of the stairwell, most of the crowd veered off to the mainline platforms to continue journeys home on trains that wheezed through the vast suburban hinterland south of London. Jenny and Alice walked out into the cool evening air on Balham High Road and headed south as a train clattered over the bridge above their heads.

When the noise subsided Jenny spoke, 'How do you fancy baked potatoes? I've got some leftover cheese.'

Alice groaned, 'It takes too long. I'm hungry now. I have some fish that needs to be used up.' She brightened, 'We could use your cheese to make a sauce.'

'Wait there.'

The greengrocer was clearing away the display in the front of his shop. Jenny ducked inside, coming out minutes later with a bunch of carrots and a green cabbage.

'Feast!' she announced.

The two women walked carefully through the thickening gloom and crossed the road. The huge bulk of the block of flats they called home loomed in the darkness above them, the serried rows of horizontal windows gleaming in the emerging moonlight reflected from the clouds.

They pushed through the doors and walked across the lobby, Alice fixing the porter with a sidelong glare, and stepped into an open lift. Jenny pressed the button for the sixth floor and both women surveyed themselves dispassionately in the mirrored back wall as the carriage whisked them upwards.

Out onto the carpeted corridor, a short walk to their door and the relief of being home swept over them. They kicked off their shoes and Jenny dropped the vegetables into the sink for washing while Alice pulled the blackouts closed. Jenny turned on the tap and searched the cutlery drawer for the peeler.

The telephone's bell jangled through the flat and Jenny paused in her work until she heard Alice lift the handset.

'Hello?

'No, it's not…

'Yes, she is…

'May I ask who's calling?'

Jenny was already drying her hands as Alice stuck her head into the kitchen, 'It's a gentleman for you,' she beamed a broad, conspiratorial smile. 'He says his name is Bryan.'

Jenny padded through to the lounge in her stockinged feet and picked up the handset.

'Hello, Bryan.'

'Hello, Jenny. I hope I'm not disturbing your dinner.'

'Not at all, you caught me peeling carrots.'

Alice sat on the couch, grinning like a witch doctor.

Jenny turned her back on her friend, 'It's nice to hear from you.'

'You said it might be fun to meet up again,' Bryan said. 'How about Sunday? I could get there in the afternoon. You don't work Sundays, do you?'

'No, I don't, and yes, that would be nice.'

'Where shall we meet?'

'I live in Du Cane Court, on Balham High Road. You can't miss it. Go to the front desk and they'll call me.'

'I'll see you then.'

The click in the earpiece cut to the buzz of a dropped line. Jenny replaced the handset and stood for a moment, arms folded, her hands clasping her sides in a self-contained hug of reassurance. When she padded back to the kitchen, Alice dashed after her.

'Well? Tell me all about it.' She pulled a chair out from under the kitchen table and plonked herself down.

Jenny resumed peeling carrots in silence.

'So?' Alice insisted.

'He's desperate,' Jenny's voice held a cold edge. 'He thinks he's going to die and he wants some fun before he does.'

Alice's face dropped, 'He said that?'

'Of course he didn't,' Jenny tutted, 'but it doesn't make it any less true.'

'Come on, Jen,' Alice implored, 'he's a fighter pilot. I'm not being rude, but I don't think they usually have much of a problem finding company.'

Jenny turned on her friend, 'And because I happen to be convenient I'm supposed to roll over?'

'He must like you. I mean he *has* called to ask you out.'

'In the pub, he didn't even know who I was. I had to tell him.' Jenny turned back to the sink, the renewed scraping of a carrot scratched at the silence.

'You *did* give him the telephone number,' Alice murmured.

Jenny dropped a clean carrot onto the draining board and started scraping the next.

Chapter 4

The wide Norfolk sky above Horsham St Faith flared with the orange glow of the descending sun as Sergeant Tommy Scott stood, with his duffel bag dangling from his shoulder, waiting for the transport. The bomber crews of 139 Squadron trudged past him on their way to the briefing room to get the final updates on weather, flight paths, flak concentration and searchlights that might be encountered on their way in and out of enemy territory. Twelve Blenheims stood dispersed around the field, heavy with ordnance and fuel for the night's bombing raid.

'Good luck, Tommy,' his pilot slapped him on the shoulder as he passed. 'I hope everything's alright at home. Give our love to Lizzy.'

'Thank you, sir,' Tommy called after the pilot's retreating back. 'I'll see you on Saturday.'

Strange forces tugged at Tommy as the aircrews flowed past him. He'd put in for this leave the moment his wife received the due date from her GP. He was bursting to see her, but standing down as his crew started a mission with a replacement gunner rubbed sorely against the grain.

'Transport to Norwich station.'

The call broke the spell. Tommy trotted towards the dark blue truck, hefted his duffel bag into the back and clambered in after it. Three other aircrew climbed aboard and sat on the benches ranged along the sides of the truck, each face graced with the beatific calm of a man leaving the firing line to visit his loved ones.

The truck growled into life and waddled over the ruts and potholes to the main gate. Once past the sentry post, the engine rattled to a pneumonic crescendo as the driver accelerated south towards the city. The truck jolted along the road in the deepening dusk, slowing down as it snarled up in the increasing traffic. Industrial buildings hunkered along the roadside, giving way to terraced houses as they penetrated the suburbs.

It was fully dark when the truck ground to a halt on the train station forecourt and the men spilled out of the tailgate. Half-a-dozen returning aircrew clambered in to take their place and the truck wheezed its way back into the gloom.

Tommy paused at the station doors and cocked his head. Rippling beneath the noise and bustle of the railway terminus he could feel the gentle throb of motors blown south on the prevailing breeze. The rumbling waxed and waned as the bombers circled, forming up and climbing. Then it subsided as the formation struck east for its long flight over the angry North Sea to targets on the north-west German coast. Tommy pulled up the collar of his greatcoat against an involuntary shiver and strode into the station. He found the next train to London on the departures board and made his way to the platform. Thoughts of navigation, bombs and the cold, uncaring sea receded. He was going to see his pregnant wife.

***

The train clanked its careful way over the points and into Liverpool Street station, gushing a cascade of steam back around its carriages as it rolled to a halt. Tommy roused from a semi-doze, shuffled to the door and stepped out onto the hard, cold platform. Eager now to finish his journey, he hurried through the station exit to the bus stop.

The London sky stood clear, rimed with silver moonlight. Anti-aircraft guns barked angry flashes into the shimmering vault and the flat thud of bomb strikes in the middle distance taunted the gunners' blind impotence.

Tommy stamped his feet against the chill for several minutes before a number 78 bus pulled up, moving with sedate care through the blackout. Tommy jumped on board and sat down. The conductor dinged the bell and walked to Tommy's seat on well-practiced sea legs.

'Where to?'

'Single to Peckham High Street,' Tommy said, wriggling in his pocket to hunt down some loose change.

The conductor wound out a ticket, tore it off and swapped it for the coins.

'Might be a bit of a detour,' he drawled. 'There's been a few sticks of bombs through there tonight. Fair amount of damage across a couple of streets.' He pushed his cap backwards and scratched his hairline. 'We, might be lucky. They might've cleared the rubble off the road by now.'

Tommy's shoulders tensed as he squinted out the window, struggling to identify landmarks in the dark. The bus lumbered to a halt, people got on, people got off, the bell dinged and the bus lurched on through the night. At length, the vehicle slowed to a crawl and passed the shadowy, crouched forms of workman heaving bricks and masonry off the road.

The conductor caught Tommy's eye and smiled, 'Them boys don't mess about. Peckham High Street's your next stop.'

Tommy skipped off the bus as it slowed at the bus stop, his momentum forcing him into a trot along the pavement. He hurried down the High Street onto Queen's Road, past the railway station and took the next left up Astbury Road, eyes darting for signs of bomb damage. His anxiety forced him back into a jog, his boots thumping the road in counterpoint to his heart.

There, at the end of the road, safe and undamaged, stood his little end-of-terrace house. His footfall slowed and he breathed deeply against the release of tension. Pushing through the gate into the tiny front yard, he paused to find his keys. With a final glance at the still-hostile skies, he unlocked the door and slipped inside. The warm smells of home flooded his nostrils as he dumped his duffel bag and shrugged off his greatcoat.

'Hello?' he called.

Footsteps sounded upstairs.

'Come up Mister Scott,' a woman's voice he didn't know. 'Your wife has a little surprise for you.'

Tommy climbed the stairs, treads creaking under his heavy boots. Candlelight glowed from the main bedroom and he stuck his head around the door. Next to the bed sat a midwife, smiling to herself with bovine torpidity. In the bed, her hair matted and tangled with dried sweat, lay Lizzy with a bundle of towels cradled in her arms.

Tommy crept closer and his wife pulled back the edge of the swaddling to show a red and crumpled face latched to her nipple, rocking to the rhythm of its sucking.

'When?' Tommy whispered.

'About two hours ago,' Lizzy smiled through her fatigue, 'but it took most of the afternoon.'

'Boy or girl?' Tommy gazed at the battered little head, raw against his wife's smooth breast.

'It's a boy.'

'It's like he knew I was coming home.'

The midwife stood up, 'Now you have company, I'll be on my way.' She slung her satchel over her shoulder. 'Mind, Mister Scott, there are some sheets and towels in the kitchen that could do with a wash as soon as you're able. I'll be back in the morning to make sure everything is alright.' She paused at the door and flashed a stern look at Tommy, 'And I don't want you bothering her for anything.'

Thursday, 10 October 1940

The clear skies persisted through the night and the new day dawned crisp and fresh. Tommy boiled kettle after kettle and scrubbed the blood and mucus stains from the bed linen, sweating over the washboard despite the chill of the room. He pegged out the dripping washing in the back yard. His hands, red-raw from the hot water and washing soap, tingled in the cold air. As he fumbled with the pegs, he tried to ignore the faint, bitter tang of burning timber that drifted across in the languid breeze.

Tommy ducked back into the kitchen and filled another kettle, this time for tea. He glanced around the cluttered room at the jigsaw of his domestic dream. On this fine morning his wife held the final piece in her arms upstairs and he knew he should be the happiest man in the district. But in his imagination, the spectre of a broken man scratched through the rubble of a house, much like the rubble the bus had skirted last night, desperate to salvage the mangled pieces of his own demolished dream.

Tommy gave the tea a final stir and poured two mugs. He dropped the cosy over the teapot and took the mugs upstairs.

Lizzy sat propped up on her pillows, gazing into the cot next to the bed with heavy-lidded eyes. She looked up as Tommy entered the room.

'Oh, thank you, Sweetheart,' she smiled, 'just what I needed.'

'How is he?' Tommy sat on the edge of the bed and planted a kiss on her forehead.

'Fed and resting,' she said. 'He seems content.'

'Have you been getting to the air raid shelter?'

Lizzy grimaced, 'It's always full by the time I get there, so I have to walk all the way back. Bad enough when you're pregnant, it'll be even worse with a new baby.'

'We live next to the railway tracks,' Tommy took her hand in his, 'and that's the kind of target a bomber is trained to look for.' He squeezed her hand. 'They hit a few properties on Hill Street last night. I saw the damage from the bus.'

'I know, I heard the explosions,' Lizzy pulled a wan smile, 'but I was busy with other things at the time.'

'And that's what makes it even more important,' Tommy pressed, 'now we've got...'

'Robert,' Lizzy gazed down again into the cot, 'his name will be Robert.'

The front door rattled under a brisk knocking.

'That will be the midwife. Let her in Tommy, love, would you?'

Tommy descended to the hallway and opened the door.

'Good morning, Mister Scott,' the midwife pushed past him, 'it's certainly a brisk one out there.'

Tommy closed the door and followed her upstairs.

The woman stopped halfway up and glared at him, 'We won't be needing you up here for an hour or so, Mister Scott.'

Tommy trailed back down to the kitchen and swilled the dregs of his tea around the bottom of his mug as he looked out the kitchen window. The sun shifted the shadows of the window frame imperceptibly across the sill towards another night-time, another bombing raid. His muscles tensed and relaxed with waves of anxiety. Unable to keep his legs still, he strode to the hallway, threw on his greatcoat and opened the door.

'I'll be back soon,' he called up and stepped out into the cold.

Action dispelled the worst of his jitters as he strode along the road, hunched into his coat against the chill of the morning air. He walked onto the main road, past the station and beyond, heading for the distant right turn into Hill Street.

Walking back along these roads seduced him towards the notion that the bomb damage was reassuringly far away from his house and family. But he dismissed that absurdity immediately. The city stretched out like a blank canvas below a night sky filled with bombers prone to scattering their loads wherever they found themselves and wheel about, relieved to be on their journey home. The crews threw the dice from too great an altitude to worry too much about the score.

Tommy's exertion warmed his blood. He loosened his coat as he came to Hill Street and walked up the gentle slope, reversing his bus journey of the previous evening. Ahead, whorls of thin, black smoke stained the clear morning air, creeping up over the roof-tops and bending away in the breeze. At its source, wardens and workmen stood in small groups on the pavement. A bus gunned passed on the now-cleared road and the men swivelled to scowl at it. Tommy slowed as he approached the tense assembly.

'Can't we get the police to set up a detour?' a warden hissed to a companion. 'Bloody buses, roaring about like it's a bank holiday in Brighton.'

The knot of men stood before a gap in a row of Georgian town houses. Where three dwellings had once completed the neat sandstone-faced terrace, there was now only rubble, timber and broken slate, heaped between the cracked and pitted walls of the neighbouring homes.

One of the workmen stood apart from the group and Tommy approached him.

'What are they doing?' he asked.

The workman put a finger to his lips, 'Listening,' he whispered. 'They believe there's someone left alive.'

'Under *that?*' Tommy muttered.

'It happens a lot.' The workman scratched his chin, 'They don't often make it out.' He looked at Tommy and shrugged, 'But we have to try.'

The silence pressed on Tommy's ears as he strained with the others to discern any sound. At length a sad-faced warden clapped his hands, 'Alright, lads,' he called, 'back to it. Careful and slow.'

One of the men climbed back onto the rubble and bent to loosen more pieces from the tangle. The others formed a line behind him and handed the bricks, one to another, away from the chaotic heap to be stacked neatly on the pavement.

The lead man lifted a lump of masonry, handed it on and then bent to brush away cement dust with gentle care. He stood, beckoned to a medic, then stepped back with hands on hips and looked up at the sky.

The medic scurried up the scree and crouched at the spot. A moment later he stood, holding what appeared to be a small bundle of dust covered rags. With a sickening lurch of recognition, Tommy saw the lifeless limbs of a broken baby dangling from its tiny body.

He stifled the gasp that jumped into his throat and averted his eyes as the medic carried the dead infant past him to an ambulance. Tommy looked back at the line of men as they resumed their delicate demolition. The workman he'd spoken with returned his gaze, his face haunted with the grim futility of his task.

Tommy lurched away on legs that wobbled under his weight, fighting the churn that gripped his guts. He turned left off the main road, following the progress of the sticks of bombs that had slashed a rent through this close-packed carpet of houses. A glance up each side road revealed more smashed and broken walls, more scattered rubble.

Tommy tottered to the next junction and staggered to a halt. He stared without comprehension at the vast empty space that opened out before him. Drawn in by the morbidity of his dread, he walked slowly up the shattered road.

Broken glass lay like dirty drifts of pack ice against the low sections of garden walls that still protruded from the dust-covered earth. Splintered roof timbers, like the broken skeletons of a defeated armada, hung together in ragged piles. Pulverised roof tiles scrawled gritty red lines across the asphalt. Here and there, dotted through the chaos, deformed saucepans and ragged toys sat forlorn of their owners, and books flapped their scorched pages in the breeze like wounded butterflies.

A policeman stood in the centre of the devastation, hands behind his back, his black cape marred with streaks of grey soot. Tommy walked towards him.

'What happened here?' he asked.

The policeman glanced at Tommy and then returned his eyes to the middle distance, 'Socking great parachute mine. Last night.'

Tommy followed the man's gaze. From where they stood, they could see over a quarter-of-a-mile along the furrow ploughed by the night raiders through residential London.

The policeman sighed, 'It's a terrible thing when it comes to this.'

***

Tommy unlocked the front door and ducked inside. The walk home had allowed his breathing to steady and the buzz behind his forehead to subside. But the worm of dread still wriggled in his stomach.

'Is that you Mister Scott?' the midwife called. Without waiting for his answer, she clumped down the stairs to the front door, wrestling her arms into her heavy coat. 'All's well with mother and baby. I'll drop by again tomorrow. Cheerio.'

Tommy shrugged off his greatcoat and went through to the kitchen. He filled the kettle and switched on the gas. He spooned the coarse, twisted tea leaves into the pot with hands that betrayed a faint tremor. While the tea brewed, he brought in the dried washing. As he pulled the towels from the line, he surveyed the yard; too small for an Andersen shelter, barely large enough for the outside toilet.

He bundled the washing onto a chair and poured the tea. Making an effort to steady his hands, he climbed the stairs to Lizzy.

She was cradling baby Robert in her arms and smiled broadly as Tommy walked in. He put the mugs on the bedside table and took his son from his wife. Standing and gazing into the still-crumpled face, a fresh chill of memory washed up his spine.

'We have to sort out a plan to get you and the boy under shelter at night,' he said. 'The bombing will likely carry on all winter. We can't trust to luck forever.'

Lizzy sipped at her tea. 'Well, let's trust in God, then. That's always seen me through in the past.'

Tommy turned to look out the window so his wife wouldn't see the exasperation that creased his brow.

'Everybody in the city is trusting in God, Lizzy. It doesn't stop a couple of hundred getting killed every night.'

'Have faith, Tommy. It all starts and ends with faith.'

The calmness of her voice made him want to share in her solid certainty, if only for a moment, but he knew that wasn't possible. So he held his tongue and kept his face to the window.

Their house abutted land belonging to the railway. Their bedroom window overlooked the wasteland separating the house from the viaduct that carried the tracks north, away from Queen's Road station. Tommy's eyes wandered over the rough grass and settled on a pile of what looked like scaffolding poles, overgrown and partially hidden by the long grass. He placed the sleeping child in its cot and reached for his tea.

'We need to be practical, Lizzy. We need to do everything we can to protect you and the baby. You can sort it out with God later.'

***

Dusk coloured the sky a darker grey as Tommy prised off the fence boards with a claw hammer and slipped through onto the wasteland. A train shambled across the viaduct, but no faces appeared at the darkened windows to observe him. Tommy moved through the long grass with exaggerated steps, like a cat stalking its prey, wary of the broken glass and rusty iron that the undergrowth undoubtedly concealed.

He reached the pile of scaffolding and pulled the bindweed and ivy away. Hefting a pole off the pile, he balanced its weight in his grip and moved back to the fence, feeding it through into his backyard. Five more trips and he judged he had enough piping to fulfil his plan. On a hunch he returned to the pile and kicked around in the nearby vegetation. Wincing as his toe struck something heavy, he bent down to disentangle the object from the brambles. He emerged in triumph with a bucket of scaffold clamps and heaved it back through the fence, crawled through after it and tapped the boards back into place.

Full darkness shrouded the neighbourhood by the time he'd finished. Away to the east an air raid warning moaned out its mournful message and the Woolwich searchlights flicked their icy tendrils into the sky. Tommy quaked with a shiver that was only partly due to the dropping temperature. Tingling within his own soft vulnerability, he went back into the house.

Friday, 11 October 1940

Lizzy awoke to the faint, but harsh grating of saw blade on metal. She checked all was well in the cot by the bed, pulled on her dressing gown and padded down the stairs. In the kitchen, she peered out of the window. Tommy stood in the yard, bent over a length of metal, cutting in even strokes with a large hacksaw. She turned away from the window and put the kettle on the stove. Pulling a bread knife from the cutlery drawer, she cut four slices from the loaf, fired up the grill and placed the bread under the flames. Outside, a section of piping clanged onto the concrete yard. Lizzy winced at the sound and cocked her head, listening for any sign of movement from upstairs. All remained quiet.

She poured the boiling water into the teapot and flipped the bread. She went back to the window and watched her husband work for a few moments before she knocked on the glass and beckoned him in.

Despite the chill of the season Tommy had a sheen of sweat on his forehead as he sat down and poured the tea.

'What on earth are you doing with metal poles?' Lizzy shut off the grill and put the toast rack on the table.

'Making a bomb shelter for you and the boy,' Tommy beamed and grabbed a slice of toast.

'A bomb shelter?' Lizzy levelled a quizzical gaze. 'And where do we have room for a bomb shelter?'

Tommy slapped his hand on the heavy oak tabletop, 'Right here.'

***

Lizzy opened the gate and reversed the pram off the pavement and into the front yard. The door opened behind her and Tommy's smiling face poked through the gap.

'Right on time. I've just finished.'

Lizzy pushed the pram into the parlour. Letting the baby sleep on, she followed Tommy through to the kitchen.

'There,' Tommy announced and stood back, hands on hips.

Between the stout wooden legs of the table, on three sides, vertical lengths of scaffold pole filled the gaps, clamped one to the next, with the end sections spliced to the legs with stout cord.

Lizzy looked from the mutilated furniture to Tommy and back again.

'That's my mother's kitchen table.'

'It gets better,' Tommy gestured, 'take a look underneath.'

Lizzy crouched by the open side. Every other vertical supported a right-angle joint that held a horizontal pole bracing the tabletop.

'It's a prison cage.' Lizzy straightened. 'I can't sleep in there.'

Tommy kissed her forehead, 'Only when a raid is close, my love. It'll keep you and the baby safe if things start flying about. Promise me you'll use it.'

Lizzy looked into his eyes and nodded, 'You're a good husband, Tommy Scott. But I'll leave you to explain it to my mother.'

Saturday, 12 October 1940

The guard at the aerodrome gate flagged down the dark blue truck. It staggered to a halt and the idling engine rattled pulses of vibration down its metal flanks. The sentry slung his rifle and walked to the back of the vehicle, sticking his head over the tailgate.

He glanced at a note clutched in his hand, 'Sergeant Scott? Is Sergeant Thomas Scott on this transport?'

Tommy raised a hand, 'Yes, that's me.'

'You're to report to the adjutant immediately.'

The guard walked back to his hut, waving the truck on. It lumbered its way to the mess buildings where it disgorged its passengers. Tommy hefted his duffel bag onto his shoulder and trudged to the office block. He walked down the corridor, loosening the buttons on his greatcoat, knocked and opened the adjutant's door.

'Sergeant Scott, reporting as ordered.'

The older man behind the desk looked up over his spectacles, 'Ah. Sit down, Scott. Enjoy your leave?'

'Yes, sir,' Tommy shrugged off the bag and took a seat. 'My wife has just had our first baby.'

'Excellent. Congratulations.' The officer smiled for a moment before his face hardened, 'I thought it best to catch you directly off the transport, save you from hearing in the mess.'

'Hearing what, sir?' sudden tension sharpened Tommy's voice.

'We posted your crew as missing on Thursday morning. They didn't return from the raid on Wilhelmshaven.'

Tommy's shoulders sagged, 'Does anyone know what happened?'

'There was no word from them at all,' the adjutant shook his head, 'and, as you know, the majority of the route to that target is over the North Sea. We can always hope they crash-landed somewhere on the German coast. But I'm afraid it's most likely they've been lost at sea.'

Tommy nodded, mute with sadness.

'Go back to barracks, Scott. Get yourself a good night's sleep. I'll put you on the rota as a reserve gunner until we can crew you up again.'

'Yes, sir.' Tommy stood and retrieved his duffel bag, 'Thank you, sir.'

'And congratulations on becoming a father.'

The words did not penetrate Tommy's numbness as he walked out the door.

Chapter 5

Bluebird Squadron climbed steadily east. The grey stains of the satellite towns rolled beneath them, first Sevenoaks and then Maidstone. Bryan levelled out at fifteen thousand feet and throttled back to cruising speed. The other Spitfires bobbed in the turbulent air on either side, organised in four fighting sections of three aircraft, the third member of each section weaving lazily around, protecting the patrolling squadron from surprise attack.

'Beehive Control to Bluebird Leader,' the wireless crackled into life, 'make angels eighteen and patrol Canterbury.'

Bryan eased his nose up to add the extra altitude and eased his throttle forward to maintain airspeed. He glanced down at the fields, uneasy about the instructions from control, fearful that fighter-bombers may be penetrating at lower levels. The minutes passed.

'Beehive Control to Bluebird Leader, thirty-plus bandits approaching Canterbury. Angels twelve.' Static filled the pause. 'They're crossing Kent coast at Deal now.'

Bryan pushed on his throttle and the squadron sped forward, the Kent Downs rolling by beneath at a quickening pace. The huge megalith of Canterbury Cathedral sat squat and solid in the centre of its city. Bluebird overflew the sprawl of buildings, seeking the raiders approaching from the east coast.

'Yellow Two to Bluebird Leader,' Bryan's wingman sounded hesitant, 'large formation at 2 o'clock. Lord knows what they are.'

Bryan eased to starboard, taking the squadron directly towards the intruders. He thumbed the transmit button, 'Bluebird Leader to Beehive Control. Are there any training flights in the area?'

'Hello, Bluebird Leader. Nothing in the area except you and your intercept.'

As the strange formation got closer, Bryan could make out more details. Eight large planes lumbered along in ragged formation. They carried a propeller on each wing and a third on the nose. Above them, but somewhat below Bluebird, flew two groups of fifteen smaller planes. One gaggle comprised chubby monoplanes with bright yellow engine cowlings, the other group were biplanes with fixed undercarriage. The strange collection of aircraft processed beneath Bluebird straight towards the city.

'Well I'll be blowed,' Bryan muttered to himself, then, 'Bluebird Leader to Bluebird Squadron. The bloody Italians have turned up at last! Yellow Section, let's break up those bombers. The rest of you take care of the escorts. Tally-ho, Bluebird, tally-ho!'

Bryan peeled into a dive and took his section down through the escorts. The Italian fighters broke in all directions as they realised the danger. But the bombers held their defensive formation and sparkles of machine gun fire flashed from dorsal gun positions.

Bryan chose a raider in the middle of the formation and thumbed a speculative burst. From the corner of his eye he caught other bombers on the formation's edge peeling away and diving. His target filled his windscreen and Bryan felt a shock of surprise to see the gunner returning his fire stood tall in a fully open cupola, slightly behind the enclosed cockpit.

Bryan fired a sustained burst. Hits slashed across the back of the bomber's fuselage, ripping through and around the gunner, and coughing shards of Perspex from the front of the enemy aircraft. Bryan roared over the Italian machine as it nosed out of the horizontal into a shallow dive. Bryan pulled up into a zoom and checked his mirror before banking hard to port.

Two of the bombers spiralled lazily towards the fields where the jettisoned bombs of their companions exploded in ragged groups. All the surviving bombers dived east, seeking safety in speed and low altitude. Bryan glanced up at the escort, also heading east in a fighting retreat. The bombers made a tempting target, but the risk of being bounced from above was not worth taking.

He jammed the throttle forward and climbed towards the battle above him. A Spitfire dived out of the melee and headed west, out of ammunition or damaged, running for home. An Italian biplane cocked into a vertical dive, rolling gently as it descended. Still labouring for altitude, Bryan watched its downward progress with suspicion until, one thousand feet below him, the Italian eased out his dive and gunned his engine. Black trails of exhaust smoke followed him in his dash for the coast.

'Crafty bugger,' Bryan muttered as he banked into a shallow, curving dive to give chase to the stocky biplane. At full throttle, the Spitfire quickly overhauled the Italian and he jinked into evasive banks as Bryan slid into firing range.

The thin strip of a sandy beach flashed by below as Bryan squeezed out a two second burst. The Italian kicked his plane into a vicious right bank, Bryan turned to follow him, throttling back to match his opponent's speed. The biplane stayed in the bank, pulling tighter and tighter. Bryan struggled with controls that became loose and flabby as he decelerated closer to a stall.

'*Shit.*' Bryan cast about for his adversary, but couldn't catch sight of him. The Italian was out-turning him. '*Shit, shit, shit.*'

The beach wheeled back into Bryan's vision. He reversed the bank and dived towards it. The manoeuvre cut through the Italian's flight path and white tracer rounds flashed over Bryan's head. The increasing speed of the dive brought the tautness back to his controls and Bryan jinked away from the menacing tendrils of phosphorus that sought to grasp him. The beach loomed in the windscreen and Bryan pulled out of the dive, making landfall at treetop height. A feverish glance into the mirror revealed his attacker had disengaged.

'Shit,' Bryan breathed to himself. 'Shit.'

***

Bumping down onto the grass at Kenley, Bryan fought to control the shivering that spasmed through his upper body. The beads of sweat seeping into his leather flying helmet, drawing a dark brown band across his forehead, belied the chill that quaked across his chest. Breathing deeply to steady himself, he pulled the canopy back as he taxied to dispersal. The slipstream dried the sweat and the crackling dryness of engine fumes steadied his nerves.

His ground crew helped him swivel the Spitfire onto the pad and he felt a jolt as Mortice jumped up onto his port wing.

'Any luck, sir?' then in softer tones, 'Are you alright, Mr Hale?'

Bryan drew another steadying breath and looked up as undid his straps.

'We ran into some Italians, Mortice,' Bryan forced his jocularity, 'queer birds, they are.' He stood and shrugged off his parachute, stepping out onto the wing. 'The bombers go down easily,' he jumped to the turf on legs that felt vaguely disconnected, 'but their fighters are saucy little bitches,'

Mortice clumped to the ground next to him.

'How so, sir?'

'Biplanes,' Bryan looked the rigger in the eye, 'higher wing loading.'

Mortice sucked his breath through his teeth, 'Giving him a tighter turning circle...'

'One of them got a good long burst off at me.' Bryan gestured at his Spitfire, 'I don't know whether there's any damage, I didn't feel any hits. Give it a once over, will you?'

'Will do.'

The rigger set about the task and Bryan stood for a moment, willing his leg muscles to come back under his control. Lighting a cigarette, he raised his face to the sound of other Bluebird Spitfires streaming back to base. Two or three waggled their wings in triumph as they swooped in for their approach. He smiled with relief and a rough affection swelled in his throat. Dropping his head in concentration, he walked unsteadily towards the readiness hut.

Sunday, 13 October 1940

Bryan pulled on his leather driving gloves and climbed into his black Humber motor car.

'Good girl,' he muttered as it sprung to life on the first turn of the ignition key.

Clunking into gear, he reversed off the gravel outside the officer's mess and drove sedately down to the station gates. The guard saluted him through the barrier and he accelerated down the road, bound for South London. Bryan glanced at his watch. It was a ten-mile journey, he'd certainly make it by mid-afternoon.

Cruising steadily north he could make out the bulbous grey shapes of the Croydon balloon barrage floating like bloated carp on fishing lines, shocked into torpidity by their unnatural inversion into the chill autumnal sky. Skirting around the west side of Croydon he noted an occasional space in the terraced shop-fronts. Many contained no rubble, the gap still incongruous, but cleared and tidied, as if the menace of the nightly terror had to be denied.

Heading further north through Thornton Heath he passed more recent evidence of the raiders' passing. A corner block lay demolished, the pile of rubble giving vent to the odd wisp of grey smoke as a buried timber smouldered away its air supply. The side road next to the ruin was roped off and a policeman stood kicking his heels next to a sign proclaiming the dangerous proximity of an unexploded bomb.

The sun broke through the grey clouds as Bryan drove on through Streatham, the Sunday afternoon walkers on the common lifted their faces to receive it like a gift. Following the signposts now, Bryan cut between the wooded fringes of Tooting Bec Common, swept down the hill and stopped at the red traffic light outside the tube station. A newspaper seller watched him lean over to wind down the passenger window.

'Du Cane Court?' Bryan called across.

'Take the left under the railway bridge,' the man drawled, 'it's down there on the right. Biggest building in town.'

Bryan waved his thanks and pulled away on the green light, a sudden knot of nerves tangling in his stomach.

Within a few seconds he recognised his destination. A huge block of flats sat squat along the edge of the road behind a low brick wall. Two entranceways breached the wall, each flanked with brick columns emblazoned with the building's name. Bryan pulled through the closest gap and parked in the courtyard.

He followed a path to the double-doored entrance and shouldered his way in. The foyer beyond the doors stopped him in his tracks. Eighty feet long and tiled with white marble it swept in an elegant curve around a large ebony-panelled reception desk. Black-painted columns topped with uplighters punctuated the floor, their light washing outwards across the white plastered ceiling. At one end, a staircase rose into the bulk of the building between curved, golden handrails. Someone cleared their throat and Bryan's eyes were dragged back to a young man standing behind the desk wearing a green uniform with silver buttons.

'May I help you, sir?' the porter asked.

'Er, yes.' Bryan advanced to the desk. 'I've come to see a Miss Freeman. She said you'd let her know I've arrived.'

The porter leafed through a small directory and picked up the telephone. After a brief, hushed conversation, he hung up and turned back to Bryan.

'She'll be a few minutes, sir,' the porter inclined his head towards a group of three leather armchairs in one corner of the lobby.

'Thank you.'

Bryan lit a cigarette as he ambled across, choosing a chair that secured an easy view of the staircase and the nearby lift doors. Tightness returned to his stomach. It was not quite fear, yet it was too craven to be called excitement. It was like waiting by the readiness hut, eyeing the telephone, knowing it would ring but unsure if, or how, you'd get through whatever happened next.

The lift door dinged open and Jenny stepped out onto the smooth marble floor. She wore a red dress and black raincoat, her outfit topped off with a bright red pillbox hat, finished with a black ribbon.

Bryan stubbed out his cigarette and jumped to his feet.

'Hello, Jenny. You look very lovely.'

Jenny's heels clacked across the stone.

'Hello, Bryan,' she smiled. 'Do you live in that uniform?'

Bryan looked down at himself and grimaced with mock chagrin.

'I tried on my suit this morning, but it's been packed away for so long it looked like I was going gardening.' He mirrored her smile, 'So this is the finest piece of tailoring I can currently muster.'

She stood on tiptoes and kissed his cheek, 'Let's hope Alice doesn't see you.'

They walked outside where the sunshine persisted in the face of a rising breeze that robbed it of its warmth.

Bryan glanced up and down the road, 'I'm in your hands, I'm afraid.'

Jenny grabbed his arm, 'I know a cafe in Clapham Common where they make the best omelettes. The owner gets fresh eggs from chickens he keeps in his garden. It's only two stops on the tube.'

They struck out towards the station.

'Your block of flats is very plush,' Bryan said. 'The foyer looks like it was lifted straight out of an ocean liner.'

'Ah,' Jenny laughed, 'the last gasp of post-war architectural optimism. At least that's how it was explained to me.'

'But seriously, I'm impressed.'

'You shouldn't be. Alice and I are there under totally false pretences,' Jenny confessed. 'Most residents moved out as soon as war was declared. So the landlord dropped the rents and the rest is history.'

'Still,' Bryan mused, 'uniformed porters...'

They ducked down the stairs at Balham station and Bryan bought two return tickets. Down on the platform, a dozen or so shelterers sat draped in blankets against the curved walls.

Bryan glanced at his watch, 'It's a bit early for that, isn't it?'

The train whirred into the station and the doors opened.

'It's never too early to feel safe, I suppose,' Jenny said, sitting down in the near-empty carriage.

Bryan remained standing, uncomfortable about the intimacy that sitting next to Jenny might imply. Instead he allowed his eyes to wander, following the curve of her thigh against the close-fitting fabric of her dress, the drape of her fine, dark hair, hanging free over her shoulders, gleaming with chocolate tones, and the sheen of her red lipstick.

'I didn't ask you,' he said.

She looked up, blinking, 'I'm sorry?'

'If you have a gentleman friend.'

Jenny gave a short shake of her head, 'I'm not looking for a relationship,' she said. 'I'm too busy with work. There's too much uncertainty…'

The train slowed and, for the second time, the dark tunnel gave way to a brightly-lit station.

'Here,' she stood, 'this is our's.'

They emerged from the stale underground air into the sudden noise of traffic skirting the common.

'This way,' Jenny tugged his sleeve and they crossed the road to a parade of shopfronts. Jenny paused in front of a whitewashed window.

'This used to be a very friendly Italian restaurant,' she said. 'They were fine people, built up their business over many years. The authorities interned the whole family in the summer, every single one of them.'

Bryan bit his lower lip. 'I…' He searched for the right words. 'I came across some Italians yesterday, over Canterbury,' he said quietly. 'They may have been fine, but they certainly weren't at all friendly.'

Jenny's hand came to her mouth and she looked into his eyes, measuring the truth of his words.

'Well,' she linked his arm, 'I don't suppose there are any easy subjects anymore. Come on, let's go and talk about omelettes.'

The bell above the cafe door tinkled as they entered. The waitress waited for them to choose a spot and placed two menus on their table.

'Do you ever go back to Hampstead?' Jenny asked.

Bryan glanced up from his menu, 'Not if I can help it.'

'Are your parents still there?'

Bryan snorted, 'My father is a vicar. They move through neither space nor time.' He glanced up and frowned, 'You're not reading your menu.'

She smiled, 'That's because I already know what I want; a cheese and ham omelette.'

'That settles it, then.' Bryan leant back as the waitress arrived, 'Two cheese and ham omelettes and a pot of tea, please.'

Jenny watched the waitress return to the kitchen with their order, 'My parents are still there too,' she said. 'I'll probably go up to stay over Christmas.'

A silence hung between the pair as the waitress delivered the teapot and cups, lifting them from a battered, green metal tray and arranging them in the middle of the table.

'Sauce with the omelettes?' she chimed.

'Yes, Daddies, please,' Bryan said. Jenny shook her head and the waitress retreated once more.

'What are your plans for Christmas?' Jenny asked.

'I tend to avoid making plans if I can.' Bryan pulled a wan smile, 'It's a bit difficult to predict what the work situation will be.'

'Well, if you happened to be in Hampstead over the season, I could call on you when I need rescuing from my parents and their bridge table.'

'Is this my function in life, now? Rescuing Jennifer Freeman from people she no longer wants to spend time with?'

'It could be worse,' Jenny smiled, 'a girl's Best Alternative isn't a bad job, really.'

The omelettes arrived and Bryan poured the tea. As they ate, they reminisced about schooldays and friends that had become lost to them both in the folds of time.

The sun dipped below the treetops on the Common opposite as Bryan got up to pay.

'If we walk across the Common we should get to The Windmill for opening time,' Jenny suggested. 'It's my round.'

As they strolled along the path, the light mellowed out into the orangey texture of a dying day. Jenny glanced up at Bryan, his features highlighted in the warmth of the sunset, his face neither noble nor ordinary, neither kind nor harsh.

'What would you be doing if there wasn't a war on?' she asked.

'Probably waiting for one to start.' He chuckled at the look Jenny shot him, 'I joined the Air Force in 1932, so I'd been waiting for this war for seven years.'

She smiled in her turn, 'I was hoping for something like poet or artist.'

'Or vicar?'

She laughed, 'It's a steady job.'

As they approached the pub door, a monotonous wail rose in the distance as another district of the city raised an air raid alert. Bryan paused and looked at Jenny, eyebrows raised.

'Come on,' she said, opening the door, 'let's not let the Germans spoil the afternoon. What do you want to drink?'

They ordered their drinks and Jenny paid.

'Come this way, I want to show you something.'

The bar opened out at one end into a large rotunda. Several tables stood against the curved walls. Jenny headed to one of these and the pair sat down.

'It's like the whispering gallery in St Paul's,' Jenny grinned, 'you can listen to other people's conversations from across the room as if you were sitting right next to them.'

'The cathedral of careless talk,' Bryan observed. 'Aren't you worried people will eavesdrop us?'

'Let them,' Jenny sipped at her gin and tonic, 'these are dangerous times and tomorrow it will be Monday morning.' She laughed at her own gaiety, 'Cheers for a lovely afternoon.' She clinked her glass against his pint and took another sip.

'You know, it's funny,' Bryan said lighting a cigarette, 'I've spent most of the summer watching air raids from altitude. To me, bombs were little puffs of smoke way below me on the ground.' He took a draught from his beer. 'I've seen what bombs did to my airfield while I wasn't there. But, up until now, I haven't been underneath the bombers, I haven't been as helpless or felt as vulnerable as I do when I'm in this city.'

Jenny leaned forward, 'You don't strike me as a man who is easily frightened.'

Bryan rolled his cigarette around in his fingers, 'Maybe a man's level of bravado is related to how much he thinks he has to lose.'

'I think that might be true,' Jenny said. 'Sadly, I believe there's little in store for us but loss and more loss, as least for another year or so. We can only face that with whatever bravado we can muster.' She smiled, 'Which is why we're sitting in a pub, enjoying a drink, while there are bombers flying about in the sky above us.'

Bryan placed his hand on Jenny's, 'I've been worrying about what might happen to you.'

Jenny's eyes narrowed slightly and she pulled her hand from under Bryan's, 'You'd forgotten I existed until a week ago.'

Bryan shrugged, 'Yet, here I sit.'

Jenny leant back in her chair and sipped her drink in silence.

'I wasn't supposed to be on that train,' Bryan continued, 'I wasn't supposed to be in London on the night we met.' He stubbed out his cigarette, 'And you didn't want to be out that night at all.'

Jenny smiled at him over her glass, 'Yet, there I sat...'

'Exactly.'

'Right, finish your drink. We should go. Alice will be worried about me, what with the air raid warning and everything.'

They walked out of the pub into the thickening darkness, heading towards Clapham South station. The traffic had faded away and the breeze had dropped with the sunset.

Bryan cleared his throat 'I'm sorry if I've embarrassed you—'

'Shush,' Jenny interrupted, 'don't spoil it.' She smiled up at him, 'It was a lovely thing to say.'

They arrived at the station entrance and Jenny paused, 'It's only one stop from here, but we could walk it if you like, it's such a nice evening.'

They started south down the hill towards Balham, past shuttered shops and blacked-out pubs. In the background, the boom of distant anti-aircraft fire ruffled the air. The road was all but deserted, the few pedestrians they encountered tipped their hats or nodded as they passed. The hill flattened out and the shops became more substantial as they reached Balham's main street.

Bryan placed a restraining hand on Jenny's arm, 'Listen'.

Underneath the rumble of big guns, a different reverberation lurked and throbbed.

'Engines,' Bryan breathed. 'Sounds like a bomber.'

They both gazed up into the black velvet void.

A sharp hiss shredded the background drone and a thin column of silver grey flashed through their vision, a momentary thread connecting the ebony sky to the roadway two hundred yards ahead of them. A dull *thunk* echoed down the street and resonated into silence.

Then the pavement heaved and the air sucked away from their faces, tugging at their eyes and pulling them forward onto their toes. A huge spout of fire and earth erupted in a vertical column and a flat wall of blast swatted them backwards onto the ground.

Bryan struggled to his feet. 'Jenny, get up,' he shouted through the ringing in his ears, 'we need to get under cover.'

He grabbed her arm and hauled her upright. Together they lurched the few steps to the nearest shop doorway. Bryan pushed her into the deepest corner, pressing his body against hers. Clods of earth and pieces of masonry thudded and clunked onto the road amidst the staccato rattle of pebbles and wood splinters. Behind that, the rushing crash of collapsing walls, one following another like the breaking of huge waves.

'What's happening?' Jenny's voice was stretched with fear.

'A bomb,' Bryan shouted against the dull clanging in his ears, 'a big one. Stay still. There might be more.'

They both flinched at the crash of batteries on Clapham Common opening fire, blindly hurling vengeful metal into the empty sky.

'I saw it,' Jenny's voice wavered with incredulity, 'I saw it hit the ground.'

An ambulance bell jingled forlornly as the vehicle passed their makeshift shelter.

'Stay here, Jenny,' Bryan squeezed her shoulders, 'just for a moment while I check it's safe.'

Bryan stepped out onto the pavement and looked down a road strewn with debris towards Balham station. A smoking crater reached almost from shopfront to opposite shopfront, fifty feet across. Dark smoke curled up from its centre and two fountains of water curved away from broken water mains. More emergency vehicles clanged past him as he stepped back into the doorway.

'I think it's clear.' He gestured her out, 'We should go and see if we can help.'

Jenny stepped out of the doorway, her cheeks wet with tears.

'Are you alright?' Bryan reached out to her, 'You're not hurt?'

'No. I'm fine. A bit shaken.' She nodded, 'Yes, we should see if there's anything we can do.'

Bryan put his arm around Jenny's shoulders and together they picked their way through the debris towards the chaos at the end of the road.

As they drew closer the acrid fumes of spent high explosives scratched at their throats and dried their teeth. The assiduous stench of gas mixed in the air with the more visceral, clinging odour of breached sewage pipes. Figures in white helmets moved through the murk at the edges of the crater and another ambulance ground past them, zig-zagging through the scree of broken bricks and clods of hard earth dotting the road.

On the pavement ahead two medics knelt next to the prone figure of a woman resting amidst a scattering of broken plate glass, her body protruding from the shop doorway in which she'd landed. Her skirt and shoes had been blown off and she lay there, incongruous in her underwear, once precious stockings rent with gashes. One medic shook his head and the other pulled the woman's coat over her face. As they passed, Bryan gave as much leeway to the body as the wreckage on the road allowed, but they still had to step over the turgid flow of blood oozing from beneath the corpse and draining towards the gutter. Bryan felt Jenny's guttural sob and squeezed her shoulders tighter.

They skirted the edge of the crater, keeping close to the shop walls, their shoes crunching on crystal shards of glass. On the opposite side of the road the three-storey buildings stood frontless, like a row of opened doll's houses, with furniture and beds strewn in childlike disarray. Heaps of bricks lay piled at their footings, speckled with the shattered wood of window frames and shredded blackout curtains. Bryan risked a look into the crater.

'Christ, it's deep.'

Jenny pushed her face into the folds of his coat.

'It's the tube station.' Her voice trembled in a strained monotone, she sounded like someone trying not to vomit. 'The tube line runs under the road.'

Thirty more yards and they came to the crossroads where the exit to the station spewed dazed and bedraggled shelterers onto the pavement, their clothes and faces blackened with soot, their hair deranged by blast. Some pressed palms to cuts and gashes, one man, suspended between two helpers, lost blood from his ears in a languid pulse. Around them, and between them, the firemen and ARP wardens scurried, intent on imposing some order amidst this tiny slice of Armageddon.

Bryan grabbed a warden by the arm, 'What's happening? Can I help?'

The man's face was stretched with stress, 'The bomb breached the tunnel, north end of the platform. There's a lot of 'em. They're underneath the mud and shingle.'

'So, give me a shovel, let's get down there.'

The warden shook his head, imploring horror filled his eyes; 'It's filling up with sewage. They're drowning in shit and there's no way to shut it off.'

Bryan stared aghast into the man's face.

'But thank you,' the other's features softened slightly and he squeezed Bryan's shoulder. 'The best thing you could do is get the lady home safe.' He nodded towards Jenny, slapped Bryan's shoulder and hurried away.

Two more ambulances clattered to a halt as Bryan surveyed the people standing and sitting on the pavement. Many cried, shaking in spasms of shock. One old man, alone and dazed, stared into the middle distance and walked up and down the pavement as if searching for something lost. A woman, dishevelled and grimy, noticed the wandering man and moved to marshal him towards an ambulance. A mud-caked fireman emerged from the dust billowing up the stairwell, retching against the rising miasma, and the whole scene was overlain with the sobs of terrified children.

'Let's go.'

Bryan placed his hand on Jenny's head, holding her close against him as he guided her through the rubble and refugees, under the railway bridge and away towards her flat. Another fire engine clanged by, rushing to help from the south, but no other person walked the dark street as they retreated from the bubble of hell sitting atop the tube station.

It took only two minutes to reach Du Cane Court. As they walked through the entrance gates into the courtyard, Jenny disentangled herself from Bryan's embrace.

'I must look a complete state.' She forced a smile as she straightened her jacket and wiped the damp grime from her skirt. 'The porter's a terrible gossip.'

They stood together for a moment on the loose shingle of the courtyard, Bryan waited while Jenny reassembled a fragile normality in the space of three or four deep breaths.

'Right,' she said, her voice small and strained, 'I'm ready.'

They pushed through the curtained doors into the dimly-lit foyer. The porter's desk stood unmanned.

'Emergency lights,' Jenny noted. 'No electricity and a long walk up the stairs to the sixth floor.'

'We can take it steady,' Bryan murmured. 'No rush.'

'Better without these.' Jenny flipped her shoes off, picked them up and headed for the staircase.

Bryan followed and they climbed the carpeted flights without speaking. The plush silence cocooned them as they walked and Bryan felt the adrenalin of the last half hour drain out of his blood to be replaced with a familiar tingling fatigue. He watched Jenny's figure sinuating up the stairs ahead of him and plodded along behind her, unable to define the feelings she stirred.

'Sixth floor,' Jenny murmured and padded down a corridor, fishing in her handbag for keys. She unlocked Number 21 and went in. Bryan followed.

'I need a drink,' she dropped her shoes in the hall. 'Would you like one?'

'Yes please.' Bryan shrugged off his coat and stood uneasily in the gloom. He heard a match strike in the living room.

'Come and sit down,' Jenny called.

Bryan walked into the lounge where Jenny was lighting candles around the room, quiet tears ran gently down her cheeks, glistening in the candlelight.

'Are you alright?' he asked.

'Sit down,' she repeated and walked to the kitchen. 'Will brandy do?'

'Seems appropriate.'

Jenny returned with two wine glasses and a squat green bottle.

'Would you pour? My hands are a bit shaky.'

Bryan poured two small measures and pushed one glass across the coffee table towards Jenny. She picked it up with both hands and took a sip.

'Alice left a note; she's in the basement shelter.'

'Shouldn't you join her?'

Jenny shook her head, 'Imagine if this whole building came down,' she took another sip, 'how much rubble there'd be piled on top of that basement.'

Bryan dropped his eyes to the brandy in his glass and said nothing.

'There's only one floor above us here.' She glanced at the ceiling, 'At least I'd be near the top of the heap...' her voice trailed off and a fresh tear welled onto her cheek.

'You can't think like that, Jen-'

'We could've been down that hole,' Jenny cut across him, 'if we hadn't decided to walk, we could've been in that station.' She looked into Bryan's face, trying to connect with the eyes that were still downcast. 'Under that earth.'

Bryan's eyes flicked up to hers and he gazed into their chestnut depth. 'Yet, here we sit,' he said with a gentle smile.

Jenny leant forward and poured herself more brandy. She stood and took her drink into the bathroom. Bryan heard the match-strike as she lit more candles, followed by the gush of water into the bath.

He poured himself another large measure; sleeping in the car and setting off at first light was a far safer prospect than driving through the blackout against the flow of emergency vehicles in a hurry, and he was enjoying the spirit's warm glow spreading through his taut nerves. He closed his eyes and listened with semi-detached interest to the sound of Jenny undress and step into her bath.

***

Bryan drifted out of a gentle doze with the feeling he was being watched. He opened his eyes to see Jenny standing in the room brushing her still-damp hair. The candlelight made the dark blue silk of her dressing gown shimmer with her movements.

'I'm sorry.' He pulled himself upright in his chair. 'I dropped off.'

Jenny smiled, her head tilting against the brush-strokes. 'It was nice to watch you sleeping. You looked almost angelic.'

Bryan snorted a laugh and reached for the last of his brandy. 'That will be from my father's side.' He drained his glass and stood up. 'So, if you're all settled, I'll be on my way.'

Jenny shook her head, 'I want you to stay.'

'Stay?'

'Yes.' Jenny went from candle to candle, blowing them out. She picked up the last one, walked over to Bryan and took his hand. She led him into her bedroom where she released her gentle grip on his fingers.

'Shut the door.'

Bryan closed the door with exaggerated care, as if afraid to break the moment. When he turned back, Jenny was on the other side of the bed, near the window. She put the candle on her bedside table, blew it out and pulled back the blackouts. A dark vista of London spread out into the night, its edges teased with wisps of desultory moonlight. Jenny paused for a moment, watching distant searchlights playing their light across the cloud base. She let her dressing gown fall to the floor and climbed into the bed, settling with her back to Bryan.

'I don't really...' Bryan's voice trailed away into his discomfiture.

'Come to bed and hold me.'

Bryan eased his shoes off with his toes while he undid his jacket and shirt. Laying them across a chair, he unhitched his belt and removed his trousers. He hooked a thumb into his sock and pulled it off, cursing under his breath as he teetered on the edge of imbalance. He sat on the chair to pull off the other one. He balled the socks together and bent to place them in one of his shoes. He paused for a moment, standing in only his underpants, wondering how much to read into Jenny's invitation. Deciding to risk a misunderstanding, he dropped his underwear to the floor and climbed into bed.

He settled facing Jenny's back, careful to keep a few inches of space between their bodies. He reached out his right arm and rested it over Jenny's waist. The smooth warmth of her skin and the curve of her hip under his forearm sent a thrill of urgent desire through his temples. Her breathing took on a lower undertone and Bryan flattened his palm gently against her abdomen, his middle fingertip resting in the hollow of her belly button.

Jenny arched her back, moving her buttocks to close the gap between them. Bryan's hand applied a gentle pressure on her belly, pulling her up, back, and onto him. He pushed forwards gently with his hips and her soft warmth enveloped him. Jenny placed her hand over Bryan's and together they pushed and rocked her pelvis, undulating her body against his penetration, breathing in counterpoint against the low rumble of anti-aircraft guns booming far away across the city.

'Oh.' Bryan stopped the movement, 'We should be careful, we need to stop.'

'No!' Jenny pushed hard against him. 'Don't stop.'

Bryan thrust once more, the clench of his climax curled his spine forwards, pushing his face into her hair. She screwed her head about and bit him on the chin, their bodies stiffening together in the rictus of passion.

The moment ebbed. Bryan put both his arms around Jenny, holding her close, and she relaxed into the embrace. He rested his forehead against the back of Jenny's skull and felt his subsiding erection slip from her body. She clasped her hands over his, pulling him tighter against her back.

'I'm sorry.' Tentacles of guilt already tightened around Bryan's heart, 'I meant no disrespect.'

'It's not you, Bryan.' Jenny's voice was quiet but resolute as she gazed out at the searchlights still seeking vengeance amongst the dark clouds. 'The bombs have made me want to take risks' – she twisted her neck to nuzzle an ear against his face – 'made me want to enjoy taking risks.'

Bryan propped himself up onto his elbow and looked down into her face, 'Is that all I am?' he asked. 'A risk?'

Jenny studied his face for a moment and turned to watch the searchlights once more.

'I don't know, Bryan. That's the shame of it.'

Chapter 6

Monday, 14 October 1940

Jenny stirred as the strengthening light of the grey dawn rolled back the darkness in the room. Behind her, the sound of Bryan dressing brought her fully awake. She turned and smiled at him.

'Good morning,' she said.

Bryan grimaced as he struggled to fasten the top button on his shirt, 'Morning. I'm sorry, I didn't know what time you had to be up.'

'Just about now, as it happens.' Jenny yawned, leaning over to grope on the floor for her dressing gown.

'God, now it looks like I was sneaking off.'

A mischievous edge tweaked Jenny's smile, 'Isn't that what you are doing?'

'No, not at all.' Bryan walked around the bed, retrieved the dressing gown and handed it to her. 'I hadn't planned on staying in London overnight. I've got a bloody fighter squadron to run.'

He faced out the window as Jenny rose and put on her gown. Movements on the road below caught his eye. People streamed along the pavement, heads down against the early morning chill.

'Look at them,' Bryan murmured. 'Carrying on as if nothing out of the ordinary is happening.'

Jenny stood next to him, leaning into him as she craned her neck to see.

'Of course they carry on. Of course they go back to work. No-one gets paid for staying at home. They have to eat, you know.' She bent to making the bed. 'What are *you* going to do today? What am *I* going to do today? We're going to carry on.'

Bryan reached out and touched her arm, 'Are you alright. After last night, I mean?'

'Are you talking about the bomb, or the sex?'

'I...' Bryan floundered, his face reddening.

Jenny took his hand between hers, 'Nothing's changed, Bryan. I meant what I said at the beginning of the evening.' She let go of his hand and walked to the dressing table, bending to peer at her face, pawing critically at the skin under her eyes. 'I don't want to mislead you.'

'Well, as long as you're alright,' Bryan gestured to the door, 'I really have to go.'

Jenny didn't look up from the mirror, 'Yes,' her voice carried an edge, 'you do.'

Bryan left the bedroom and stepped across the hall. The sound of a spoon against a cereal bowl drifted from the kitchen. He eased the latch open and slipped out the front door. The abrupt cessation of cutlery noise suggested his exit had not gone unnoticed.

'Hallooo. Who's there?'

Jenny stared into the reflection of her own eyes as she listened to Bryan leave.

'It's alright, Alice,' she called. 'It's only Bryan.'

A timid knock sounded at her door and Alice peered in, 'Bryan?'

'Yes.' Jenny's gaze stayed locked on the mirror, 'Bryan.'

Bryan trotted down the last flight of stairs and crossed the lobby. Nodding to the porter as he passed, he pushed through the doors and hurried out into the courtyard. His stomach growled with hunger and his breath held the taint of stale alcohol. He crunched across the shingle to his car. The black paint held a faint patina of cement dust blown from the collapsed buildings around the tube station. Bryan unlocked the door and climbed in. Rummaging in the glove compartment he retrieved a stray boiled sweet. Grunting with relief as the citrus tang of the sweet cut through the clag on his tongue, he turned the ignition.

The engine growled into life, but Bryan let it idle. He sat flicking the gearstick backwards and forwards in its neutral position. The memory of Jenny's warmth invaded his mind and with it came chagrin, like the remorse of a petty thief caught in the act of his first crime. He shook his head to clear the notion. Today could not be different from any other day, because today might be his last, and he had no space for any other distraction.

He jammed his foot on the clutch, put the Humber into gear and pulled out through the gates. He glanced left, towards the station. The road was blocked off and behind the barriers men moved in weary concert, some shovelling rubble, some busy in the maw of the bomb crater and some lifting wrapped bundles into an army truck parked under the railway bridge. As he watched, a train chuffed across the bridge heading towards Victoria, carrying passengers from the southern suburbs on their way to work. Bryan blinked against the absurdity of the tableau, turned south and accelerated away from the city, vainly fleeing the clinging tendrils of sex and fear.

***

Harry Stiles sat next to Bryan's desk, glancing from the squadron leader's empty chair to the telephone next to the blotter. Technically Bryan was absent without leave already and it wouldn't be long until the adjutant's delay in reporting it would count as aiding and abetting. Stiles had sent 'B' flight up to cover the day's first patrol, but if a full squadron scramble was called in, there'd be big trouble.

The crunch of tyres on the gravel outside prised a sigh of relief from the adjutant's chest. He stood up and straightened his cap as Bryan entered the office and strode across to his desk.

'Thank the stars, Bryan. Where have you been?'

Bryan slumped into his chair.

'I got caught up in an incident.' He scrabbled in a drawer for a fresh pack of cigarettes, 'It's a bit much when you can't take a lady out for a stroll without someone trying to blow your bloody head off.' He lit a cigarette and hunched over his desk. 'My car got blocked in a side road,' he lied, 'I had to wait for the army to clear away the rubble.'

'You should've telephoned, Bryan,' the adjutant said. 'Anyone else would've been on a charge by now.'

Bryan looked up, 'Did I miss anything?'

Stiles shook his head, "B' flight have it covered for the moment.'

'There we are then, no damage done.' Bryan stood up, 'I'm off to clean my teeth.'

'You should be with the squadron at readiness. Your name is on the board. What sort of example is this to be setting?'

'Example?' Bryan cocked his head, 'What's wrong with you, Madge? Sometimes you act like you're the head boy at your own bloody public school, flapping around looking for something to witter about. There's a war on, I got caught up in a bombing raid, it made me a bit late. Now, I need to clean my teeth and have a shit. I'm sure Goering can wait another fifteen minutes.'

Bryan shouldered past the older man and stalked to the door. The adjutant flinched as the door slammed shut.

'Roll on bloody Scotland.' He muttered under his breath.

***

Bryan gargled with cold water and spat into the cracked porcelain basin. He rinsed his toothbrush and scrubbed the fur from his tongue. Rinsing and spitting again, he watched the yellow-tinged water circle the plughole twice before disappearing.

He stowed his toothbrush in his toilet bag, grabbed a newspaper from the dresser and walked down the corridor to the toilets. Choosing a cubicle, he dropped his trousers and underpants. Settling himself on the rough, wooden toilet seat, he lit a cigarette and scanned the frontpage of the paper.

'Northern Town Suffers Light Raid – Casualties as yet Unknown.'

'Light raid…' Bryan muttered to himself and flipped the page.

'Port on South Coast Suffers Heavy Raid – Nearly 100 Killed and Over 200 Made Homeless.'

Bryan folded the newspaper and dropped it onto the floor. He tried to picture one hundred dead bodies lying in and around the houses they'd called home. Jenny's words came back to him; *'Imagine if this whole building came down…'*

Bryan dropped his cigarette between his knees and it extinguished in the fouled water with an angry hiss. Bryan finished and stood, fastening his belt and pulling the chain. The cistern clanked, flushing a guttural surge of water that sluiced the yellowing bowl.

Stepping over the paper on the floor, Bryan walked to the locker room. Minutes later he left the officers' mess and clumped across the airfield in flying boots, his sheepskin flying jacket slung over his shoulder, oxygen tube and wireless cables swinging across his chest to the beat of his footsteps.

Bryan chose a circuitous route to the readiness hut that took him within hailing distance of his Spitfire. His whistle pierced the morning air and his rigger turned to locate the noise. Bryan stuck up a questioning thumb. The rigger stuck up two thumbs in affirmative response. Bryan nodded and curved his path away from the dispersed machines and towards the pilots lounging outside the hut.

This was his life: This was where he lived. Bryan Hale and Bluebird Squadron had been the two halves of a dovetail joint when he'd left on Sunday lunchtime. Now, on Monday morning, an uneasiness rested on his shoulders, an otherworldliness chafed and gnawed at his being.

The solid, detached growl of Merlin engines built like a breaking wave in the chill autumnal air. Bryan glanced up at the six Spitfires of 'B' flight swooping into the landing circuit, the yellow patches still intact over the ports of their unfired guns.

As Bryan walked closer, the other five pilots outside the hut hauled themselves to their feet. He waved them down and slumped into a deck chair slightly apart from the others.

"Bugger," he muttered under his breath.

Tuesday, 15 October 1940

Bryan sat in the mess, pushing his scrambled egg around the plate with his fork. The adjutant came in, poured a mug of tea, walked to the table and sat down opposite him.

'Morning, Madge.' Bryan did not lift his eyes from the plate, instead he forked a lump of the egg breakfast into his mouth, forcing it down with a grimace.

'Look, Bryan, I'm sorry about yesterday. But I can't help it if it's my job to point out the rules. You can't run a bloody air force if you don't have rules.'

Bryan looked up, 'Do you know Balham tube station at all?' he asked.

The older man nodded, 'Been through it on my way up to the Oval cricket ground.'

'I was there on Sunday evening,' he laid his fork on the table, 'or I would've been, if Jenny hadn't suggested we walk back from Clapham Common rather than take the Underground. There's probably a rule that prevents me talking about it, but to Hell with it.'

The adjutant said nothing.

'It was a single bomb, a bloody big one. We saw it fall, like a lightning strike. God only knows how many people got trapped in that station.'

'They have wonderful rescue teams. I'm sure they did their best to get them out.'

'No, Madge,' Bryan shook his head, 'not this time. The explosion ruptured the main sewer pipes. The poor bastards drowned in filth, pinned down under the rubble.'

The adjutant straightened his back and exhaled a long breath, 'We'll be away from all this in a week, Bryan. When we get to Scotland there'll be a chance to relax and forget all the bad things.'

Bryan dropped his eyes back to his eggs and picked up his fork.

'Who is Jenny?' the older man asked.

Bryan raised his head and stared through his companion.

'I'm not sure yet.'

He got up and walked out the door, the fork still dangling from his hand.

***

Bryan's Spitfire climbed steadily away from the rough grass of Kenley's landing strip. He flew at the head of 'A' flight, five other Spitfires climbing in formation around him.

He thumbed the transmit button, 'Flight Leader here, course one-zero-zero, angels three thousand. We'll stooge over as far as Maidstone and then double back and drift south until we get to the seaside. Watch out for 'B' flight on their way home. We don't want any hunting accidents. Loosen up, stay alert.'

The group levelled out at three thousand feet. Four pairs of eyes scanned the terrain below for low-level fighter-bombers, the other two pilots peered into the grey blankness of the autumnal English sky, wary of danger from above.

'Yellow Three to Flight Leader,' Simmonds' voice crackled onto the air. 'That's 'B' flight above us. They'll be crossing over from the starboard quarter.'

Bryan glanced up and smiled as the leader of the other flight dipped his wing to get a better view of the 'bogeys' below him, then waggle his wings in recognition.

The dark smudge of Maidstone's crowded buildings, grey against the brown landscape, rolled out over the horizon's edge.

'Beehive Control to Bluebird 'A' flight. Observers are calling twenty hostiles crossing the coast south of Folkestone. Low and fast, repeat, low and fast.'

Bryan glanced at his compass and calculated the heading.

'Flight Leader to 'A' flight, follow me onto vector one-two-five. Let's lose some height, that should bring us head-on with the bastards. We engage in sections. Green Section loosen up a bit, Yellow Section stick with me.'

The three aircraft of Green Section drifted away to port as the whole flight banked to starboard and sunk closer to the rushing fields. Their descent lifted the horizon and Bryan discerned a few tiny black specks against the sooty clouds, clawing for more altitude.

'They called twenty,' he muttered, 'where are they?'

Bryan squinted against the blur of his propeller. There! A speck of yellow moving against the dun earth… and another.

Bryan stabbed transmit, 'Bandits ahead and below. Green Section break left, Yellow Section break right. They've got top cover so watch your tails. Engage the lower formation. They have the bombs. Tally-ho!'

Bryan flipped off the safety and dipped his nose another fraction. The German fighter-bombers barrelled towards him at no more than five hundred feet, their angry yellow cowlings growing larger at an alarming speed. He stabbed the firing button for a second before the enemy flashed below him.

'Break!'

Bryan kicked his Spitfire onto its starboard wingtip and hauled the stick into his belly. G-force squeezed the air from his lungs and his vision blurred with tears. Then he was around, levelling out and ramming the throttle flat out in pursuit of the raiders. Gritting his teeth, he leant against his harness, willing the gap to close.

Voices exploded into his headset; '109s coming down now…'

'Green Section, break, break, break…'

'Watch out, he's firing…'

'On your tail… On your tail…'

Tracers bent over Bryan's canopy. He sensed Agutter, on his right, peel away steeply to starboard. The tracer curved and sparkled, sliding past Bryan's port wingtip towards Simmonds… A blast of orange flame deflected Simmonds upwards and his Spitfire rolled onto its back. Somehow his transmitter clicked on and his banshee howling rang in Bryan's ears for long seconds until the transmission was silenced by the hard earth.

Bryan kicked his aircraft into a violent jink to the left, then the right. The tracer had stopped. His rearview mirror was clear.

Ahead, in loose formation, twelve bomb-laden Messerschmitts roared towards the capital, one Spitfire laboured to catch them.

The first fringes of the suburbs rolled away underneath and the Germans fanned out across the rooftops.

Bryan wrestled with a moment of indecision, then stuck with the raider nearest to his nose. Closing to firing range Bryan's thumb hovered over the button. Low industrial buildings gave way to houses and a church spire reached up out of the cityscape. Bryan lurched up instinctively, putting his Spitfire squarely in the centre of his quarry's rearview mirror. The Messerschmitt reacted, screaming up into a violent climbing turn, hanging from its propeller. Bryan banked in the same direction, watching his adversary climb to the point of stall. An object detached from the 109 and a parachute unfurled behind it. The fighter hung motionless for a sickly moment, then dropped towards the ground. Bryan gurgled in hopeless rage as the machine, laden with its bomb, dropped onto a terrace of houses, exploding in a ball of flame amongst the collapsing walls.

***

Fagan, the intelligence officer, scribbled in his notepad. 'You say there were six escorts?'

'Six or eight.' Agutter scratched at his tangled hair.

'And they jumped you?'

'We had seen them above us,' Agutter explained, 'but they came down faster in the dive than we expected, I suppose.'

Fagan's gaze turned to Bryan.

Bryan sighed, 'We chased the bombers on their way to London. There were twelve of them. We had to try stopping them.'

'You're claiming one destroyed?'

'No,' Bryan shook his head. 'I didn't fire at him. I was closing in, he got windy and bailed out.'

'And' – Fagan glanced at his notes – 'the other eleven?'

'They dispersed. There were no other defending aircraft.' Bryan's eyes dropped to his shoes, 'I assume they released their bombs and ran.'

Fagan finished scratching on his paper, looked up and smiled, 'Don't let it trouble you, Bryan. Between them it hardly makes up a Heinkel bomb load, and there'll probably be a hundred of those over the city tonight.'

'Do you know anyone in London?' Bryan's monotone rang hard and flat.

Fagan laid down his pen, 'I understand what you're driving at, Bryan. But these tip-and-run raiders are little more than a nuisance, however absurd that sounds. The Germans are bombing London at will practically every night and the only thing we can hope for is bad weather. It's not the best defense plan in the world.'

Bryan chewed his lower lip in silence.

'And next spring,' Fagan continued, 'we can look forward to round two of Winston's Battle of Britain.' His face softened, 'You'll be away to Scotland very soon, Bryan. Enjoy the rest. Get your head straightened out.'

Bryan stood up. 'Come on, Agutter. Next patrol is in fifteen minutes.'

The two men clumped to the door and out onto the grass.

Fagan also stood, walked to the blackboard on the wall and retrieved a cloth from the shelf. He paused for a moment in reflection, then wiped the name 'Simmonds' away with one firm stroke.

Wednesday, 16 October 1940

Tommy Scott opened his eyes and blinked against the low-slanting sunlight that scythed through the windows and flared off the crisp, white material of his pillowslip. The last wisps of an already-forgotten dream fled out of his grasp and the real world solidified around him. He clamped his eyes shut and pressed his face into the pillow.

The sound of bristles on leather teased at his ears and he raised his head to trace the noise. A few beds down, on the opposite side of the Nissen hut, an airman sat on the edge of his mattress, a boot perched on his left hand while he polished the toe with his right.

'Is it getting any better?' the young man asked without looking up from his work.

Tommy swung into a sitting position and scrubbed his face with the palms of his hands, chasing away the last of his slumber.

'I became a father, and lost my crew on the same night. It gets no better, and it gets no worse.'

The other nodded in silence.

Tommy regarded the polishing airman for a long moment. 'You're the first person to start a conversation with me since it happened. I don't really understand why I deserve the big cold shoulder.'

The other man put his gleaming boot on the bed and shuffled the other onto his hand. Dabbing his brush in the polish tin, he pursed his lips and looked across at Tommy.

'I reckon you've scared everybody,' he nodded as he thought it through. 'We all know the law of averages; there's hardly a mission flown where everyone comes back. But we all believe it won't happen to us. We all think we'll be the golden boy who avoids the chop.

'And then you pull the longest straw. You get to go home to your warm, soft wife while your crew goes to the bottom of the sea. Somehow you made it a lot more unlikely that anyone else in this barrack is going to be anywhere near as lucky as you.'

'That's not fair,' Tommy said. 'I booked that leave months ago.'

'It doesn't need to be fair. It's what the lads believe that counts. Some of them think what happened makes you a jinx. No-one wants to associate with a jinx. A jinx steals away whatever luck you've got left.'

Tommy grabbed his towel and toilet bag from his locker and walked out of the hut to the shower block.

***

The airman's words still rankled in Tommy's mind as he shuffled along with the queue towards the serving hatches in the mess. The conversation ahead of him drifted back in snatches;

'…could be an easy posting…'

'…it's a gimmick. You'll end up on heavies when it fails…'

The man directly in front of him piped up, 'Never volunteer for anything, that's my rule.'

Tommy leant forward and tapped the man on the shoulder, 'Volunteer for what?'

'They're putting together crews for a couple of special squadrons,' the man said over his shoulder. 'They're looking for gunners willing to retrain as radio operators. They've been asking around. No takers so far.'

Tommy collected his meal and sat down at a trestle bench. He chewed on his food and weighed the option. The episode that morning had bruised his emotional ties to the squadron. As a reserve gunner that no-one wanted to fly with, he might end up trusting his life to a bunch of green airmen fresh out of training camp, or a rag-tag scratch crew that needed a last-minute stand-in. Retraining would put a few weeks between him and the next operation over enemy territory. That meant more time for his son to have a father. Under the circumstances, it might be worth a bash.

Chapter 7

Friday, 18 October 1940

The telephone jangled on the sparse wooden desk, eager fingers snatched the handset from the cradle halfway through the second ring. The pilots outside the hut stopped what they were doing. Conversations lulled to silence. Newspapers and books lowered into laps as heads cocked to catch the news.

The orderly stepped out onto the grass, 'That's it, gentlemen. Bluebird is ordered to stand down. The next time you take off, you'll be bound for Scotland.'

Bryan stood up from his deckchair and quelled the mounting chatter with his upturned hand, 'Well done, Bluebird Squadron.' Bryan smiled from face to face. 'Enjoy your weekend leave. I'll see you all back here on Monday.'

A ragged cheer burst from the pilots and they trailed off to get showered and changed. Bryan lit a cigarette and watched them go. Then he cast his gaze around the aerodrome. A Hurricane squadron started their engines across the field, off to play cat-and-mouse games with the piecemeal intruders. Over in dispersal, the news of the stand-down reached Bluebird's ground crews and men slapped each other on the back, or stood looking at their aircraft, hands on hips, like they were beholding them for the first time.

'We'll never see such days again, I'll warrant.' The adjutant's voice disturbed his reverie.

'Hello, Harry.' Bryan blew out a trail of smoke. 'At least not until next spring. Do you fancy a beer?'

The older man nodded and the pair strolled towards the mess.

'What are your plans for the weekend pass?' the adjutant asked.

'I may well go for a look around London while most of it is still there.'

'And that young lady you mentioned? Jenny? Is she part of the plan?'

Bryan stayed silent.

The adjutant back-pedalled: 'You can be proud of yourself, Bryan.' His gesture took in the whole airfield. 'It's been one hell of a summer.'

The pair strode through the mess door, straight to the bar.

'Two pints of bitter, please.' Bryan turned to the adjutant. 'We lost too many and killed too few, Madge. That's the brutal mathematical truth of it. Now we're moving our best guns out of the front line. It makes no sense.'

The older man took off his cap and reached for the pint set before him, 'To be honest, Bryan, if you look at the maths, you've been pushing your luck for several weeks now. Living under the stresses of running a fighter squadron… you can't fathom what it's done to your nerves. This move will probably save your life.'

A wry smile creased Bryan's face. 'Last week I nearly got the chop from a bloody Italian biplane. A day later I was making love…' his voice trailed off.

The adjutant placed a hand on Bryan's shoulder, 'Hopefully this girl will give you pause for thought. Having someone to love makes a man put a greater value on his own skin.'

Bryan picked up his pint and took a long draught. 'In all probability I have nothing to offer a woman except the prospect of bad news delivered in a telegram. Jenny knows that. I don't think she sees me as any more than a fling.'

'Why don't you try changing her mind? You might both be pleasantly surprised with the results.' The adjutant drained his pint, 'Right I've got a bucket-load of paperwork to get tied up. Think on it, Bryan. God knows, you deserve it.'

Bryan watched the other man leave and finished his own pint. The steward approached to clear away the empty glasses.

'Whisky, please. A large one.'

Bryan signed the chit for the drinks and walked, whisky in hand, back to his office. Seated behind the desk he sipped the amber liquid and glanced at his watch. Nearly 6 o'clock. Jenny would have left work and she'd be on a bus heading for Victoria. There she'd jostle in the crowds to find a space on a southbound train and stand crushed into the backs of strangers all the way to Clapham Junction, where most travelers disembarked to catch other trains on other lines. She may even get a seat for the last five minutes until the train clattered across the bridge into Balham station. He wondered if they'd begun fixing the hole in the road as he stared at the chipped bakelite telephone on his desk.

※※※

Jenny sighed with relief as the doors swung open at Clapham Junction and the carriage disgorged its human load onto the twilit platforms. A man standing next to her stepped aside and indicated a vacant seat. She smiled her thanks and sat down. The man's hungry eyes lingered on her. She gave him a moment to stop, but his gaze remained insatiable. She stood and walked to the other end of the carriage, found another seat by the window and sat with her back to the man. Outside, the shapes of buildings loomed past in the gathering gloom. The train slowed on its approach to Balham station and the dark, brooding silhouettes yielded a gap as the track crossed the bridge over the road. Below, dimly lit with red lamps, the crater in the street yawned like the maw of a sleeping behemoth. Men in dark blue overalls worked around its edges.

Jenny stood, and a shiver of sensuous memory prickled down her spine. Moving to the door she chanced a glance at the man with the avaricious eyes. He was engrossed in reading his newspaper, squinting in the dimness, and did not register her look. The train shuddered to a halt and Jenny alighted, the strange tingle persisted.

Trotting down the steps she averted her gaze from the blocked-off entrance to the tube station as she passed. Out onto the pavement she slowed her step and breathed deeply of the chill evening air. It had been a hectic week and she had lost herself in the reams of reports flooding across her desk. Now the man on the train and the desire in his eyes had snagged a hook into her mind and her thoughts wandered to Bryan and the memory of strong hands on her skin.

She crossed the road with exaggerated care and her heels skittered along the opposite pavement to scrunch into the shingle as she walked into the courtyard bounding Du Cane Court. Pushing through the doors she hurried across the lobby. Keeping her head down as she passed the porter, she stepped into an open lift. The doors closed behind her and she caught her reflection in the mirrored wall. Her cheeks glowed red with a wanton flush and her pupils dilated at the sight of it. She turned and faced the blank doors, feeling the teasing whirr of the lift cables through the soles of her shoes. The bell dinged and the lights clicked up until the lift slowed and stopped at the sixth floor. Trotting down the corridor she opened the door to her flat.

'Alice, are you here?'

There was no answer, so Jenny walked to the living room, pulled the blackout curtains closed and groped along the wall for the light switch. The bulbs flickered to life. She checked the curtains were properly closed and slipped into the bathroom to turn on the bath taps.

The telephone jangled, tearing through the silence. She picked it up at the third ring.

'Hello…

'Oh. Hello, Bryan. It's nice to hear from you…

'Yes. As it happens, I'm at a loose end…

'That's fine. I'll see you tomorrow afternoon…

'Yes…

'Goodbye.'

Jenny replaced the handset as if it were fragile, and took a deep, steadying breath. She walked to the bathroom, lit a few candles and shut off the taps. The flames softened and blurred through the steam rising from the tub. A small and tender ache started in the base of her stomach and worked down as she peeled the clothes from her body, delighting in the faint chill of the cold bathroom that tickled over her skin. Naked, she eased into the hot water and flipped her long hair over the edge of the bathtub. Settling down into the warmth, she pressed and stroked her belly where the ember of desire glowed and strengthened.

Saturday, 19 October 1940

Alice sat on the edge of Jenny's bed watching her friend apply red lipstick. The stick was worn down to a stub and Jenny dibbed it with a small paintbrush and dabbed the dwindling remnants carefully onto her lips.

'What're you going to do when you run out?'

Jenny paused in her work. 'Look slightly less gorgeous I suppose.' She resumed her dabbing, 'Or borrow yours.'

'Why should I help you keep a Spitfire pilot?'

Jenny frowned, 'I am not keeping him. I'm just *seeing* him.'

A wicked grin creased Alice's face, 'Are you planning on *seeing* as much of him as you did last time?'

Jenny glanced sideways at her friend, 'You're not exactly Florence Nightingale, yourself.' She paused and wrinkled her brow, 'I don't know. I feel like I want to. I know that I shouldn't and it sort of makes me want to even more. I suppose I'll see how I feel when he's here.'

'How would you feel about a cup of tea?'

'Oh. I'd love one.'

***

Bryan parked up in the courtyard and climbed out of the Humber. He straightened his overcoat, checked his tie in the wing mirror and walked towards the entrance. Jenny's final words to him on Monday echoed in his mind.

'Yet here I am,' he breathed to himself and pushed through the doors. He stood by the desk while the porter called Jenny, then sat and waited for her to arrive.

The lift door pinged and Jenny emerged.

'You should've come up,' she called as she walked towards him. 'Alice was most keen to meet you again.'

Bryan stood, 'I didn't want to presume anything.' He bent to kiss her cheek, 'You look lovely.'

Jenny smiled, 'Good. That's exactly what I was aiming for.' She linked her arm in his, 'Come on, I thought we'd take the train into town, have a drink in Covent Garden and take stroll.'

Bryan held the door open for her, 'Sounds like fun.'

'And tonight,' she continued, 'a special treat.'

Bryan relinked their arms as they walked across the courtyard, 'Should I guess?'

Jenny giggled, 'No. There's a club on the seventh floor of the building. They have a restaurant and a piano player. I've booked us a table.'

They walked towards the station. Beyond it the workman toiled around the crater. As they drew nearer a warden held up his hand.

'Could I ask you to wait a moment, please?'

Two soldiers emerged from the entrance to the shattered tube station. Between them they carried a stretcher on which lay a body wrapped entirely in tarpaulin. They lifted their load into the back of an army ambulance and closed the doors. The warden waved the pedestrians to continue on their way.

Bryan glanced down at Jenny, 'Are you alright?'

Jenny nodded, 'I walk past this mess every day.' She glanced up with a wan smile, 'Let's go and live a little.'

They climbed the stairs to the mainline platforms, boarded a train to Victoria and sat down.

'They're still not sure how many people got trapped down there,' Jenny said. 'I've heard it might take a month or more to dig them all out.' She sighed, 'Try imagining, your husband' – she paused – 'or your lover… simply didn't arrive when you were expecting them, and no-one could tell you where they might be. It's too much to contemplate.'

Bryan placed his hand on hers, 'I'm afraid I'm developing what you might call a 'surgeon's view' of suffering.' He grimaced, 'I have to sleep at night, after all.'

Jenny squeezed his hand, 'Enough. Let's talk about something else.' She smiled with mischief, 'Do you remember Beaky Jones at school?'

Bryan snorted a laugh, 'The music teacher? He told me I was tone deaf, which obviously stymied my plans for a career in opera…'

Their laughter punctuated the rest of the journey into town. From Victoria they took a taxi to Covent Garden. Bryan paid the driver and they spilled out onto the Piazza.

The columns and arches of the main building were stuffed with sandbags and an old man sat on an upturned bucket playing an accordion. Passers-by occasionally dropped coins into a tin mug between his feet.

'Come on,' Jenny urged, 'I know a pub you'll like.'

She grabbed his hand and led him away from the Piazza and around a corner. A small stone-paved alleyway cleaved a gap between the buildings and at the end stood The Lamb and Flag.

They pushed through the doors and ordered a drink at the dim, wood-panelled bar. Then, finding a table, they sat down.

Bryan sipped his pint, 'You're very at home in the city.'

Jenny nodded, 'I love it. There's something about being anonymous in the crowd that makes me feel… I don't know, sort of powerful. When I was younger I used to travel down from Hampstead with my friends almost every weekend. We became proper little city rats.'

Bryan shook his head, 'My parents didn't allow me that kind of freedom. I've always felt like a bit of a sore thumb in London. And now the place is being torn apart piece by piece.'

'They say you never know what you've got…' Jenny smiled. 'Finish your drink. Let's take a walk down The Strand and visit Nelson.'

***

Twilight nibbled the edges of the sky as they walked away from Balham station. Sentries stood easy at the steps to the tube line, but recovery work had ceased for the day. They strolled the short distance to Du Cane Court and entered the lobby where the porters busied themselves blacking out the windows.

'You said you'd booked a table?'

'Yes.' Jenny glanced at her watch, 'Not for half an hour or so, yet. But that doesn't matter,' she smiled broadly, 'there's a cocktail bar up there too.'

On the seventh floor they walked into the restaurant. Sleek, shiny black furniture contrasted sharply with light polished oak on the floors and walls. Bryan stopped for a moment and surveyed the luxurious décor.

'I know!' Jenny said. 'I told you, if it weren't for Hitler and the war I couldn't afford to live here.'

They ordered two Martinis and found a seat.

'Thanks for a wonderful afternoon, Jenny. To be honest, I wasn't sure I'd get to see you again.'

Jenny stirred her drink with the olive, 'Think about what you're saying, Bryan. Neither of us can be sure about anything. They're dropping bombs on me and they're trying to shoot you out of the sky. It's like a game of Russian Roulette where somebody else is pulling the trigger.'

'I meant I didn't know whether you'd *want* to see me again.'

Jenny's eyes flitted up from her drink and a wry smile spread across her face, 'See previous answer.'

A moment's silence stretched between them as Jenny swirled her olive around the glass.

'I have some news,' Bryan continued. 'Bluebird Squadron is moving up to Scotland on Monday.'

'That is such good news.' Jenny reached across and squeezed his hand, 'It will be a lot quieter up there, a lot safer.'

'I had hoped you might be a little upset.'

Jenny looked into his eyes, 'Let's go through, I think our table's ready.'

***

They were the last to leave the restaurant and the waiter smiled and nodded as he gave Bryan their coats. They pushed through the doors into the dimly lit corridor, descended one flight of stairs to the sixth floor and came to Jenny's door.

'So, Squadron Leader, can I interest you in a nightcap?'

Jenny opened the door and kicked off her shoes. Bryan laid their coats on the chair in the hallway and held the door open with an outstretched arm so the lights in the corridor penetrated the flat.

'Good girl,' Jenny purred. 'Alice closed the blackouts before she went out.'

A table lamp came on in the living room and Bryan let the door close.

'What kind of war is this that makes an enemy out of the light?' she sighed. 'Take a seat. It's brandy again, I'm afraid.'

He sat down, 'I can live with that.'

He heard the clink of bottle on glass from the kitchen and enjoyed the feeling of sexual tension creeping into his stomach.

Jenny returned and crouched next to his chair, handing him his drink. She took a sip from her own and placed the glass on the coffee table.

The lamp backlit her and chocolate tones glinted in her hair. Bryan reached out to stroke it.

'Maybe,' he said softly, 'if we'd met earlier, before the war…'

'We did. Remember?' she smiled, 'and you didn't even notice me.'

Bryan frowned and gazed down into his drink. Jenny lifted his chin and leant over to kiss him. The tenderness of her lips overlaid a breathless passion and Bryan felt the blood quicken in his temples.

She pulled her head back to regard him. 'But here we are.' She stood, scooped up her drink and walked along the hallway to her bedroom. Bryan finished his drink, placed the glass on the coffee table and followed her.

He found her standing by the window in the darkened bedroom staring out across London, watching the searchlights slash and probe the sky across the capital. Her head dipped slightly as she heard Bryan enter the room behind her, then she returned her gaze to the tenebrous expanse of the city.

'I watch the raids every night until I can't stay awake anymore.' She took a sip from her drink, 'I'm glad you called. I'm glad you're here.'

Bryan stood behind her and put his arms around her middle. 'I'm sorry,' he said. 'It's the fact that you so obviously don't love me that makes the whole thing somehow… awkward.'

Jenny snuggled back into his embrace, 'It's not really so complicated. This whole war is a monstrous act of misplaced passion. People are dying for reasons they don't understand and we'll all have to take a bit of the blame. So why should we feel any guilt for the things that make us know we're alive?' She squeezed his hands clasped against her belly.

Across the dark sky, in the middle distance, three searchlights latched onto a raider, holding it in their icy glare as it traversed the city. Another battery of lights swung upright to join the cone, pinning the bomber like a specimen against the night. Moments later shell bursts blossomed around the beleaguered plane as it weaved in a frantic attempt to escape the dazzling fingers of light. Suddenly it bucked from the force of a direct hit and a cascade of prematurely exploding incendiaries spilled from its belly. Broken, it dropped into a burning spiral of destruction, down and away into the swallowing darkness.

'Jenny, I think I-'

'Shush, Bryan.' Jenny began undoing the buttons of her blouse, 'Don't get obsessed with me, I'm really not worth it.'

Sunday, 20 October 1940

Jenny woke to the dawn light slanting through the open curtains. She pulled a stray strand of hair from her mouth and arched her back against the stiffness of her muscles. She reached out to find the other side of her bed empty. A piece of paper, neatly folded, lay on the other pillow. She grasped it and flattened it out. Written there in pencil were the words *'I'm not going.'*

PART 2

MERIDIEM

Chapter 8

It was still early morning when Bryan's Humber swept past the guard hut at Kenley Aerodrome and cruised to a halt outside the officers' mess. He rolled out of the car and strode towards the station offices. Through the window he noted the adjutant's desk lamp illuminated a figure hunched over the desk. Trotting up the steps he pushed through the entrance and clopped the short distance along the boarded corridor to the adjutant's door. He knocked once and went in.

Harry Stiles raised his head from the chaotic spread of papers on his desk, 'Hello, Bryan. You're back early. Anything wrong?'

Bryan slumped down into a chair and scrabbled in his pockets for his cigarettes, 'You said they needed pilots for night-fighting.'

The other man nodded.

Bryan lit a cigarette, 'How do I go about volunteering?'

Stiles leant back in his chair, 'Should I ask what's brought this on?'

'No,' Bryan's eyes flashed, 'you should tell me how I go about volunteering.'

The adjutant opened a drawer and shuffled amongst some forms, 'Do you want to take some time and sleep on this? The admin people won't be around until Monday, so it makes no odds. You might want to consider the implications.'

'And they are?'

'Well, you relinquish leadership of a squadron, so that will stick on your record…'

Bryan nodded.

'And it's goodbye to single-seat fighters.' Stiles leant forward, 'And, quite frankly, Bluebird Squadron will miss your example. There's still a lot of work to be done on the newer pilots, and we'll probably be heading back to the south coast by Easter at the latest. You've got many friends in this squadron, don't discount that.'

'I can't leave…' Her name stuck in his throat and he gritted his teeth against the guilt. 'I can't leave London.' He gestured at the ceiling, shaking his head disconsolately, 'The bombers…'

'Alright, Bryan.' The adjutant picked up his pen, 'Let's get the form filled out.' He paused in his scribbling and looked up, 'I really hope everything works out for you.'

Monday, 21 October 1940

Bluebird's Spitfires coughed and choked into life around the dispersal pens of Kenley. One by one the squadron's full complement of eighteen aircraft taxied out onto the grass strip and roared into the air. The first flight to take off banked into the circuit to await the others. Once all became airborne, the squadron formed into six vics of three, dipped in salute over the aerodrome and climbed away northwards into the grey October sky, away from the Channel, away from the menace of German raiders.

Bryan and the adjutant watched them go.

'I telephoned your transfer request through this morning,' Stiles said, 'and they'll post the paperwork direct to your new station.'

Bryan's eyes lingered on the sky, squinting at the dots receding against the grimy clouds, 'And that's where?'

'You're joining 604 Squadron at Middle Wallop.'

'And that's *where*?'

'In between Salisbury and Winchester. Lovely part of the world by all accounts. You're required to report by midday on Wednesday.' He smiled, 'I'm packing off the ground crews this afternoon, but I'm not away until the morning. So, if you fancy a couple of beers this evening?'

The sight and sound of Bluebird Squadron faded into the distance.

Bryan nodded, 'It doesn't seem like there's much else left to do.'

Tuesday, 22 October 1940

Bryan brushed his teeth, screwing his face against the pounding in his forehead. He threw his toilet bag into his suitcase and fastened the leather straps. One last check around the room and out, down the corridor to where his Humber sat waiting, grimy and black. A flight of three Hurricanes buzzed the field and banked away into the landing circuit. Bryan sucked in the faint taste of cordite in their backwash, a testament to recent combat.

He threw his suitcase into the back seat and climbed in. The engine started on the first turn and he pulled away down the drive. The guard on the gate saluted as he passed. Bryan gunned the engine and swung north, towards London.

***

Bryan pulled up into the courtyard of Du Cane Court and looked at his watch. It was just past lunchtime. He locked up his car and strolled towards the railway station.

The crater still gaped between the wrecked shops on the High Road. He walked past the station and peered over the barrier at the crater's edge. Ladders poked up from its depths and the sounds of hammering and digging echoed up to the road. An army guard eyed him with lazy suspicion.

'I saw it hit,' Bryan said, nodding at the chasm.

The guard wrinkled his nose and returned to eyes front.

Bryan strode back to the station, climbed the stairs to the mainline and boarded the next Victoria-bound train. Under the benign arch of broad daylight, the general public displayed a kinder outlook to his uniform. Women smiled at him with pleasant, bovine warmth, and men nodded, sometimes touching the peaks of their hats. A young boy sat on the opposite side of the carriage, apparently alone, staring at Bryan with unblinking eyes.

'Shouldn't you be at school?' Bryan said.

'Bombed out,' the boy replied. 'Are you a fighter pilot?'

'Yes, I am.'

'I bet you don't fly a Spitfire.'

'No, I'm afraid I don't.'

'You can't be very good, then. Not if you don't fly a Spitfire.'

The boy, satisfied he had put the world to rights, turned to stare out of the window at the slate roofs gliding past below the elevated track.

Belching great furls of steam, the train sighed to a halt at Victoria. The doors swung open, clattering a tattoo along the side of the carriages as people flowed out of the train and hurried on their way.

Bryan had no appointments to keep, so he loitered on the platform to light a cigarette and look around at the cavernous station. Surprisingly, there was no bomb damage to be seen, and he could imagine no bigger target. Shaking his head, he sauntered off in search of food.

The steamy windows of the Station Café drew him across the concourse and he was soon hunched over a hot mug of tea and a round of toast, sparingly scraped with butter. His eyes rested on the girl behind the counter who had served him and taken his money.

'Doesn't it worry you?' he asked.

The girl looked up from polishing cutlery, 'Doesn't *what* worry me, sir?'

'Working in the railway station,' he grimaced skyward, 'when there are bombers about.'

The girl smiled, 'I don't think that much about it, to be honest. We had a bit of a scare last month when one of them crashed in the forecourt.' She furrowed her brow, 'But I'm more scared at home. We don't have a shelter so we have to sit under the stairs.' Her smile dropped away to introspection and she bent to polishing again.

Bryan finished his tea and stood to leave. He dropped a penny in the tips jar as he passed the counter. The girl watched him go in silence.

Bryan emerged from the station and walked across the forecourt. He ignored the taxi rank with its expectant cabdrivers and started east on foot towards the river. Halfway down the tall funnel of buildings bounding Victoria Street was a large ragged gap, newly punched into the tall façade. Bryan slowed as he approached. The fetid aftertaste of brick dust and burnt timber clung around the remains of two buildings. One still thrust its metal girder skeleton upwards from the pavement, although blast had stripped it of its once elegant flesh. Its neighbour had succumbed completely, sitting in a heap of layered masonry in the open grave of its own basement. Bryan strode on, fastening his overcoat against the chill creeping over his skin.

He strode on into the sedate bustle of Parliament Square. Khaki-uniformed sentinels with fixed bayonets dotted the long walls, in between the squat megaliths of grey sandbags, stacked in moss tinged regimentation around doorways, guard huts and the fine statues of Empire. Bryan hurried past, through the shadow of The Clock Tower, its bulk looming in naked vulnerability as if offering Big Ben to the care of the gods.

A river breeze ruffled the air as Bryan crossed the road and dropped down to the walkway on the north bank. His pace slowed to match the ebbing tide and the physical tensions that had stiffened his muscles for the past two days slackened with the river's languid flow.

Stepping up his pace again he followed the curve of the Thames eastwards and crossed to the south bank at Blackfriars. He continued east, watching the tugs battling the tide until the urge took him to strike out into the labyrinthine streets lined with the homes, shops and pubs of the city he'd stayed to defend. Through Southwark towards Elephant and Castle, he meandered his way south. Dogs sniffed at his trousers as he passed and damp, unswept leaves stuck to the soles of his shoes. Occasional broken tiles and cracked panes bore testament to the blast wave from nearby bomb strikes in neighbouring roads.

Aircraft noise teased at the edge of Bryan's hearing and he stopped walking, cocking his head to better catch the sound. It was more than one engine, but the echoing baffle formed by the rows of terraced houses blurred its direction. A short, spluttering burst of machine gun fire sliced through the growl of pistons, seeming almost delicate with distance. Bullets clattered into the roof and wall of a house further down the road.

'Bloody hell.' Bryan scurried to the opposite side of the road and crouched in the lee of a garden wall scanning the sky beyond the ridge tiles. The engines swelled to a crescendo and a yellow-nosed Messerschmitt fighter careened into view only one hundred feet above the rooftops. As it passed over, a large black shape swung down from its fuselage and, with an audible 'clank', disengaged from its cradle to begin its wobbling downward arc. The German hauled into a climbing bank and the racket echoing between the houses redoubled as a pursuing Hurricane skidded outside the intruder's turn and accelerated into the chase.

'*Boom…*'

Bryan's attention snapped away from the battle above as the suck and blow of blast wave compression rattled the windows and doorknobs around him. A black, boiling smoke cloud rolled over itself into the sky two hundred yards behind the terraced houses. Bryan ran along the road in the direction he'd been walking, searching for a left turn that would take him closer to the bomb strike. An alley opened up between the houses. He dashed down its length, body-swerving dustbins and rabbit hutches. The alley dog-legged left into an enclosed yard. Dead end.

'Shit.'

Bryan retraced his steps to the road and ran in the other direction. The black smoke cloud had detached itself from the earth and drifted away in the breeze, elongating as it went, like a dark, spindly finger pointing back at the doom it had delivered.

Bryan accelerated to a sprint, skittering to a halt at a crossroads and turning right. Running hard, he cursed the blank end walls of the terraced rows as he pounded down their length. Another crossroads, another right turn, and there it was ahead of him.

Glass and rubble fanned out into the road in a ghastly mix with broken cups and cutlery. The tea room's sign swung lopsided on its bracket from a single hook. Breathless now, Bryan loped along the pavement towards the wrecked façade. The road was empty, but Bryan heard coughing and raised voices coming from inside the building. He slid to a halt and peered through the shattered front wall. From the billowing dust two soldiers emerged dragging a younger man between them. Fear danced on the man's features and his voiced cracked with terror; 'Please, no. You don't understand. She's my friend, I know her.'

'What's happening, lads?' Bryan's confusion coloured his own voice with tension.

The larger of the soldiers turned to him. 'Looter,' he said. 'This tasty gentleman was helping himself to a lady's jewellery and her purse.'

'But he knows her. He's just said so.'

'We saw him slinking in there after the bomb hit. He doesn't know her. She's got no face left.' He turned to his companion, 'Around the back. In the yard. That'll do.'

Bryan stepped forward, 'What are you going to do?'

The soldier raised his arm and placed the flat of his palm squarely on Bryan's chest, 'Like I said, he's a looter. You've seen the public notices. I suggest you run along and leave us to it.'

The soldiers dragged the sobbing man along the pavement and down the side of the broken building into the yard behind.

Bryan stood frozen for a moment, then cast his frantic gaze up and down the street. A police car approached the junction at the end of the road. Bryan ran towards it waving his arm and shouting.

'Hey. Hey, it's down here. Come quick. They're going to shoot him.'

The police car crossed the junction and accelerated towards him. As it drew level it stopped and the officer in the passenger seat wound down his window.

'The tea room,' Bryan pointed, 'it's been hit. Two soldiers have collared a looter. I think they're going to bloody well shoot him.'

The police car drove on and Bryan strode after it back towards the wrecked building. The policemen got out as the soldiers emerged. Bryan couldn't hear what they said, but he could see the soldiers handing over the looted property. He came level with the group as the policemen started towards the yard and the troops turned to leave. The bigger soldier levelled cold eyes at Bryan as he slung his rifle and walked away. Bryan swallowed hard and stumbled after the policemen.

The trio entered the shop's yard. Empty wooden crates stood in neat piles, a handcart and a sack barrow stood next to the back door. In the middle of the space knelt the thief. Sobbing wracked his body and drool hung in a sickly curtain from his lower lip. He peered at the newcomers from under rapidly swelling brows, and his nose, skewed sideways across his face, dripped blood into the dust. With his left hand he cradled his right wrist close to his chest. The fingers on his right hand bent backwards at horribly unnatural angles.

***

The police car drew up on the road outside Du Cane Court and the driver twisted in his seat to smile at Bryan, 'Here we are, sir. Thanks for your help this afternoon.'

'It doesn't feel like I did anything.'

'Well, you might've saved that looter's life.' His smile evaporated, 'For all it's worth.'

'Isn't it the bombs?' Bryan asked. 'Isn't it possible the bombs change the way people behave? Lead them to make bad choices?'

'Maybe, sir,' the policeman pursed his lips, 'or maybe they give London's vermin the opportunities they would be waiting for anyway.'

Bryan climbed out and walked into the courtyard. It was well past 6 o'clock and the sky darkened around the brooding mass of the building. Blackout curtains already blotted out many windows. Some glowed with light, the occupants of the flats, perhaps distracted, still unaware of the deepening gloom outside.

Bryan strode through the entrance, entered the lift, and within moments found himself in front of Jenny's door. His uncertainties uncoiled to fill his stomach. The unfamiliar feelings that had stalked his recent days, and the vulnerability they pressed upon him, summoned loveless spectres from the depths of his leaden youth. But the brute force of elemental desire had dragged him here once more. He raised his hand to knock.

'Hello, Bryan.'

He started at the voice behind him, composed himself, and turned.

'Hello, Jenny,' he smiled, 'I was in town…'

A wry smile twisted on Jenny's lips, 'All we have is vegetable soup, and that's mostly potatoes. You're welcome to share if you're hungry.'

She stepped between him and the door, the scent of her hair teased into his nostrils and her proximity traced a tingle down his neck.

'Vegetable soup sounds perfect.'

Jenny unlocked the door and strode into her bedroom. She threw her handbag onto the bed and pulled the blackouts closed. Bryan walked down the hall to the lounge and closed the blackouts there.

'Thank you,' Jenny said as she flicked on the lights and breezed into the kitchen. She lit the gas under the large, covered pot that stood on the stove, 'I am *so* hungry.'

Bryan sat down at the kitchen table while Jenny stirred the soup.

She glanced over her shoulder and smiled, 'We must make sure we leave some for Alice.'

Silence settled between them for long minutes and Bryan's knots of anxiety loosened as he watched Jenny taste the food, add a pinch of salt and turn off the gas.

She pulled two bowls from a shelf, ladled in the soup and placed them on the table.

'You left a note.' She avoided eye contact as she fetched two spoons.

'Yes. I'm not going to Scotland. I've asked for a transfer.'

Jenny handed him a spoon and sat down.

'A transfer?'

'I'm joining a squadron in Hampshire.'

Jenny frowned, 'I thought rotation was meant to give pilots a rest.' Her voice roughened at the edges, 'How can they let you hop over to another squadron and simply carry on?'

'They asked for volunteers. It's a new development.'

Jenny cocked her head in silent question.

'Night-fighters,' he took a sip of the hot soup, 'we'll be operating against the bombers at night.'

Jenny regarded him in silence for a moment, her eyes flicking over his features.

'So instead of taking the break you deserve, you've chosen to fly about in the dark over London trying to shoot down bombers.'

'Someone has to-'

'But why you, Bryan?' Her voice hardened in tone but dropped in volume, 'You *deserve* to step back from it. You've done your bit. You've been at the sharp end *all summer*. What were you thinking?'

Bryan dropped his eyes for a moment, 'I suppose I was thinking about the things I've seen. The shelterers in the tunnels. The gaps in the terraces.

The rubble in the roads. The bodies they're still pulling out of the tube station.

'I went into town this afternoon for a walk. A year ago, that would've been a wholly unremarkable thing to do. Today, I saw a tea room blown to hell and two soldiers beat a looter halfway senseless. A tea room for Pete's sake. I can't walk away from all of that.'

Outside the mounting wail of the air raid sirens nibbled at the tension hanging between them.

Bryan reached across the table to take Jenny's hand, 'And I was thinking about you-'

'Don't you dare,' Jenny snapped, pulling her hand away, 'I'm not prepared to carry a weight that heavy to your funeral, nor do I expect you to carry it to mine. It's not fair.'

'I'm sorry…'

'No. Don't be…' Her tone softened and she reached back to grasp his hand. 'It's not your fault that I can't say what you want to hear. But I *don't* want you to get killed.' She squeezed his hand. 'Let's live for as long as we're allowed to. Let's live without debts or anchors.' Her eyes glistened with infant tears, 'And let's die without regrets.'

The windows rattled to the opening salvoes from the Clapham anti-aircraft battery, prising the night apart to throw speculative explosions into the inky London sky.

Jenny let go of his hand and returned to her soup.

'I *know*, Bryan,' she murmured, 'but please, don't say it. Just be content that I know.'

Wednesday, 23 October 1940

The feeling he was being watched tickled Bryan out of his slumber. He opened his eyes to see Jenny's face. She was propped up on her elbow, regarding him with an unreadable expression.

'So where is this new station?' she asked.

'Mmmm?' Bryan squeezed the bridge of his nose and blinked the sleep from his eyes.

'The one you're moving to?'

'You know I shouldn't tell you that.'

'I work for The Ministry, Bryan. I could tell Hitler much more interesting things than where you're going to be hanging your hat.'

Bryan regarded her for a moment, but her expression didn't change.

'It's called Middle Wallop…' he conceded.

Jenny snorted a laugh.

'…and it lies midway between Over Wallop and Nether Wallop.'

Jenny dropped back onto her pillow and melted into giggles.

Bryan sat up and reached for his watch.

'I have to go. They're expecting me to report there before lunch.' He looked down into Jenny's eyes, 'When can I see you again?'

'I don't know, Bryan,' she smiled, 'what with you having to work nights and everything…'

Bryan grinned in spite of himself. Jenny reached up and pulled him down towards her.

'…so, you need to say goodbye properly.'

***

Alice sat sipping her tea, listening to the murmured farewells exchanged at the flat door. She heard a kiss planted on Jenny's cheek or forehead and the click of the closing door. Jenny trailed into the lounge and leaned back on the sofa.

'You've got 'perfect couple' written all over you,' Alice said.

'We're not a couple. We're just friends.'

'Come on, Jenny. Anyone can see how much he means to you.'

Jenny regarded her friend with a steady gaze, 'It doesn't matter what he means to me. Once the fire and the bullets have finished with him, he'll be gone. Then no amount of feeling will make a difference. He could've transferred to Scotland and been safe. But he's chosen to be a hero, he's chosen the front-line, he's chosen the war.' She closed her eyes as if picturing a face. 'I have an auntie who still loves a man who got squashed into the soil on The Somme. There was nothing left for the army to send home to her. But she loves him still. She gets through her days by clinging on to a photograph and a ghost.' Her brow furrowed, 'Bryan won't stop until the war ends or he gets killed fighting it.'

'But he's alive now,' Alice whispered.

Jenny's eyes snapped open, 'Yes, and that's why I loved him this morning.'

Chapter 9

The sentry at the gate eyed Bryan with suspicion through the guard's hut window as he made the telephone call to confirm a new pilot was expected at Middle Wallop. At length he approached the Humber and leant down to the open window.

'All cleared, sir. Follow the signs to the officers' mess. The squadron leader's office is in the next building along.'

Bryan nodded his thanks and crawled his car up the drive. He pulled up outside the mess and glanced at his watch. Still over an hour before he needed to report for duty. Time for a stroll.

The mess commanded views over the whole aerodrome. Many twin-engine aircraft stood dispersed around the field's perimeter, some under tarpaulin covers, some with maintenance crews tinkering in opened engine panels. Bryan grunted as he lit a cigarette. Bristol Blenheims - the exact same bus he'd been flying at the declaration of war over a year ago. He sucked the smoke deep into his lungs and walked towards the nearest aircraft.

The plane wore its chipped and faded camouflage paint like a spinster aunt at a fashionable party, willing to join in, but sadly behind the times. As Bryan approached, he noticed the top turret had been swapped with a featureless Perspex dome. Getting closer he noted the familiar gun pod on the bottom of the fuselage, its face pierced by four machine gun barrels. He grimaced; only half the punch of his Spitfire. He ducked under the fuselage, examining the unfamiliar aerials poking from the nose and wings.

'Hello, sir?' a rigger approached, rolling a cigarette between grimy fingers.

Bryan straightened, 'Flight Lieutenant Hale. New on squadron. These kites are a bit the worse for wear.'

'We only use the Blenheims for familiarisation and operator training.' The rigger licked and sealed the paper, then pointed with the finished cigarette, 'Our proper kit is away down the other end of the field.'

Bryan squinted in the direction of the rigger's gesture towards some squat, twin-engine machines in the middle distance.

'Now those are Beaufighters. Different proposition altogether.'

'And why should I like those any better?'

The rigger's smile widened, 'There are four 20mm cannons in their bellies.'

Bryan mirrored the rigger's smile, 'That sounds like a good enough reason. Right, I'm off to check in with the squadron leader. Carry on.'

***

Squadron Leader Lawson rose as Bryan entered his office. He offered his hand, Bryan saluted and accepted the shake.

'Sit down, Hale.' Lawson sank back into his leather chair and regarded his new arrival. 'You've come to us from single-seats, I see,' he glanced down at the papers on his desk, 'with quite an impressive operational record, I have to say. Well, we're gearing up to play a different kind of game on this station.' He paused and chuckled, 'You might even call it 'murder in the dark'. It won't be to everyone's taste.'

'I've spent the summer shooting Germans in the back, sir. I have no qualms about carrying on with the job.'

'Good,' Lawson said. 'You'll spend the next couple of days reacquainting yourself with the Blenheim before you start training on interceptions during daylight.

'Tomorrow, we'll team you up with your operator and you'll get the basic instruction on the Airborne Interception equipment.' Lawson leant forward, 'It's all top-secret stuff. We need the Germans to think they're still safe coming over in darkness.' He smiled, 'It'll make them easier to hunt. Here,' he pushed a document across the desk, 'sign this.'

Bryan scanned the document, 'Official Secrets Act?'

Lawson nodded, 'Like I said…' He waited while Bryan signed and then scooped the paper into a drawer. 'Welcome to 604 Squadron, Hale. Our code name is Blackbird. Report to the adjutant at 8 o'clock tomorrow morning.' He stood and offered his hand again, 'Good luck.'

Thursday, 24 October 1940

Bryan and the adjutant, a portly man named George Campbell, walked together towards the lecture hall. Newly-built hangars bounced back a dull gleam from the watery autumn sun and the hoarse roar of engines crackled along the breeze as mechanics tested and tweaked their tuning.

'Your operator is a non-commissioned airman,' the adjutant explained, 'a young sergeant named Tommy Scott, he's been reassigned from air gunner so he's knows the Blenheim inside out. I reckon you'll make a good team.'

They pushed through the door of the large wooden hut. Inside, a few dozen chairs were arranged in uneven rows in front of a desk. On top of the desk stood a large black box with two round screens, gazing blankly over the chairs like a robot owl. Behind the desk stood a tall man in civilian clothes, wearing glasses. In the front row, standing to greet them, was a slight man with an Air Gunner badge on his tunic.

Campbell locked the door behind them and ushered Bryan forward.

He gestured towards the tall man, 'This is Albert Beckwith, our civilian science officer,' then nodded at the uniformed man, 'and Sergeant Thomas Scott, your designated operator.'

Scott smiled, 'Most people call me Tommy, sir.'

The three men sat down and Bryan eyed the strange contraption on the desk with interest.

'This is a demonstration model of the Airborne Interception device, Mark IV,' the scientist began, 'but before I show you how to read the screens, let me define the basic theory.

'You are familiar with echoes. If you shout across a valley and measure how long it takes for the echo to return, you will be able to calculate the width of the valley, knowing the speed at which sound travels. If you used a sound locator to detect the echo, you could also estimate the direction from which the echo has bounced. Essentially AI does this with radio waves instead of sound waves.

'The information thus deduced is displayed on the two cathode ray screens on this machine which is located at the operator's station in the aircraft's fuselage,' he tapped the top of the owlish box. 'The screen on the left shows the contact's bearing in relation to your direction of travel. The other shows the elevation of the contact, in other words, the relative height difference between you and your target.

'The operator,' he nodded at Scott, 'interprets the two readings and conveys instructions to the pilot until the target is sighted and an engagement is made possible.'

'Does it work?' Bryan's question interrupted the scientist's monotonous flow.

Beckwith regarded him over pursed lips, 'Within limitations.' He adjusted his glasses. 'The biggest object in the environment reflecting radio waves is obviously the Earth itself. And it reflects them so well that they will tend to overpower reflections from smaller targets. The lower your altitude, the worse it is.

'If you are flying at ten thousand feet, the ground reflections will limit your detection range to ten thousand feet in *all* directions. Much lower and the equipment becomes, for all practical purposes, ineffective. But this shouldn't cause a problem as most raiders cross the coast at, or above, fifteen thousand feet.'

Bryan looked into the scientist's benign, smiling face, 'Any other limitations?'

Beckwith blinked twice. 'Er, yes. Although the AI switches very quickly between transmit and receive, there is a problem with echoes arriving during the 'transmit' phase of the cycle. In short, they will not be received. This is far more likely to happen at close range when echoes are returning at a higher rate. So, overall it's far more accurate at longer range.'

Bryan leaned forward, 'So what actually happens as we close in?'

'The AI will be rendered ineffective by what we call 'instrumental disturbance' at between one thousand and six hundred feet. To put this in context: on a moonless night, a pilot with good eyesight should be able to spot a medium bomber's silhouette at about one thousand feet.'

Campbell stood up before Bryan's intake of breath turned into another question, 'Thank you Mr Beckwith. I think that just about covers it.'

Beckwith threw a cover over the machine and tidied up the desk.

The adjutant turned to Bryan, 'Sergeant Scott has passed through basic AI training on the ground simulator. So as soon as you've got yourself a few hours flying time on the Blenheim, you'll start interception training together.'

Friday, 25 October 1940

Tommy Scott watched the Blenheim taxi smoothly along the perimeter and swing into the wind at the end of the runway. The engines' roar subsided as the pilot throttled back to complete final checks.

'Who's that?' a rigger sauntered up.

'Flight Lieutenant Hale,' Tommy answered. 'I've been assigned as his operator. He's transferred here from Spitfires.'

'Well, this should be interesting.'

'That's why I'm watching.'

The engine noise swelled once more and the Blenheim surged forward, its rudder twitching from side to side to maintain a straight course. The tail lifted and the engines' roar redoubled as Bryan pushed the throttles fully open. The main wheels left the grass and the aircraft yawed into the crosswind as the landing gear retracted.

The rigger whistled under his breath, 'That's a very tidy take-off. Looks like you've got a good one.'

'Flying's only half of it,' Tommy lit a cigarette. 'He was a bit rude with the boffin yesterday.'

The rigger shrugged, 'As long as he gets you up safely and brings you home in one piece. The rest you can live with.'

Tommy wandered off towards the operations hut. The growl of engines approached the aerodrome and Tommy spun on his heel to face the sound. Bryan's Blenheim broke over the perimeter fence, dipped low to the grass and roared away in a climbing bank.

When Tommy reached the hut, the adjutant was leaning on the doorjamb scratching his chin.

'Hello, Scott.' He nodded at the receding aircraft, 'He can certainly fly.'

'Yes, sir. That he can.'

***

Bryan banked the Blenheim onto the landing circuit and throttled back into his approach. Gear lever down, throttle tweaked to prevent yaw, rudder held steady. The wheels bumped down and the familiar rumble of flying machine over rough grass vibrated the control column in his gloved hands. He taxied up to his dispersal bay and shut down the engines. The flight instructor, wedged against the airframe behind the pilot's seat, slapped him on the shoulder.

'That was excellent, Hale. Have you done any night-flying?'

Bryan continued his shut down procedure, 'Not as such.' He paused in reflection, 'I've flown through heavy clouds on instruments only. That was never a problem.'

'Right. I'll come back for your night-flying assessment tomorrow evening. When you've finished shutting up shop here, I'll see you in the ops hut to update your flying log.'

***

Bryan walked out of the officers' mess into the chill dusk of the late autumn evening. The sound of engines had drawn him out. The noise came from two Beaufighters warming up across the field. Bryan walked along the perimeter track, skirting around behind the aircraft until he reached the end of the grass runway. Here he stood and lit a cigarette in cupped hands to avoid attracting attention to himself.

This was his first close look at the aircraft he was expected to take into combat against the intruders of the night, and he smiled to himself in satisfaction. It was about the same size as the Blenheim but its snubbed nose sat fully behind the propellers, lending it the pugilistic air of a street-hardened prize fighter. The pilot sat hunched in the centre of the cockpit, underlit by the faint glow from his dimmed instruments. The man straightened up, checked the darkening sky for stray aircraft and knocked the throttles forward, swinging onto a runway defined on each side by a line of small lights. The pilot increased his revs and the propwash tore at Bryan's hair and flapped his trouser legs like flags behind his calves. The Beaufighter raced across the grass and clawed into the air.

The buffeting dropped for a moment before the second machine wheeled into position. After a brief pause, its engines screamed to a crescendo and it slid away across the field, climbing into the deepening gloom. Bryan grinned fiercely into the wake of their throbbing chorus as the hunters curved away to hunt their quarry. The lights clacked off on one, then the other side of the runway and Bryan stood alone in the night.

Saturday, 26 October 1940

Bryan sat in the corner of the mess, bunched up in a worn leather armchair, staring balefully at the mug of tea going cold in front of him. He glanced at his watch and sighed. Barely 10 o'clock. His thoughts drifted to Jenny. Perhaps she was taking a leisurely bath after a lie-in, looking forward to her weekend. His muscles bunched against the urge to get up and find a telephone box. He lit a cigarette and shifted his weight to relieve his suddenly restless legs.

The door swung open and four pilots ambled in. They nodded to Bryan in his corner and he followed them with his eyes to the bar. The steward busied himself for a few minutes then placed a tray of drinks on the bar. Three of the men grabbed mugs of tea and squabbled over the sugar bowl. The fourth picked up a pint of beer and took a long draft. This man strolled over to Bryan.

'Flight Lieutenant Alan Carson,' he said as he sat down. 'Welcome to Blackbird Squadron.'

'Bryan Hale. Thank you.' Bryan gestured at the pint, 'That's a bit rash isn't it?'

Carson set his pint down on the table. 'I'm not on ops again until Monday. It's two nights on and two days off, around here. Particularly nice when it coincides with a weekend.'

'Two days off?'

'They say it conserves the night vision. Stops your peepers getting exhausted.'

'And does it work?'

'I have no clue. I haven't seen a single Jerry bomber since we started this lark. Control tells us one is in our vicinity. My operator tells me it's in front of my face. But it's never there.' He shrugged and picked up his beer, 'It's all a bit of a pantomime, really.'

Bryan's frown deepened. 'Is it the equipment or your operator that isn't working properly?'

'Lord only knows.' Carson raised his glass, 'Anyway, chin, chin. No more faffing about for me until Monday.'

***

Dusk descended across the field as Bryan clumped his way through the damp grass to the operations hut. The first of the Beaufighters had left for their patrols, so the runways would be clear for a while.

Bryan swung into the dimly-lit hut and dropped his kit next to the door. A scuffle of boots greeted him and he made out Sergeant Scott standing to attention in the room.

'Good evening, Flight,' the smaller man greeted him.

Bryan waved him back to his seat, 'As long as we're working together, you can forget that nonsense.' Bryan bent to retrieve his logbook and pencil from his kitbag, 'Anyway, what are you doing here? I thought this was a night-flying test.'

'I'm your navigator as well as operator.' Scott relaxed into his chair. 'There's a radio beacon on the station. It's my job to get you back here at the end of the sortie.'

'Right.' Bryan sat down opposite his crew member. 'What do you make of this Air Interception kit? Is it a goer?'

'I've passed all the simulation tests on the ground, and I don't mean to blow my own trumpet, Flight, but it was shockingly easy to get it right. All the operators said the same thing.'

Bryan leant back and scratched his chin, 'It beats me how they can train you to use it when you're sitting in a hut, when they admit the bloody thing doesn't work properly until you get to ten thousand feet.'

Bryan fished out his cigarettes, lit two and handed one to Scott.

'They tell me you served as a gunner on Blenheims before this.' Bryan pulled on his cigarette, 'Why the change?'

'I was on leave when my crew went missing on an op.' Scott's eyes dropped down for a moment. 'They would have re-crewed me, but I heard about this night-fighting lark so I volunteered to come here and retrain as an operator.' He looked up and smiled, 'I reckoned it would be better for me to stooge around over England trying to protect my wife and baby, rather than fly over to Berlin and drop bombs on other people's.'

Bryan considered the other man's face for a moment. 'Well,' he said, dropping his cigarette on the floor and scrunching it out with his heel, 'in that case, we owe it to your wife and baby to make this thing work.'

***

Full darkness blanketed the airfield as Bryan swung the Blenheim onto the end of the runway and waited for clearance. The runway lights ran like two strings of pearls away into the murk before him.

In the fuselage, behind Bryan and the flight instructor, Tommy Scott sat hunched in his seat, muscles tensed. He reached down and pulled his lap belt a notch tighter as the familiar queasy fear of take-off penetrated his intestines. Finally, the engines roared to capacity and Tommy rocked in his seat to the bump and shudder of the airframe as the craft rushed across the grass. His buttocks tightened with the awful lurch as the twin-engine Blenheim lost the friction of the sod and yawed into the ethereal embrace of the air. Tommy sucked in a deep breath and held it while he ticked off in his mind the ascent through the first two thousand feet, the most dangerous minute of space where little mitigation could be expected if something went wrong.

The smooth climb continued and Tommy allowed his bursting lungs to suck in the cold, fresh air that whistled its way into the aged fuselage through ill-fitting hatch seals and the holes left by missing rivets.

'Intercom check, can you hear me operator?' The flight instructor's calm voice intruded in his ears.

'Operator here, loud and clear.'

Tommy shivered as the aircraft's climb reached ever-colder air. His eyes streamed and his nose dribbled into his mask, freezing it to his face. He pulled the mask off, squeezed it and shook out the broken ice. The flat cadence of the flight instructor's voice, calling out course and altitude changes for Bryan to execute, droned in his headphones. He glanced up at the Perspex blister where the spider legs of sub-zero temperatures weaved their sparkling cobwebs in the lee of the howling slipstream. The cold gnawed through the layers of his clothing and finally sunk its teeth into his flesh in search of his very bones. A miserable lethargy descended on him, urging him to surrender to the warmth of sleep.

'Hello, operator,' the flight instructor's voice roused Tommy with a jolt, 'we'll have the bearing for the home beacon when you're ready.'

Tommy creaked his arms and fingers into protesting motion and switched the AI from standby to on. A dull hum intruded on the intercom as the machine flickered to life. He dipped his head to the leather visor and watched the sullen green glow of the cathode ray tubes resolve into a picture he could interpret. At this altitude the ground returns were flat and the radio beacon stood out clearly.

'Operator here, bearing one-five-five please, Flight. It's thirty-five miles to a mug of hot tea.'

Chapter 10

Sunday, 27 October 1940

'Cup of tea?' Alice called through from the kitchen.

Jenny, sitting by the window, broke her reverie to answer, 'Yes, please.'

Her gaze focussed on the grey expanse of the city. Away in the distance a snake of sea mist, pulled westwards by the incoming tide, betrayed the hidden course of the Thames. This silken wraith, encroaching inland from the North Sea, subsumed the buildings on the riverbanks, erasing their solid certainty from the world, like the dreams of an abandoned bride.

Alice put the tea tray on the coffee table and addressed the back of Jenny's head, 'What are you doing?'

Jenny stood and walked to the sofa, 'Exactly what I promised myself I wouldn't do.' She sat down, avoiding eye contact.

Alice stirred the tea. Satisfied it had brewed sufficiently, she poured two cups, 'I'm sorry, my love. You'll have to explain.'

'I'm worrying about Bryan.'

Alice placed the teapot back on the tray and picked up her cup, 'No biscuits, I'm afraid.'

Silence hung between them for long moments.

'They won't know who I am,' Jenny said. 'They won't know it's me who should be told if anything happens.'

'I'm not so sure,' Alice ventured, 'I think most of them write a letter. You know, the one that gets sent if they don't come back.'

'No.' Jenny shook her head, 'Bryan won't do that. He would never dream of apologising for getting killed, not to anyone.'

'But it's obvious he loves you.'

'Yes, it is.' Jenny picked up her teacup, 'But I'm afraid I told him not to.'

Alice sipped her tea, 'How do you fancy a walk across the common? It's Sunday after all. We should get out into the fresh air.'

Jenny looked up, 'Yes, alright. That would be nice.'

***

Bryan and Tommy entered the adjutant's office and sat down. Campbell offered them each a cigarette from an ornate silver box on his desk.

'Well, gentlemen, you've been passed to begin Air Interception training this afternoon. You'll be going up with another training flight where you'll take turns flying as target.'

'In daylight?' Bryan asked.

'Yes.' The adjutant lit his own cigarette, 'It makes no odds to the operator whether it's night or day, he's staring at his little screens anyway. Just make sure you don't let slip any clues to him over the intercom,' he waggled his finger by way of emphasis. 'You'll be carrying one of our special signals officers who be marking Scott's performance, so naturally, as referee, the signals officer will need to maintain visual contact with your target, no matter how far away it might remain.' He smiled benignly and looked from one man to the other.

'How long before we get onto active combat patrols?' Bryan asked.

'There's no guarantee you will, Hale. This whole thing seems to be quite difficult to get right. We're letting a lot of operators go, posting them back to Bomber Command as air gunners. So, if Scott fails muster, you'll have to start again with a new operator and take it from there.'

***

The watery October sun banished the last damp tendrils of the morning mists as Jenny and Alice strolled arm-in-arm along Balham High Road. They cut west through the terrace-lined backstreets and struck north towards the railway station at Wandsworth Common. An engine chugged lazily up to the platforms as they approached. It belched thick bundles of hot steam into the chill autumn air while passengers jumped from the carriages and slammed the heavy doors behind them. The driver gave a short toot on the whistle and the train heaved its weight away, continuing its long trek into the southern suburbs. The disembarked passengers flowed around the two strolling women as they crossed the road, skirted The Hope and Anchor and walked onto the common.

Jenny smiled at the shouts and laughs escaping the pub's windows.

'It's nice to hear people enjoying themselves.'

'I don't think people change,' Alice replied. 'The saints will continue with their good works, the sinners amongst us will enjoy our devilments and the drunks will carry on drinking, war or no war.'

'But it's always there at the back of your mind, isn't it?' Jenny sighed. 'The uncertainty.'

Set back from the path, a ring of sandbags surrounded an anti-aircraft gun emplacement. The long olive-green barrel protruded through camouflage webbing and gaped its silent threat at the quiet sky. Two soldiers leant against the sand-filled hessian sacks, rifles slung and cigarettes dangling, their eyes glued to the sway of the two women as they sauntered past.

'It's a big city to flatten,' Alice smiled wryly, 'and if you believe Mister Churchill, we can take it for a long time yet.'

'Leave poor Winston alone,' Jenny chided. 'It's his *job* to be our lighthouse in the storm. Maybe, in his heart, he's as scared as the rest of us, but he's the only one who can never admit it.'

The path led them to a pond. A motley crew of ducks and geese paddled towards them, hopeful for a gift of bread.

'Maybe this isn't as bad as it gets,' Jenny said. 'Some people say the night raids are meant to keep us on notice during the winter; to keep us hiding in our holes until the invasion comes next spring.'

Alice remained silent. The waterfowl jockeyed for position, cocking their heads in vain anticipation.

'At least we'll have one last Christmas in freedom,' Jenny mused.

Alice snorted a laugh, 'Don't you think Christmas is a bit too German for its own good, what with all the *Santa Claus und Tannenbaums*?'

Jenny giggled at Alice's theatrical Berlin accent. 'No, I believe we're going to have a brave little British Christmas.'

***

The two Blenheims climbed in loose formation to eight thousand feet and levelled out, heading north to get beyond the range of German fighters. Bryan pulled into a long starboard bank, circling around and back onto the same heading, to put some distance between the target plane and himself. The signals officer clambered back from the cockpit, crouched next to Scott's position and reattached his oxygen and intercom lines.

'Right, then,' he said 'Switch on and let's get our pilot onto the bogey's tail.'

Scott pushed his forehead against the visor and peered into the green glow. Ground returns blotted out half of each screen and fringes of dancing lines, pulsating from around the edge, obscured much of the rest. Scott pulled away from the visor.

'What's all this?' he asked, pointing at the interference.

'We call that 'grass',' the officer replied. 'It's like the background hiss on the shipping forecast. Learn to look through it.'

Scott bent his brow to the visor and squinted hard at the screens. A faint blip crept out from the ground returns and flirted with the grass on one side of the screen. Scott waited a few moments to be sure it wasn't a ghost.

'Contact at one thousand yards. Seventy-five yards high. Turn twenty degrees to port.'

Bryan banked into the new heading and Tommy watched the blip edge across the screen, slowly at first, then accelerating abruptly until it crossed the centre and threatened to bury itself in the grass on the opposite side.

'Reverse turn, thirty degrees starboard.'

The fuselage rolled as Bryan brought the aircraft onto the new heading. The blip refused to move.

'Add another ten degrees starboard.'

The blip wobbled, then raced back across the screen.

'Reverse turn, forty degrees port.' Sweat prickled into Tommy's eyes as the blip bounced back across the screen and vanished into the confusion of interference at its edge.

'Damn. Sorry, Flight. I've lost contact.'

'Stand-down operator.' The officer's order compounded Tommy's disappointment, 'Pilot. Fly straight and level, we'll take over as target plane.'

***

Jenny and Alice veered west across the grass. In the middle distance, the squat outline of Wandsworth Prison hunkered against the skyline.

'Do you fancy a quick drink in The County Arms?' Alice asked. 'Then we should catch a bus home before it gets any chillier.'

They quickened their pace along the path, admiring the primly kept front gardens of the large houses bounding the common, residences of an erstwhile Victorian merchant class. Crossing the main road, they pushed through the heavy wooden doors of the saloon bar into the comfortable fug of the panelled pub. Stripping off hats and gloves they walked to the bar.

'Whisky and green ginger, please,' Alice ordered.

'Oh, that sounds nice. Make that two.'

Alice paid for the round and they carried their glasses to a corner booth, away from the bar.

Alice sipped her whisky and regarded Jenny from under arched eyebrows.

'So, why did you tell him not to?'

Jenny's eyes dropped to the amber liquid that she swirled around the glass and she remained silent.

'Jenny, you have a lovely man who cares about you. Why shut him out?'

Jenny's brow furrowed against the reprimand and she cleared her throat.

'I was very much in love with a lovely man when I was eighteen.' Her voice stayed steady, but when they lifted from her drink, her eyes glistened with nascent tears, 'I don't ever want to be hurt that badly again.'

***

Bryan and Tommy trailed back to the operations hut behind the scientific officer. Bryan cast a wistful glance across the field to where the Beaufighters rumbled and coughed their way through engine tests in preparation for the coming night's patrol.

'What sort of evasion was he pulling, Flight?' Tommy asked.

'None. He was flying straight and level right down the line.'

'Strewth… Really?' Tommy dragged his leather helmet from his head. 'I'm sorry, Flight. I was working exactly the way they taught us in ground training. What a bloody shambles.'

'I'm not sure it was,' Bryan murmured. 'You're not an idiot, and the boffins seem convinced their magic box works. So, we must be missing something.'

The trio clumped into the operations hut and the officer flicked through the training roster.

'Back here tomorrow at the same time, please,' he said. 'We'll give it another crack.'

The man walked out and Tommy made to follow him. Bryan reached out and tugged at Tommy's sleeve.

'Wait a moment, Scott. Sit down and let's have a think about this.'

Tommy took a seat opposite Bryan's.

'The whole point of this game is to get our kite into the right bit of sky directly behind the target, going at more-or-less the same speed in exactly the same direction.'

Tommy nodded.

'I'm sitting up front doing what *you* tell me to do,' Bryan continued. 'So essentially *you* are trying to knock down the enemy using our plane as a missile.'

'In a way, I suppose.,.'

'You trained and served as a gunner, Scott. What's the most important principal when aiming at a moving target?'

'Deflection.'

'Precisely,' Bryan leaned back in his chair.

Realisation lightened Tommy's features, 'So, I need to direct you towards the place the target is *going* to be, rather than where he *is* when I read his bearing.'

'That's the key,' Bryan smiled. 'If he's off our bearing by thirty degrees, call a fifteen degree turn and then concentrate on getting our speed the same. Call another ten degrees and take time to check our speed again. Then call the last five degrees and we should be right up his arse.'

***

The bus swung left down the High Road between rows of shops closed and shuttered against the deserted pavements of a Sunday afternoon. Jenny travelled in silence, the smooth warmth of the whisky buzzing in her stomach, a counterpoint to the jagged edges of old memories. Alice sat mute beside her, digesting the revelation and adjusting her mental image of her friend. Alice reached up to ring the bell and the two women stood as the vehicle shuddered to a halt outside their block. The conductor tipped his hat as they alighted.

Alice offered her arm as they crossed the pavement and Jenny accepted with a faint smile.

'I can't fully understand the way you feel,' Alice began, 'but you can't punish Bryan for something that someone else did to you.'

The pair crossed the lobby and stepped into an open lift. They endured the porter's furtive glances until the door slid closed.

'He's not a child, Alice. I've told him it will never be a serious relationship. How he deals with that is his choice.'

Alice pulled a wan smile, 'I don't know that he has a choice anymore.'

The lift whirred upwards and Jenny stared in silence at the door.

***

Bryan strolled into the officers' mess and headed for the bar. Carson was there already, leant on the gleaming wood surface, chatting with another pilot.

'Ah, Bryan. The new boy. Come and join us.' Carson waved him across, 'Meet my good friend and fellow knight of the darkness, Leslie Moss.' Carson's voiced dropped to a conspiratorial level, 'He's a bit of an arse, but you'll find he grows on you.'

Carson giggled at his own joke while Bryan ordered a round of drinks.

Moss offered his hand, 'How is your training coming along?' he asked. 'Have you divined the secrets of the black magic box yet?'

'It's the bloody operators,' Carson interrupted. 'Mine's little more than a grease monkey made good. He's obviously in above his depth.'

Bryan glanced sideways at Carson, 'If the RAF trained Einstein to be your operator, you'd be doing no better.'

Moss leant forward, 'How do you mean?'

Bryan took a swig of his pint, 'Me and my operator have been thrashing this out. Tell me, when you're flying at night or in heavy cloud, do you feel comfortable relying on the aircraft's instruments.'

The other two nodded.

'So, if you're happy to believe those instruments are telling the truth,' Bryan continued, 'why are you disbelieving the AI box? Simply because it's a new invention?'

'But it's obvious it doesn't work,' Carson said. 'My operator tells me the target is in range, and it's patently bloody well not in range, because I can't bloody see it.'

Bryan placed his pint on the bar, 'You've gone past it.'

'What?' Carson frowned in confusion.

'It's not only about direction, it's as much about speed,' Bryan continued. 'I reckon you're approaching too fast. We know the operator loses the trace at close range. In between him telling you that you're on the bandit's tail and you actually searching for the target, you've gone *past* it.' Bryan smiled into Carson's face. 'So you end up flying next to it, or worse, in front of it.' Bryan took another swig of beer. 'To be quite honest, I'm surprised you haven't been shot to pieces already.'

A contemplative silence descended on the trio for a moment.

'Right.' Carson, the colour draining from his cheeks, broke the spell, 'Call of nature. Excuse me, gentlemen.'

Bryan watched the shaken man stumble towards the latrines and drained his pint. He turned to Moss, 'So, telephone calls off base. What's the rigmarole?'

'Strictly against the rules, of course,' Moss said, 'however there's a public telephone outside The George in the village. As long as you don't say anything that might encourage the Luftwaffe to come and bomb us tomorrow, no-one seems to mind too much.'

Bryan winked his thanks and strode to the mess door.

The first creeping fingers of dusk tugged at the horizon as he climbed into his Humber. The shouts and laughs of riggers and mechanics drifted across the field as the never-ending task of checking and maintaining the squadron's fighting machines ground on.

Bryan waved to the guard at the gate and turned left for the short drive along the edge of the airfield to Middle Wallop village. Parking in front of the pub, he climbed out and walked to the red telephone box at the corner of the car park, fishing around in his pocket for change. The door creaked closed on its thick, leather hinges and he dialled the operator to connect his call.

***

The dull tones of the October skies began their descent towards darkness over the washed-out grey of London's grimy buildings. Jenny squinted at the typeface on the bone-yellow paper, struggling against the fading light. She sighed and dropped the newspaper.

'I'm sorry,' she called. 'I need the lights on.'

She stood up, closed the blackouts and skirted the sofa to the light switch.

'Already?' Alice lay in the bath, shaping her fingernails on a decrepit emery board, 'I hate winter.'

Jenny sat down and retrieved her paper. Small articles filled the inner pages, glossing over the bombing raids that were categorised as light or heavy, on anonymous towns and cities hinted at by their rough location, northern or coastal. Only London was named. But the news always lagged a few days behind the events; casualty figures in stark black and white that, for all their implied horror, had already become mass burials in hard-pressed local graveyards.

A small knot of anger gripped the base of Jenny's throat. This new world of prosaic destruction tore her between what she wanted and what she was ill-prepared to suffer. The anger in her breast cooled and tightened to a smaller ache of despair, a longing for it to be over so she could be Jenny again.

The telephone's jagged ring ripped across the room. Jenny leant across and picked up the handset.

'Hello? Jenny Freeman.'

The operator instructed Jenny to hold and connected the caller.

'Hello?' Bryan's voice sounded metallic through the miles of cable.

'Hello, Bryan.' The muscles across Jenny's shoulders loosened, 'How are you?'

'I'm well. I was calling to say I won't be heading your way for a while. They are very keen to teach me an awful lot of things over here, and I think they'll keep me at it until I've learned them all.'

'That's alright, Bryan.' Jenny lowered her voice and turned her back to the bathroom door, 'It's probably just as well, I'm busy at work too. I'm simply glad to hear you're safe.'

'Don't worry about me. Things are less hectic here than the job I came from.'

The small talk wilted into a heavy pause.

'Damn,' Bryan cursed, 'no more loose change. I'll call again when I can-'

The strident beeps counted down the last seconds of the call to be replaced with the self-satisfied purr of the dropped line.

Jenny placed the handset in its cradle and returned to the sofa. The gentle *zip-zip* of the emery board lacerated the silence and the knots of tension retied across her shoulders.

Chapter 11

Monday, 11 November 1940

Bryan and Tommy trailed after the signals officer back to the operations hut, slumping into chairs as the man flipped back through his log book.

'Right gentlemen,' he looked up and smiled, 'you've achieved 90 per cent interception success on target planes that are flying straight and level, which is excellent.' He paused to allow his compliment to sink in, 'And 55 per cent interception success where the target plane is engaged in evasive flying. Of course, by success, we mean the aircraft is close enough to the target for a reasonably competent pilot to score some hits.'

Bryan sucked his teeth in contemplation, 'So what happens now?'

The signals officer snapped his log book shut.

'Well, I'm done with you,' his smile broadened, 'so you'll be sent back to the flight instructor for conversion to Beaufighters.'

'At last,' Bryan breathed to himself.

'Hale, you report here tomorrow at 10 o'clock. Scott, you'll remain on station at standby until conversion is completed. Then there'll be a few familiarisation flights and they'll let you loose on the enemy.'

He walked towards the door.

'By the way,' he said over his shoulder, 'a little bird tells me you've been assigned Blackbird C-Charlie.'

As the officer left the hut, Bryan looked at Tommy and his eyes narrowed.

'Shall we go and take a squint at C-Charlie?'

The two men walked side-by-side across the grass towards the dispersed night-fighters. Scott stood a good few inches shorter than his pilot and whistled self-consciously, kicking at tufts of thick grass with his flying boots.

'Well done, by the way,' Bryan said. 'It's your solid performance that's got us this far.'

'Thanks, Flight.' Tommy's cheeks reddened, 'I always try to do my best.'

'There's a couple of pilots in the officer's mess who don't have a great deal of affection for their operators.'

Tommy remained silent.

'And I'm guessing that's a two-way street?'

Tommy nodded, 'I've heard a couple of grumbles in the sergeants' mess.'

'Well, we're both after shooting down bombers before they get to their targets, so let's focus on that and leave the bitching to the others.'

They arrived at Blackbird C-Charlie, standing in its blast pen outside the perimeter track. Once more Bryan's senses thrilled to see the pugnacious, round-nosed aircraft sitting squat and fearsome on its sturdy undercarriage.

'Shall we take a peek inside, Flight?' Tommy whispered. 'There's a hatch under the fuselage.'

Tommy unlatched the hinged panel and Bryan climbed the steps built into its topside. Tommy followed and pulled the hatch closed behind them. Bryan elbowed his way along the fuselage towards the cockpit, Tommy lingered to view his own station.

Forward of the access hatch, the fuselage housed a Perspex dome. Set high under the dome was a swivel seat with backrest and safety harness.

Tommy glanced down in front of the seat. Four 20mm cannons sat underneath the catwalk, slightly below floor level, their thickly greased breeches glimmering with murderous intent. Smiling, he climbed into the seat and swivelled to face the tail. Grunting with pleasure at the largely unobstructed rear view, he turned his attention to the 'magic box'. It sat suspended from the fuselage roof behind the dome. He could look into the visor and back to the sky with a small movement of his head. The box itself was a newer version of the equipment he'd used during training. Next to it was a dedicated altimeter and an airspeed indicator to assist his interpretation of data on the screen. He noted with some pleasure a hot air duct on the fuselage wall set to discharge straight at the seat.

Tommy squeezed forward through a pair of armour plate doors to the cockpit and found Bryan musing in the pilot's seat set in the centre of the compartment. The sloping windscreen had the oily translucency of bulletproof glass, while lighter, Perspex panels offered unrestricted views to the sides and above.

'How do you get out in an emergency, Flight?'

Bryan shot a withering glance at his operator. 'There's a hatch behind the seat, thanks for asking. You're standing on it.'

Tommy braced his feet either side of the hatch, released the latch and dropped down onto the ground. He walked out in front of the aircraft, surveying its shape and form like a stable boy assessing new horse flesh. The Beaufighter's air of muscled aggression made up for the extra weight her lines might carry. He ran his hand along the sensuously scalloped slots under the nose that vented the cannons' fire, and smiled. As a tool for the job in hand it was unlikely to get much better than this.

Tuesday, 12 November 1940

The Beaufighter curved gracefully onto the landing circuit, dropped towards the grass and flared out for a perfect three-point landing. Tommy watched the man he'd started to think of as *his* pilot taxi smoothly away to dispersal, gunning and cutting the engines to steer the big aircraft off the runway.

He pulled up the collar on his overcoat and wandered back towards the sergeants' mess.

***

'If it was up to me, I'd put you on operations tonight.' The flight instructor scribbled the training flight down in the log and closed the heavy leather cover. 'But rules are rules and there's nothing I can do about it.'

'It makes no sense,' Bryan pleaded. 'Bombers are getting through unmolested while I have to jump through hoops to prove to you that I can fly a bloody aeroplane.'

'Listen, Hale,' the other man jabbed his pencil into Bryan's chest, 'if I let you go into combat with only a couple of hours of familiarisation, *and you don't come back*, then it's my neck on the block.' He jammed his pencil into his top pocket. 'Get as many hours in your log book as the maintenance crews will let you.'

The instructor strode out of the hut. Bryan sank into a chair and cupped his face in his hands, 'Shiny-arsed bastard.'

***

Bryan shouldered his way into the officers' mess and threw his greatcoat across a chair on his way to the bar. Carson stood there already, scanning through *The Standard*. Bryan ordered a bottle of light ale and hunkered down next to the reading man.

'What's news?' he asked.

Carson flipped back a few pages and jabbed his finger at an article.

'It says here that Bomber Command paid a visit to some factories in Munich on Friday night.' He sucked in a long breath, 'Germans aren't happy. Says here they've promised a "reprisal in strength".'

'Bloody hell!' Bryan swivelled the paper on the shiny wood of the bar and read the headline. 'Why does Winston insist on stirring up the bloody Nazis on their own doorstep?'

Carson frowned, 'Why on earth wouldn't we? They're bombing our cities. They're absolutely creaming London. Surely we have to hit back in kind.'

'You've heard Churchill,' Bryan muttered, 'he's always saying "London can take it".'

Carson's frown deepened, 'I don't follow you.'

'Well, if he thinks London can take it, what makes him believe Munich or Berlin can't? If he expects German bombs on British heads to strengthen our resolve to resist, how will British bombs on German heads not do the same?'

Carson waved to the steward for another round.

'So, we should let them get away with it, then?'

Bryan poured the fresh ale into his glass.

'There'll be a time to bomb German cities. But first, there needs to be something else that is scaring them stiff. That's when bombing might crack their morale.'

Carson sipped his beer, 'What else could possibly scare them?'

'When we've got the British Army back onto French soil, threatening to cross The Rhine. That will be the time to clobber them.'

Carson barked a short laugh, 'Are you mad, Hale? Do you honestly think we'll ever get back onto the continent?'

'Yes, I do. But we need the Americans to wake up and join in.'

'So, what would you be doing with Bomber Command in the meantime? Send them home on leave pending an American invasion of Europe?'

'No. They should be bombing the French ports to dust to make sure *we* don't get invaded next year. And they should be bombing the Luftwaffe's airfields in occupied territory, same as the German's did to us all summer.'

'So,' Carson scratched his scalp, 'your plan to fight a bomber war against Germany would largely consist of bombing France?'

Bryan sniffed and took a swig of beer. 'Absolutely. Makes perfect sense.'

Long seconds of silence trailed between the two men.

'When are you on patrol again?' Bryan asked.

'Tomorrow night.'

'Let me come with you?'

Wednesday, 13 November 1940

Bryan braced himself against the armoured doors behind the pilot seat as Carson banked G-George away from the runway and switched off the Beaufighter's navigation lights. A few hundred yards ahead of them, Moss in M-Mother doused his lights and vanished into the cavernous maw of the winter sky.

They listened to control's course instructions to Moss and waited.

Then it was their turn: 'Night-warden Control to Blackbird G-George.'

Carson flicked to transmit, 'Blackbird G-George, listening out.'

'Blackbird G-George, heading one-four-zero, patrol Channel east, angels fifteen.'

The Beaufighter's nose lifted as Carson began the climb to patrol height and they lumbered on through the dark. Bryan's eyes, hungry for light, were drawn down to the twinned luminescence of Southampton and Portsmouth passing beneath, blacked out but clearly discernible as faint, glowing patches against the jet-black English countryside. Further south a curved line of fluorescence betrayed the waves lolling against the beaches.

'Night-warden Control to Blackbird G-George, heading zero-four-five. There is a hostile in your vicinity.'

Carson pulled the heavy night-fighter into a smooth bank to port and nudged the throttles forward. Levelling out on the new heading, they droned on.

'Night-warden Control to Blackbird G-George, heading three-four-zero.'

'I reckon the bugger is on his way to Oxford,' Carson said, 'or maybe Birmingham.'

He levelled out on the new heading and Bryan squinted into the night, willing himself to see the raider they chased.

'Night-warden Control to Blackbird G-George. Flash, repeat, flash. Handing over.'

The coded instruction to activate the onboard detection apparatus heightened the tension in the cockpit as the seconds slipped by.

'Pilot to operator. Do you have anything?'

'Nothing definite yet, stand by.'

Carson's hand drifted towards the throttles, the creeping fear of collision prickling across his skin. Both he and Bryan scanned the sky ahead and above, aching to catch a movement.

'Pilot to operator. Anything?'

'Not yet–'

The aircraft bucked with a vicious jolt, like a car hitting a curbstone.

'Damn it,' Carson cursed, 'we just hit his bloody slipstream. You must have something on that screen.'

'It's difficult to say. It's very indistinct.'

The Beaufighter lurched through another sickening thud of turbulence and Carson's nerve failed him. He pulled back hard on the throttles and the two engines coughed and belched long banners of bright orange flames from their exhausts.

'That's torn it,' Bryan shouted. 'Move! Dive!'

Dazzled by the exhaust flashes, Bryan clung on as Carson throttled forward and threw the fighter into a violent left bank. Golden orbs of tracer fire erupted from somewhere close by, licked past the cockpit and curved away, lighting an arcing tangent to the Beaufighter's turn.

Carson eased back on the power and hauled into a long, shallow circle, bringing them back onto their original heading.

'Pilot to operator,' Carson's voice betrayed a vibrato of fear. He took a breath and steadied himself, 'can you regain contact?'

Bryan tapped him on the shoulder and pointed out to the starboard quarter. A line of silver splashes stitched their way through the ebony landscape, the last one hit something that bloomed into a ghastly orange flower of fire.

'He's dumped his bombs,' Bryan said. 'He'll be hedge-hopping his way home by now. We've lost him.'

Carson's shoulder sagged under Bryan's gloved hand.

'Blackbird G-George to Night-warden Control. Contact lost, returning to patrol line. Listening out.'

Thursday, 14 November 1940

Alice slid two plates into the hot water and Jenny attacked them with a dishcloth, swilling off the remnants of mashed potato and putting them in the draining rack. She chased the knives and forks around the bottom of the sink and finally pulled the plug, studying her reddened hands as the water gurgled away.

'What do you think they're using hand cream for?' she asked.

Alice placed the folded tablecloth in a drawer. 'What are you talking about?'

'They had no stock in the shop and the assistant said it was because of the war.'

'I have some, somewhere. Wait a minute.'

Jenny rinsed the last suds out of the sink and wiped down the splashes on the draining board.

Alice plonked the small glass tub of hand cream on the kitchen table and grabbed the boiling kettle from the stove.

'Time for a cuppa' before our German friends arrive.'

Jenny sat down, unscrewed the lid and dipped into the white cream. She rubbed the salve in between her chapped fingers, enjoying the slippery smooth relief it brought.

'I shall be twenty-nine next year,' she mused, 'I'm sure my mother will remind me of that when I see her.'

Alice sat down and put the steaming teapot between them, 'Please don't say anything about being left on the shelf. You've got a perfectly fine cure for that situation.'

Jenny paused the motion of her hands, 'I haven't heard from him in ages.'

Alice poured the tea, 'And how do you feel about that?'

Jenny splayed her fingers, appraised her stretched palms and took another dab of hand cream. 'As if he'll never come back. The longer I don't see him or hear anything, the stronger the wall becomes, the more confident I am that I'll be able to deal with it when he gets killed.'

Alice sipped at her tea, 'What if he was to come through the door right now?'

Jenny glanced wistfully down the corridor, 'I'd want to hold him and kiss him and not let him leave.'

'Mmm...' Alice stood up, 'Fancy a quick game of cards?'

They moved to the lounge and hunched over the coffee table.

Hand after hand of whist was won and lost. A long session of pontoon, using raisins from the kitchen cupboard as chips, saw Jenny bankrupted twice. Then the two women wracked their brains to work out the rules of half-forgotten games from their childhoods.

Alice leant back in her chair to arch her aching back as Jenny dealt herself a game of patience.

'What time is it?'

Jenny looked at her watch, 'Just past eleven.'

'There's been no air raid warning.'

Jenny dropped the cards onto the table and stood up. Switching off the lights, she went to the window and pulled the blackouts open. London lay under the twin blankets of darkness and silence, each making the other heavier.

'Oh, my word,' Jenny whispered. 'They haven't come.'

Alice joined her by the window, 'Or they've gone somewhere else.'

Friday, 15 November 1940

Bryan and Tommy sat in the adjutant's office along with a second crew who were also undergoing training. Bryan sucked on a cigarette and tapped his foot in impatience; the afternoon was slipping away and he wanted to get a couple of hours into his log book before the sun went down. The adjutant entered and all four men stood.

'Sit down, gentlemen.' The older officer waited for the scraping of chairs to quell. 'I've received instructions to make both of your crews operational.' A wan smile passed over his lips, 'Going by the book, you both need more hours and I should oppose this in principal. But the Germans have turned the screw and we need more guns in the air as soon as possible.

'During last night's full moon, they put several hundred bombers over Coventry. The raid lasted twelve hours. We've got no official figures yet, but some estimates have two thousand civilians killed or injured. There's some speculation that Coventry has ceased to operate as a city. The Ministry is worried about the possible effects this might have on the country's general morale and wants to bring down some raiders, get some pictures of wrecked bombers onto the front pages.

'You all have leave for the weekend, reporting back to station no later than 11am on Monday. You two,' he nodded at the second crew, 'will be night-available on that day. You two,' he nodded at Bryan and Tommy, 'will join the flying rota on Wednesday. If there are no questions, you're free to go.'

The four men stood and left the office.

'Typical bloody Air Force,' Bryan muttered as they walked into the fresh air. 'They announce it's a bloody emergency and then give you a two-day holiday.'

Tommy laughed, 'I'm not complaining about that, Flight. I haven't seen my little boy for a month.' His brow wrinkled, 'But I've never travelled home from here before.'

'Where's home?' Bryan asked.

'Peckham, south-east London.'

'I'll give you a lift. Be ready in an hour.'

'I'm not sure, Flight,' Tommy tapped his sergeant stripes, 'we're not really supposed to.'

'Of course,' Bryan nodded. 'Well, I need to make a call from the telephone box outside The George. If you happen to be there, it would be rude of me not to offer you a ride.'

***

Tommy strode the last fifty yards towards The George as the big, black Humber passed him in the gloom and pulled into the car park.

Bryan climbed out and walked towards the telephone box.

'Jump in,' he called. 'I won't be a minute.'

Tommy climbed in and waited. The big car's interior smelled of tobacco-aged leather with mildew undertones. A few moments later Bryan got into the driver's seat.

'Did you want to call your wife? I have some change.'

'We don't have a telephone,' Tommy answered. 'It'll have to be a surprise for her, I'm afraid.'

***

Bryan roared along the country roads, anxious to make as much headway before the light failed completely.

'Are you married, Flight?' Tommy asked, letting his eyes unfocus on the blur of hedgerows barrelling past the car.

'No, I'm not. Unless you include the RAF.'

'I'm sorry. I thought, what with you making the telephone call…'

'I did call a woman. But she's not my wife.' Bryan chewed his lip, 'I'm not even sure she's my girlfriend.'

'Oh, so you're still wooing her?'

'It's gone beyond that, Scott. We sort of started at the other end.' Bryan sighed, 'But she doesn't want to admit there's anything in it, in case I get the chop.'

'I can see why some girls might think that way. Me and Lizzy spoke about it before we tried for a baby.' He mused in silence for a second. 'I suppose it might make you feel safer, living in the moment and not making plans. But the best things in life are the ones that grow over time, they bring the happiest moments.'

'She certainly brings me happy moments.' Bryan smiled in his turn, 'Maybe I should call her bluff and survive the war.'

***

Darkness choked out the final vestige of daylight as the long road unfurled beneath them. Brief conversations alternated with lulls of cigarette-filled quiet. As they approached the suburbs of Kingston and Twickenham, Bryan nudged Tommy from a doze. The spidery talons of searchlights scratched the sky over the centre of London and the cloud base reflected the desultory flash of bomb strikes and the dull red tinge of fires.

'The Germans are about.' Bryan's understatement belied the tension tightening his shoulders. 'Hopefully they'll be done by the time we get there.'

The only other traffic on the roads was near-empty buses, looming like the ghosts of galleons above them, and emergency vehicles, crashing heedlessly past on their way to the city. Bryan strained his eyes to stay on the road, pulling in every time an ambulance or fire bell closed from behind. Progress was slow.

As the road swung due west, the dim crimson glow over the city filled the horizon with the velvet richness of demonic theatre curtains, stitched together by the hellish flashbulbs of gunfire from the anti-aircraft batteries on Richmond Common.

Tommy stared ahead, straight-backed in his seat.

'I try not to imagine this,' he murmured. 'What kind of war is it, when the wives and children are in more danger than their soldiers?'

'It's the kind of war we have to win,' Bryan replied. 'If this,' he nodded at the fire glow, 'is part of winning it, then those wives and children will go down in history. If we lose, it will just be a sickening waste and we'll never be forgiven for not surrendering.'

The cloud cover thinned and the barely-waning moon slid lazily out from its muffling blankets to sit stark and bright on the ebony felt of the night. Its frosted rays edged the road with silver tresses as the puddled tarmac reflected the light.

'Whatever they're aiming for, they won't miss it now.'

Bryan lit a cigarette and offered one to Tommy.

'You can drop me off at Clapham Junction, Flight.' Tommy accepted the smoke, 'I'm sure I can get a bus from there.'

Bryan looked out to his right, south towards Balham. The sky over Jenny's home remained resolutely dark.

'Don't be an arse, Scott. I'll take you home, it's only a couple of miles.'

Crawling through Brixton and bearing north-east to Camberwell, the Humber whined along in low gear. The crumpled bark of bomb strikes rippled in from the middle distance. Tommy wound down his window and hung his head outside, trying to gauge the direction of the raid.

'I reckon they're over the docks again,' he said. 'Hopefully they won't drift too far this way.'

They turned onto Peckham Road and Bryan slowed. A writhing coil of smoke curled down the thoroughfare, spewing from a seething conflagration in the shop frontages. Advancing at walking pace they crept past the bomb strike, rubble and glass crunching under his tyres. They emerged on the windward side of the fire and visibility returned.

Tommy, still hanging out the window, craned his neck back to the burning building. Wardens stood on the pavement, held at bay by the gouts of leaping flames spiralling out of the shattered shop.

'Bloody hell.' Tommy pulled his head back into the car, 'That's the chip shop. They'll have a job putting that one out.'

A fire tender clanged its way along the other side of the road towards its impossible task. As it passed, Bryan caught a glimpse through the windscreen of the taught faces on the men in the cab and a stab of empathetic fear tightened his chest. For a moment, the nakedness of total exposure to the crushing force of high explosive sent a rush of panic up his throat.

'There's a railway bridge up ahead.' Tommy's voice jarred Bryan back to the moment.

He swallowed the ball of tension, 'I see it.'

'Under the bridge and first left. My house is at the top end'

Bryan pulled the Humber into the left turn and grimaced as the car slewed and wobbled.

'Feels like I've picked up a puncture.'

Bryan drove with exaggerated care to the end of the road and parked on the pavement. Both men got out and Bryan checked the wheels. One at the back sat low on its rapidly deflating tyre. Tommy came and stood beside him.

'You'll need some light to fix that,' he said. 'Come inside and wait for the all clear. Then we can get a torch on it.'

Away to the north-east a string of explosions pummelled a line of destruction through the streets of Woolwich.

'Alright, Scott,' Bryan murmured. 'I could do with a rest from driving. Thank you.'

Tommy grabbed his bag from the car and Bryan stood back as he knocked on the front door and fell into the embrace of his surprised and delighted wife.

Another stick of exploding bombs in the distance pulled a flinch across Bryan's fixed smile with each detonation. At last, Tommy disentangled himself and gestured towards him.

'Lizzy, this is Flight Lieutenant Hale. He's the pilot I'll be working with.' He turned his smile to Bryan, 'Flight, this is Lizzy, my wife.'

'Come inside, Mr Hale,' Lizzy smiled. 'I'll put the kettle on.'

Bryan followed them through to the kitchen and shrugged off his greatcoat. Being inside the house imparted a flimsy sense of security, despite the distant impacts rattling the windows. The room was lit with candles and Bryan accepted the plain wooden chair he was offered.

A baby's chuckle blurted into the room. Bryan dipped his head to one side and peered under the table. A pink, round face regarded him from a bed of knitted blankets in a rough wooden cot.

'We don't have a bomb shelter,' Tommy explained, 'so I reinforced the table.' He tapped at a scaffold pole with his foot, 'There's room for Lizzy under there too.'

Lizzy set the tea cups and pot on the table, 'I can do corned beef hash and fried potatoes if anyone is hungry.'

***

After their meal, Tommy and Bryan moved through to the living room, leaving Lizzy to breastfeed the baby in the kitchen. The cooking smells from their dinner hung through the little house like pleasant memories.

Bryan sat down on the small sofa. The persistent grumble of distant explosions underlaid the punctuating tick of the clock on the mantle, beneath it the coals in the fireplace glowed like a mimesis of the city ablaze.

'I have some of this left,' Tommy held up a whisky bottle from the sideboard. 'I'm not sure how old it is. I'm not much of a drinker. It's probably from last Christmas.'

'I don't think it goes off,' Bryan smiled. 'It's a nice home you have here. Very cosy.'

Tommy poured two glasses and handed one to Bryan.

'Wives and girlfriends,' he toasted.

A single large explosion, away by the river, jolted the windows into a desultory genuflection.

'Isn't there a proper shelter your wife could use?' Bryan asked.

'Our backyard is too small,' Tommy sat down on an armchair, 'an Andersen has to be a decent distance away from the building to be any use.'

'Isn't there a public shelter?'

'There is, but it gets full really quickly. Then you have to spend the night squashed up with seventy-five people and only half-a-dozen buckets for everyone to piss in, if you'll excuse my French. It's rather unpleasant, especially for the ladies.'

'So, you risk it at home, instead?'

Tommy sipped his whisky and his eyes drifted out of focus for a moment. 'Nothing but the biggest parachute mine can destroy a *whole* street. And they don't drop many of those.'

Bryan looked into the golden spirit at the bottom of his glass and said a silent prayer for the all clear to sound.

Saturday, 16 November 1940

'Mister Hale?'

Bryan's eyes fluttered open and his face crunched into a wince as the pain from his kinked neck lanced across shoulders. He pulled himself out of his cramped foetal hunch, swung his legs to the floor and pushed his torso upright. Lizzy stood next to the sofa holding a mug of tea and a flapjack on a napkin.

'Ah, Mrs Scott.' Bryan reached out for the tea and swilled the thick whisky slick from his tongue. 'Thank you.'

Lizzy placed the flapjack on the sofa's arm. 'The all clear went at 4 o'clock this morning. I thought it was best to leave you be.'

'What time is it now?'

'It's coming on for half-past-seven.'

'Christ, I really need to leave.'

'Finish your breakfast, Mr Hale,' Lizzy smiled. 'It's not yet light. I'll make some fresh tea.'

Bryan arched his back and immediately regretted it; cramps clenched his flanks, clamping him into agonised immobility. He reached carefully for the flapjack and munched methodically as he waited for his body to come back under his control. As he chewed, Tommy came into the room cradling the baby.

'He sleeps like a log, even with the bombing.' He bobbed the baby up and down in his arms, 'He was born during a raid,' Tommy sat down on the armchair opposite. 'That night they demolished several streets a little way west of here. It's the closest they've been.'

'I'm surprised the stork got through.' Bryan's smile wrinkled into another wince as he stood up. 'I'd like to use your WC, if I may.'

'Of course, Flight. It's in the back yard.'

Bryan walked on stiff legs through to the kitchen, put his mug and napkin on the table and went out the back door. The wintry chill of the dawn air re-stiffened his muscles and his gasp of shock hung before his face in a cloud of vapour.

Built onto the back of the house was a brick and tile lean-to. The blue-painted door reached neither the top nor bottom of the doorframe, leaving a two-inch gap at both ends. For some unfathomable reason a diamond-shaped hole adorned the centre of the door at eye level. Bryan unhitched his belt and opened the door.

The toilet pan and overhead cistern stood against one wall. Against the other leant a variety of long-handled tools and offcuts of timber. Bryan lifted the lid and lowered himself onto the wooden seat. The shock of cold on his buttocks was short-lived and Bryan relaxed in the gloom, gazing across at the rusting tools draped in the tangled tracery of last season's cobwebs. The inexorable scent of damp brickwork crept over him as the death-cold concrete floor sucked his warmth out through the soles of his shoes.

'Home, sweet home,' he muttered to himself, pulling a square of newspaper from the looped string nailed into the wall and leaning sideways to wipe.

***

Tommy grasped the hubcap containing the wheel nuts in one hand and a mug of tea in the other while Bryan wrestled the spare wheel onto the Humber.

'Are you nervous about starting ops, Flight?' Tommy took a swig from his tea, squatted down and proffered the hubcap.

Bryan looked into the face that appeared suddenly at the same level as his and picked out one of the wheel nuts.

'I'm always more worried on the ground than in the air,' he sniffed in the brittle scent of far-off burning, 'and I'm always more worried on the ground in London than anywhere else.'

A shadow of strain flicked across Tommy's face and Bryan immediately regretted his connotation, 'Still, there'll be no-one chasing *us* around the sky, so we can get on with our job without looking over our shoulder all the time.' He winked at the other man, 'We'll be the wolves in *their* sheep-pen.'

Bryan finished attaching the wheel, clicked on the hubcap and gave the tyre a sturdy kick.

'Shit. It's as flabby as a nun's arse.'

Bryan retrieved a foot pump from the boot and pumped vigorously, leaning heavily against the car and grimacing against his still-complaining muscles. Once satisfied the tyre was solid, Bryan unhooked the pump.

'Right,' he pulled a flat smile across his unshaven face. 'Please thank Mrs Scott for me, she's been more than kind.'

'I will do, Flight. See you back at base on Monday.'

Tommy extended his right hand. Bryan stared at it for a moment, cocking his head in surprise as if it were a small woodland creature that had jumped between them. Then he leaned forward and grasped the hand for a single shake, taken aback by the firmness of the other's grip.

'Yes, Monday,' he said and climbed into the car.

Pulling away, Bryan glanced into the mirror. Lizzy had joined her husband outside and the couple watched him leave, like he was a favourite uncle or family benefactor. Bryan shook his head and pulled onto the main road, heading west.

Loops of greasy smoke still spewed from the chip shop. Its ravenous burning had devoured the properties next to it and heavily damaged the ones next to those. Now the fat had been consumed, fire engines damped down the blackened devastation with desultory plumes of water. Bryan drove slowly over the debris littering the road, conscious he couldn't afford another puncture.

Once past the area affected by the raid, Bryan's progress quickened and he soon turned on to Balham High Road, heading south. He pulled into a small garage, dropped off his wheel for repair, then finished his journey to Du Cane Court, arriving more than twelve hours late.

His passage across the lobby no longer attracted the interest of the porter who stared with sedate, unfocussed boredom into space.

The lift climbed to the sixth floor and he found himself knocking gently on the door of Number 21.

The door opened a crack and Alice peered out.

'You!' her eyes narrowed.

'Yes,' Bryan said. 'Is she in?'

Alice opened the door and stepped back. She gestured down the hallway.

'She's in the living room.'

Bryan stepped into the flat and waited as Alice pulled on her coat and wrapped a scarf around her neck. She treated Bryan to another withering look and left, swinging the door shut behind her.

Bryan pulled off his coat and walked through to the living room.

Jenny sat staring out of the window with her back to him. Bryan looked at her hair pooling across her shoulders and the arch of her petite back as she sat erect on the hard, wooden chair. He felt a familiar stirring.

'I'm sorry. I got delayed,' he said into the gulf between them.

'Delayed,' she echoed, her voice was small and soft.

'In Peckham,' Bryan continued. 'I gave my operator a lift home and got a puncture. I had to stay there until the all clear. I'm told that was at 4 o'clock.'

'I know,' Jenny sighed. 'I was sitting here when it sounded.'

Bryan laid his coat across the arm of the sofa. 'They don't have a telephone in their house, and it really wasn't safe to go searching for a public box. I'm sorry.'

Jenny's shoulders sagged a degree and she rubbed her forehead with the fingers of one hand.

'This is exactly what I wanted to avoid. I've spent the whole night imagining all the ghastly things that could've happened to you.' She turned to face him, her eyes pushing fresh tears over her reddened eyelids, 'And now I'm too exhausted to be happy that you're safe.'

Bryan started towards her, but she held out a palm and he stumbled to a halt.

'I was content,' she sniffed hard to control her crying, 'living and working and carrying on as normal, and then you telephoned to say you were coming.'

'I'm sorry-'

'Don't you see, Bryan?' a frown creased her brow. 'You forced me to expect you,' she hugged her arms across her breast as if in response to a deep pain, 'and you didn't come.' She wiped the wet streaks from her cheeks with the heel of her hand and turned her face back to the window.

'Would you rather I left?' Bryan's voice came out harsher than he'd intended.

'I don't know what I'd rather.' Her gaze remained pinned to the cityscape stretching out beyond the glass. 'Sometimes I think it would be easier if you got killed. Once you're dead, I can stop feeling. And if I stop feeling I can hope to survive, to grow old, alone if need be, but to grow old in peace.'

She turned her head halfway towards him, her eyes unfocussed, 'You have to promise me you'll live… or get on and die. I need to be sure, or I need to be free.'

Bryan crossed the room and laid his hands on her shoulders.

'Are you asking me to give up flying?'

'No, I'm asking you to give up fighting. Stop putting yourself in harm's way. Transfer to a training unit, be a flying instructor' – she twisted her head to look up at him – 'anything that gets you through the war alive.'

'I couldn't train young men to do a job I've walked away from.' He gestured towards the window. 'I can't sit back and let the Nazis bomb people simply because it's dangerous to get in their way.'

'You've done enough, Bryan.' Her voice carried an undercurrent of tremolo as she struggled to master her tears, 'No-one will know or care why you've stepped back from it.'

'That's not strictly true, Sweetheart.' Bryan bent to kiss her neck. 'I'll always know.'

Chapter 12

Wednesday, 20 November 1940

Bryan sniffed the air as he strolled along the perimeter track. It was only mid-morning, but the importance of this day had levered him from his bed early. A full month away from combat flying had chiselled at his previously calloused outlook and something akin to stage fright bubbled around in his vitals. He paused to light a cigarette and pulled his greatcoat closer about his neck to ward off the chilled northerly breeze.

Another figure moved through the morning. Bryan recognised the adjutant, ploughing a determined course through the damp grass from the stores back to his office. The other man noticed the smoker on the perimeter and deviated his track.

'Morning,' Campbell called as he approached. 'Did you hear the good news?'

'Not that I'm aware,' Bryan called back and waited for the adjutant to close the gap.

He arrived, slightly breathless and beamed Bryan a wide smile, 'Moss bagged a raider last night.' Campbell's gloved hand bunched into a fist that he shook in his excitement. 'A Junkers 88,' Campbell continued. 'The cheeky bugger came in with his navigation lights on. Moss tracked him in and put a burst into his belly. Crashed in flames somewhere near Chichester. That'll teach him.'

Both men set off walking in the direction of the office block.

'Moss picked him up on a visual?' Bryan frowned, 'What about the AI set?'

Campbell gave Bryan a sidelong glance, 'Well, obviously the AI helped him stay with his target and close in to killing range.'

'So, what's our score so far?' Bryan asked.

'That's our first.'

'And the other night-fighter squadrons?'

'They've had no joy so far; young Moss has broken our duck.'

'How big was the raid?'

'Between Birmingham and Leicester, they estimate several hundred.'

Bryan grunted, 'And we got one.'

The two men walked in silence for several yards.

'It seems the Germans might be catching on to the same game,' the older man offered, almost apologetically. 'On Saturday night, one of our Wellington bombers reported coming under attack from a fighter over Germany. They made no more transmissions. They're posted as missing.' The adjutant brightened, 'Still, it's *your* first crack at them tonight, isn't it?'

Bryan nodded and lit a fresh cigarette.

'I've heard good things about your crew, Hale.' The man's fist waggled again, 'I'm sure this is the beginning of great things.'

***

Bryan's eyes reflected the faint glow of the dimmed instrument lights as he ran through the pre-flight checks one final time.

He flicked on the intercom, 'Comms check, operator?'

'Loud and clear, Flight.' Tommy's voice crackled back, 'Strapped in and ready to go.'

Bryan switched to transmit, 'Blackbird C-Charlie, awaiting clearance. Listening out.'

Static hummed against a backdrop of silence for long moments, then the controller's smooth voice filled his earphones.

'Good evening, Blackbird C-Charlie. You are clear to take-off. Patrol Channel, angels fifteen.'

Bryan scanned the darkening sky above and ahead of the Beaufighter's stubby nose in a last check for descending aircraft, then pushed the throttles forward. Power surged through the airframe, dragging the fighter across the field and up into the void. Bryan waited for the jolt of the retracting undercarriage settling into their bays, then he banked onto a south-easterly course and eased into a shallow climb. He flicked off the navigation lights and pressed the intercom, 'Pilot to operator, switch guns to fire.'

Thirty seconds later, a reply, 'Safety catches off, Flight.'

The warm drone of the two engines bracketed Bryan's senses as they crossed the coast and swung onto their patrol line. Blackbird C-Charlie was on the prowl for the first time.

Tommy switched on the AI apparatus to warm up the cathode ray tubes and his harness buckles glowed with the reflection of their sickly green light.

'Night-warden Control to Blackbird C-Charlie,' the controller's voice was calm, but the words racked up Tommy's tension; 'We have a bandit approaching your patrol line. Turn onto heading two-six-zero, maintain angels, prepare to flash.'

'Two-six-zero.' Bryan's confirmation rung flat and emotionless, 'Turning now.'

The Beaufighter's fuselage tipped, yawed and levelled out, groping into the darkness ahead where its quarry lay cloaked in black.

'Night-warden Control to Blackbird C-Charlie. Flash, repeat, flash. Handing over.'

Tommy swallowed a knot of nerves and flicked on the transceiver. He ducked his head to the visor and peered at the screens. A tangled web of lines leapt across their surface.

'Flashing now, Flight.' Tommy held his voice as steady as he could, 'No joy yet.'

The aircraft sped into the unknown towards the unseen. Despite the chill in the fuselage, beads of sweat pricked into Tommy's eyebrows as he strained to untangle the ground returns. Then the scratchy lines bundled themselves together and a blip coalesced from the chaos, moving at speed down the trace.

'I have contact, Flight.' Tommy's voice rose with his triumph, 'We're approaching very fast. Throttle back.'

Tommy felt the aircraft's vibration change its timbre as Bryan eased back smoothly. Still the blip closed at pace.

'Too fast!' Tension compressed Tommy's words, 'Throttle right back. We're on top of him!'

The Beaufighter dipped with a sudden, sickening lurch. The negative gravity threw Tommy up against his straps and rapped the bridge of his nose against the visor's leather edge. The Perspex dome over Tommy's head banged with the percussive impact of somebody else's slipstream and a huge object flashed horribly close overhead, travelling fast in the opposite direction.

'Fuck!' Bryan hauled the Beaufighter onto one wing in a tight turn to follow the raider out into the Channel. 'Bloody great Heinkel,' he gasped, 'we nearly ended up in the cockpit with the bloody pilot.'

Tommy held onto the superstructure with one gloved hand as the fuselage tipped into the turn, and rubbed the stinging skin on his nose with other.

'Sorry, Flight,' he said. 'My fault.'

Bryan levelled out and the engines' whine mounted a notch as he pushed the throttles flat out.

'Keep a watch on the screen,' Bryan's voice was stretched but controlled, 'if he's kept to the same course, we should be right behind him.'

Tommy bent to the task. 'No contact.'

The minutes passed. 'No contact.'

Bryan fishtailed the aircraft in a desperate and futile attempt to sweep more of the sky.

'No contact.'

The engine note dropped back as Bryan slowed down and broke off the phantom chase.

'He must've seen us and changed course,' Bryan said. 'Hardly surprising, he was close enough to count my fillings.'

The Beaufighter rolled gently into a shallow bank, heading back to the British coast.

'Blackbird C-Charlie to Night-warden Control. Contact lost, returning to patrol line.'

***

Bryan dropped into a perfect three-point landing and taxied out to the dispersal bay. Tommy unhooked his straps and knelt over the gun breeches in the fuselage floor, re-engaging the safety catches on the unfired cannons.

The aircraft jolted to a halt, the engines cut and the propellers windmilled to rest. Tommy checked the AI apparatus was off and exited through the rear hatch. The night air chilled his face, but the shivering that pulsed through his body had its genesis in his core. He stood, miserable and alone in the dark, waiting for his pilot to finish the shutdown.

A few minutes passed before the hatch under the cockpit fell open and Bryan dropped to the ground. He banged the hatch shut and walked towards the operations hut for debriefing. Tommy fell into step beside him.

'I'm really sorry, Flight.'

'What for?' Bryan pulled off his gloves and flying helmet and fumbled inside his jacket for his cigarettes. 'You did your job perfectly.'

'I nearly got us killed.'

'Control didn't think to tell us the bandit was outgoing, and I didn't think to ask.' Bryan lit a cigarette and sucked greedily at the smoke. 'We'll tell the intelligence officer and he'll send a memo to the control room. We're all still learning after all.'

Tommy noticed the orange end of Bryan's cigarette wobbling in the darkness, tracing out the violent trembling of his hand.

Thursday, 21 November 1940

Bryan sat alone in the mess, mopping the dregs of his eggs from a metal plate with an anaemic corner of toast. The door scuffed open. Carson and Moss strode over, scraped out two chairs and shuffled their knees under the table. Bryan picked up his mug, glancing from one face to the other as he sipped his tea and waited.

'I hear your monkey tried to kill you last night.' Carson broke the silence as a steward delivered plates to the newcomers.

Bryan set his mug on the table.

'His name is Scott. He has a rather pretty wife called Lizzy, a bright pink baby called Robert and he lives in Peckham, an area not noted for its primate population.' Bryan lit a cigarette, 'And it was Night-warden that sent us barrelling inland after an outgoing bomber. Scott's performance was spot on. Unfortunately, we found a nose where he was led to expect a tail.'

'Christ,' Moss muttered around a mouthful of toast. 'I hope someone gets put on a charge for that.'

Bryan shrugged, 'Shiny-arsed bastards *are* as shiny-arsed bastards *do*. I imagine the memo has been drafted. Incidentally, I'm told *you* had some luck the other night.'

Moss nodded emphatically, 'Ju 88. I put a good long burst four-square into the ventral gunner. She rolled over and went straight in.'

'Did they switch off their navigation lights before they hit the ground?' Bryan crushed his cigarette out on his plate.

Moss looked up, a shadow of chagrin passing through his features. 'They all count,' he murmured, scooping a lump of congealing egg onto his fork.

'It's not good enough.' Bryan lit a fresh cigarette. 'We need to do better. We have to be terrifying the bastards every night they come over.'

'I don't follow you.' Carson picked up Bryan's cigarette packet and stole a smoke. 'Why is shooting down an enemy bomber not good enough.'

Bryan hunched forward, setting his elbows on the table, 'Aeroplanes will never be an effective defence against aeroplanes. Determined pilots in large numbers will always get through. If nothing else, we learnt that during the summer. Certainly, shoot down the ones we find, but we also need to get into the heads of the crews in the planes that we never see. We have to make sure every Luftwaffe crewman flies with fear in his guts.

'Your Junkers pilot with his navigation lights,' he nodded towards Moss, 'obviously thought he was on a milk run. He was more scared of mid-air collision with one of his own than any threat from us.' He took a long pull on his cigarette. 'Over two hundred bombers in the air and we bag one of them. Hitler will take those odds, every night, all winter.'

'I noticed the boffins are back,' Carson offered. 'They're working out at dispersal with the ground crews. Something about upgrading the AI sets.'

'Good,' Bryan said under his breath. 'We're all still learning, after all.'

***

Jenny peeped out between the blackouts to the impassive darkness beyond, 'Seems quiet again.'

Alice looked up from her book, 'I heard a rumour they'd bombed Birmingham last night. Perhaps they've gone there again.'

Jenny let the drapes fall back into place and returned to the sofa. She sat with a straight back and hands clasped in her lap, heedless of her friend's concerned gaze.

Alice put down her book.

'Why don't you put the radio on, Jen? Find some nice relaxing music and I'll make a pot of tea.'

From the kitchen, Alice listened as Jenny dialled through the channels, pausing for a few moments whenever music swelled out of the static, only to move on in search of something different. Snatches of dance melodies and stentorian newsreaders came and went while the kettle worked up to a whistle. At length Jenny settled on a light classical channel and Alice took in the tea tray to the gentile backdrop of chamber music. Jenny greeted her with a thin smile.

'Bryan isn't the nub of the problem, is he?' Alice poured the tea and handed a cup to Jenny. 'I'm guessing it has a lot to do with that old flame you mentioned.' She poured her own cup and levelled a look at Jenny. 'Would it help to talk?'

Jenny pushed an errant strand of hair off her cheek and took a sip from her cup.

'Richard,' she said at length. 'His name was Richard.'

Alice settled back in her chair, remaining silent.

Jenny looked up to meet her gaze, 'I was an office junior in a small import business based in Highgate. He was… a fair bit older than me. He worked as a salesman and regularly visited the shipping department. Our office adjoined the warehouse. I often worked there alone, especially when shipments were coming in or going out. Richard brought in the orders he'd written up for me to type and he'd generally stay to chat for a while.

'He wasn't particularly handsome, but he looked safe and solid, like nothing could defeat him. And he had a wonderful smell. He didn't smoke, so he smelled of coal tar soap and skin. He always smelled clean.'

Alice shifted her weight in the chair as Jenny took another sip of tea.

'One day, as he was about to leave the office, I caught his sleeve and kissed him.' Jenny's eyes unfocused to the middle distance.

Alice leant forward, 'And then?'

'He very gently pushed me away and told me to think about things, to sleep on it and decide whether this was what I really wanted. Then he stroked my cheek with his fingertips and left.

'A week later he visited the warehouse again. He came in and simply raised his eyebrows. I kissed him again, and this time he kissed back.

'That evening after work I waited for him outside and we went for a drink. He insisted on driving across to Hampstead, to The Holly Bush. It was off the beaten track but close to where I lived with my parents. Lovely little place with open fires, and I didn't have to stand at the bus stop to get home.

'After a few weeks of doing this, mostly on Wednesdays as I remember, he told me he had a little flat in the city. He suggested we should spend the weekend there, maybe go to a show or something.'

'And did you?'

Jenny nodded, 'Several times over the course of the next year.' She finished her tea and placed the cup back on the tray. 'I loved him. It felt so right. It was the natural thing to do.'

'Did he love you?'

'Yes, he did. Or at least he started saying he did, soon after I began sleeping with him.' She chewed her lower lip, 'I suppose I'll never know for sure.'

'Why? What happened?'

'My mother worried about the age difference, even though she could see how happy he made me. In the end, she asked about a bit, for her own piece of mind really. No-one seemed to know very much about Richard, but eventually she discovered where he lived and paid him a call.'

A frown furrowed Jenny's forehead and she looked into Alice's eyes, swallowing against her rising emotions.

'His wife answered the door.'

'Good Lord.'

'The next morning, my mother telephoned my boss and told him I wasn't going back, and she made sure he understood why. I never saw Richard again.' Jenny's face crumpled into fresh tears. 'It broke my heart, Alice. It broke my heart to pieces.'

***

Cigarette smoke embroidered the air in the sergeants' mess, swirling around the shoulders of the men striding to the desk, responding in turn to their shouted name at mail call.

'Thomas Scott!' The orderly held up a small manila envelope.

Tommy jumped from his chair and grabbed the letter like a trophy. He walked back to his table, prised open the flap and began to read.

'From your girlfriend?' Two operators sat down, each clutching their own mail.

Tommy glanced up from his letter, 'It's from my wife, Lizzy.'

'Nice,' the second man piped up. 'You're Hale's operator, is that right?'

Tommy folded the letter and let his hands sink to the tabletop. He looked from one face to the other, 'Mr Hale is my pilot, yes.'

'You seem to be terribly friendly with him, what with him being an officer and everything.'

Tommy held out his right hand, 'My name's Tommy.'

The speaker was taken aback for a moment, then shook Tommy's hand, 'My name's Donald, and this here is Desmond.'

'I prefer Des,' the other man nodded.

Tommy smiled at them both, 'I did a fair number of missions on bombers. I suppose it's natural for me to be friendly with my crew. Mr Hale flew Spitfires from Kenley all summer, so I suppose he's used to getting along with groundcrew.'

'I doubt he chauffeured them around, though.' Donald's words hung in the air, only a slim tone from becoming a threat.

'He has a girlfriend in Balham. My family lives in Peckham. A lift with Mr Hale saves me the train fare, which gives my wife a few more shillings to spend on our baby.'

Tommy again looked from face to face, this time without a smile.

Des pushed back his chair and stood, nudging Donald's shoulder as he turned to leave.

'Well… alright…' Donald stood and followed his companion to the door.

Tommy watched them go, unfolded his letter and finished reading. With a broad smile breaking across his face, he tipped the envelope on end and a small object fell onto the table.

Chapter 13

Sunday, 24 November 1940

Bryan sauntered across the field, hands in pockets, squinting through the misty air at an unfamiliar aircraft standing on the perimeter.

'Morning, Flight.' The condensation hanging in the air softened the edge of the call.

Bryan turned to see Tommy striding towards him.

'Hello, Scott. What the hell is that thing over there?'

'It's called a Defiant.' Both men started towards the plane together. 'At least that's what I heard in the mess.'

They arrived at the hardstanding and walked around the machine. It had the squat demeanour of a Hurricane but behind the pilot's canopy sat the substantial dome of a traversable turret, bristling with four guns.

'Whoever dreamt this up?' Bryan shook his head in slow dismay.

Tommy shrugged, 'A gunner who wanted to be a fighter pilot, perhaps?' He scratched his head. 'It's difficult enough to hit anything from a bomber flying straight and level. What it's like in this I can only imagine.'

Bryan walked around the front of the wing, running his hand down the gun-less leading edge, whistling his disapproval. 'What's it doing here?'

'They were up last night and the turret jammed. You can't bail out if the turret jams.' Tommy joined Bryan at the nose of the craft, 'I heard the gunner went into a blind panic, so his pilot put down at the nearest airfield.'

'What the hell were they doing going up at night in this thing?'

'I'm told they're using these as night-fighters,' Tommy said. 'Stationed down near Portsmouth, I think.'

'I don't see any antennae,' Bryan said, scanning the nose and wings.

'I believe it's all visual, Flight.'

'Good Lord,' Bryan breathed. 'Heaven help the poor bastards. It makes you wonder if we deserve to win this bloody war.'

Both men walked back towards the station buildings.

'I got a letter from Lizzy the other day,' Tommy rummaged in his tunic pocket and pulled out the envelope. 'She asked after you.'

'She's very kind. You're a lucky man to have a woman like that.'

'She says she feels a lot happier knowing I'm flying with you. She used to be a bundle of nerves when I was on bombers. I think meeting you has set her mind at rest.'

Bryan cast a sideways glance but said nothing.

'She sent me a memento as well.' Tommy brandished a lock of hair tied up in bright red ribbon. 'It's a mixture of Lizzy's hair and Robert's. Maybe it will bring us some luck, maybe we'll bag something tonight.'

Bryan nodded, 'Maybe. We'll see.'

***

Bryan and Tommy sat staring disconsolately out of the open operations hut door. Carson and Moss sat together on another bench with their operators standing behind them, rocking on their heels, absorbed by tension.

The morning mist had stayed all day to become desultory cushions of fog that rolled across the field, blotting out the horizon and silencing the chill air with its damp, ethereal grip.

'I don't understand why we're not allowed up,' Carson broke the miserable silence. 'It can't be much different to flying in the dark.'

Moss tilted his head back and closed his eyes, fatigued by staring at the billowing greyness. 'Probably not,' he said, 'until you're coming in on the circuit. Have you ever had to land in fog? It's a bit scary when cloud base suddenly turns into a concrete runway.'

'The fog here is immaterial.' Bryan dragged off his flying helmet and scratched his scalp. 'It's the fog over there that makes the difference.' He waved his hand in the general direction of Europe, 'If they can't take-off, we'll have nothing to shoot at.'

'And,' Tommy interjected, 'the moisture interferes with the AI'

Carson frowned at the sergeant's contribution and opened his mouth to speak, but his rebuke was stalled by an orderly clumping into the room.

'The Met boys say this pea-souper probably goes all the way to Moscow. There are no plots on the table at control, not even the usual mine-layers in the Channel. So, we're to stand down for the night.'

'Well,' Bryan smiled at Tommy, 'It seems everyone got lucky tonight.'

Thursday, 28 November 1940

The tepid afternoon sunlight filtered through the lecture hall's grimy windows as Squadron Leader Lawson tapped his pen on the desk to quell the soft hubbub of conversation amongst the crews.

When silence fell, he cleared his throat and began.

'It's always been a relatively easy job for a German navigator to get his bomber over the capital. A quick jaunt over the Strait of Dover, a sharp left turn and then follow the Thames Estuary straight to London.' He pursed his lips, 'Sometimes I wonder why they bother with a blackout at all.'

A murmur ran through his audience.

'But now that the Luftwaffe has opened up attacks on Coventry, Birmingham and the rest of the Midlands, their crews are faced with a seventy-mile crossing over the sea and an even longer flight over blacked-out countryside. Even when the moon is out, this is a very different proposition.' He paused and looked around the faces upturned before him.

'But it seems the Germans have their own team of backroom boys. A few weeks ago, a Heinkel fell to anti-aircraft fire and the pilot managed a forced landing on the Dorset coast. Luckily, the bomber came down in shallow water so the crew couldn't fire their aircraft. From what we've salvaged from the wreck, it's obvious they've developed a magic box of their own.

'Although we're not entirely sure how it works, we think we know how it's used: We believe that only the best crews are equipped with this gadget and that it guides them to the selected target by some means of RDF. They fly ahead of the main force, loaded exclusively with incendiaries and flares. Once their ordnance has marked the target, the accuracy of the main force is practically guaranteed.' He paused again to allow his words to sink in.

'If we can intercept these fire-starting aircraft, we can achieve two things: the elimination of an expert crew, and considerable disruption to the accuracy of the raiding force. In short, we'll be getting the best possible return on investment.

'Your patrol lines remain the same, mid-channel at the furthest, stay between Weymouth and the Isle of Wight. You'll take-off at dusk, an hour earlier than usual, so be at readiness by 3 o'clock. Good luck, gentleman.'

The crews stood with a scraping of chairs. Bryan and Tommy walked out into the waning afternoon. Bryan lit two cigarettes and handed one to Tommy.

'This could be interesting,' he said. 'Make sure you bring your lucky charm.'

***

Long fingers of gloom seeped across the horizon as Bryan hauled the Beaufighter off the runway and into a shallow climbing turn towards the coast. As the aircraft gained altitude the dusk retreated, driven back by the re-emerging afterglow of the sunset blazing low in the western horizon. The distinctive hook of Portland Bill slid away underneath them and Bryan banked into a long slow turn to port, losing altitude as he went.

He flicked on the intercom.

'Pilot to operator. I'm going to fly the patrol line at a lower altitude. If they're coming in at their normal height, we might be able to pick one out against the last of the sunset. Keep your eyes peeled to landward.'

'Understood, Flight.' Tommy flicked on the AI set and polished the port side of the observation dome with the back of his glove. 'Looking out.'

Bryan levelled out at ten thousand feet and eased the throttles back to cruising speed. The minutes ticked by as the faint glow of the dying sun gave ground to the thickening darkness.

Tommy searched the sky above the night-fighter's port side with unfocussed eyes, sweeping back and forth at an unhurried pace. A suggestion of movement tickled at his periphery vision. Locking his gaze onto a scrap of darker blackness, he thumbed the intercom.

'I think I see something, Flight. Turn ninety degrees to port and climb. Keep it steady.'

The fuselage tilted as Bryan made the course adjustment and Tommy swivelled his chair to keep the anomaly alive on his retinas.

'On course now.' Bryan's voice lay flat and calm in Tommy's earphones. 'What altitude do you estimate?'

'I would guess he's about three thousand feet above us. I'm switching to AI now.'

Listening to Bryan report the sighting to control, Tommy rested his forehead against the leather visor and relaxed the aching muscles in his eyes. The chatter of ground returns progressively quietened as the Beaufighter climbed away its altitude deficit. As the spiky interference receded, a strong blip appeared at the top of the trace.

'Contact! I have a contact.' Tommy took a deep breath and steadied his voice, 'Turn ten degrees starboard and continue climbing.'

As their height increased the sunset's magenta afterglow rallied against the dark and Bryan caught their quarry's outline against the shimmering blue-black of the heavens.

'I see him, Scott. Not sure what he is, though. I'll get closer.'

Tommy lifted his face from the screens and gazed up into the night. After a few moments his eyes adjusted and the black smudge five hundred feet above them broadened out into a distinct silhouette as Bryan edged into position immediately below it.

'What do you think, Scott?'

'It's a Heinkel, Flight.'

'Exactly what I thought. Attacking now.'

Bryan allowed the German bomber a full minute to pull away ahead of them and then tilted the nose upwards.

The Beaufighter bucked as the four cannons in its belly barked explosive shells into the sky. A dozen hits flashed on the Heinkel's underside before it exploded, splitting open like a rotten fruit, showering incandescent incendiaries and yellow marker flares in its wake like the blooming petals of malevolent flowers.

Bryan throttled back and banked around as the stricken bomber lurched over into a vertical dive. The broken aircraft twisted grotesquely as it plunged into a cloud layer which muted its garish burning to the eerie glow of a distant furnace: a ghostly, dissipated light that contracted back on itself as it surrendered to darkness.

Three parachute flares remained suspended in the void, swinging balefully to-and-fro as they followed their mother ship, lighting the now-empty scene of slaughter with incongruous sparkle.

Bryan circled until the flares too disappeared into the cloud and their harsh golden glow flickered and died.

'Blackbird C-Charlie to Night-warden Control,' Bryan's voice was clear and calm. 'Bandit destroyed. Returning to patrol line. Listening out.'

***

Bryan and Tommy clumped back towards the operations hut where the intelligence officer sat, dozing over his blank combat reports, awaiting the crews' return.

'That worked a treat, Flight,' Tommy still floated on the exultation of their success. 'I had him bang-to-rights straight down the middle of my trace.'

'Don't forget we saw the poor bugger first. I'll be happier when we can find them blind.'

'He was definitely a firelighter,' Tommy's buoyant mood refused to deflate. 'All those flares and incendiaries. Exactly like the squadron leader said.'

'Yes, Scott. I believe we finally made a bit of a difference tonight.'

Friday, 29 November 1940

'So, what should we do to celebrate your first kill, Hale?' Carson shuffled the cards, squinting against the sting of tobacco smoke curling up his face from the cigarette clenched between his teeth.

'Let's catch the milk train to London,' Moss picked up each dealt card as it skidded across the table towards him. 'As soon as we land tonight, scrub up, get changed and drive to Andover. Get the first train into Waterloo and we can be in Covent Garden for a late breakfast. What do you think, Bryan?'

Bryan pushed a shilling bet out onto the table. 'I suppose it could be more fun than hanging around here wearing sunglasses and eating carrots.'

'Capital. That's a plan, then. See you and raise.' Carson pushed out two coins in front of his cards. 'Don't you have a girlfriend in London?'

'No.' Bryan folded his hand, 'I don't think I do.'

***

C-Charlie shuttled back and forth on the patrol line, both its crew scanning the blank purple vault for the faintest flicker of movement. Bryan tracked the waning afterglow with incremental hikes in altitude, climbing to preserve the last vestiges of daylight he needed to trap the intruders they hunted. Wheeling round at the western end of their patrol line, Bryan glanced at the altimeter and then out at the blanket of darkness around them.

'Pilot to operator, we're at eighteen thousand feet. If any firelighters have come in, we've missed them. So, it's back to staring at the magic box for tonight.'

The Beaufighter banked into its easterly leg and Bryan became aware of a small mushroom of light invading the darkness far off in the north-east.

'Can you see the glow at 11 o'clock, Scott?'

'Yes, Flight. London is taking it again.'

Bryan cursed under his breath and hit the transmit button.

'Blackbird C-Charlie to Night-warden Control.'

'Hello C-Charlie. Receiving you.'

'There's nothing doing out here, request permission to break off patrol and move north-east. We suspect there is trade over London.'

'Hello C-Charlie. Negative, I'm afraid. Blackbird's orders are to cover approaches to Liverpool and The Midlands. Maintain patrol.'

Static whirled in their earphones as Bryan and Tommy gazed helplessly at the point of light on the horizon that bore witness to the flames that were devouring dreams and curling bodies into ash.

Saturday, 30 November 1940

'It's bloody hopeless.' Bryan's gloved hands gripped the steering wheel as the Humber careened along the deserted Salisbury Road heading towards Andover. 'Did you see hide or hair of any bombers?'

'Not a sausage,' Carson mumbled around a stifled yawn.

Bryan glared at Moss in the rearview mirror.

'No,' Moss intoned. 'Nothing.'

Bryan thumped the wheel with the heel of his hand, 'What's the point of hauling guns around in an empty sky?'

Moss shrugged in case Bryan was still watching him.

'Ours is not to reason why…' Carson sighed. 'Can't we just enjoy our day off in London?'

'Yes, of course,' Bryan breezed. 'We watched it getting bombed last night while we flew in circles somewhere else and today we'll look for a pub that's still got windows.'

'Good.' Carson said. 'You need to take the next right for the railway station.'

***

Carson and Moss had already fallen asleep as the train pulled into, and then away from, Basingstoke. The strengthening dawn light had delivered an embarkation of commuters.

'May I sit here?'

Bryan looked up into the face of a young woman.

'Yes, please do.' He shimmied up the seat to give her room.

'Your friends look exhausted.' She sat down, handbag in lap.

'We work nights and we haven't been to bed yet.' Bryan smiled, nodding at the other two, 'These impetuous youths wanted breakfast in London.'

'Oh, are you on bombers?'

'No, not really… similar, though.'

'My husband is on bombers. He's a rear gunner.' She looked past Bryan and through the train's window at the naked trees dashing past. 'Funny to think of him coming home and going to bed at the same time I'm setting off to work.'

'Do you worry about him?'

'Sometimes.' She glanced into Bryan's eyes, 'But I know he'll do his best to come back to me. He's a good man and I love him very much.'

'Have you been married long?'

'A little over two months.' She held her chin slightly higher, 'We married as soon as he finished his gunnery training. We only had one night before he got posted away to his squadron.'

'That must've been difficult.'

'Yes.' She blushed and giggled, 'Mind you, I think he hit the target on his first mission.'

'I'm sorry?'

She stifled her giggles with one hand and patted her belly with the other.

'Oh, I see,' Bryan twigged. 'The pattering of tiny feet?'

'I believe so.' Her blush deepened, 'Isn't it terrible? You're the first person I've told and I don't even know your name.'

'It's Bryan.'

'Hello, Bryan.'

***

The train clanked to a halt in Waterloo and Bryan mouthed '*Good luck*' to his travelling companion as she disembarked and became lost in the crowds. Carson and Moss slumbered on, and for a brief moment Bryan considered abandoning them and taking a train to Balham. The moment passed and Bryan kicked their shoes.

'Wake up, girls. Time for breakfast.'

The three men walked up the platform and through the ticket barriers. The chill of the morning air, amplified by the cavernous station and the cold stone floors, pinned their breath in the air behind them, like drifting clouds of disconsolation.

'Where are we heading?' Moss blinked against his tiredness.

'Down to the River Thames and then along the bank until we get to a bridge, Westminster is the closest.'

Bryan ducked down a narrow street and dog-legged over another road to a lane that led down to the bank of the Thames.

All three of them stopped in their tracks as the river vista opened up before them. Across the water to their left, huge plumes of smoke wheezed from burning buildings in Whitehall, individual columns snaking together, conspiring to blacken the sky. Orphan fires punctuated the scene, north and east, and behind them the skyline floundered under a roiling conflagration centred on Blackfriars.

'What's happened here?' Moss's brittle voice betrayed his genuine shock.

Bryan put a hand on his shoulder. 'Last night's raid is what happened here. And it happened while we were arsing about over Hampshire and Dorset.'

'This is unstoppable.' Carson shook his head at the extent of the destruction.

Bryan slapped him on the back, 'Well, we've been given the job of stopping it.'

They stood for a moment in silence and Moss began shivering with the cold.

'Come on.' Bryan started off. 'Breakfast won't hunt itself.'

They dodged between the riverside path and the alleys in between warehouses until they reached Westminster Bridge. Climbing the wide stairway, their eyes were drawn to the grimy bulk of the Palace of Westminster. Although draped in smoke from nearby fires, it showed no sign of major damage. They crossed to the north bank amidst the flow of office workers, many of whom wore anxious masks of concern, uncertain if their destination would be intact when they arrived.

Coming off the bridge beneath Boadicea's imperious gaze, they walked past the silent Saint Stephen's Tower towards the edge of Parliament Square.

'We need to head north,' Bryan said.

But the junction to Parliament Street was roped off and guarded by policemen. The trio approached the barrier, squirming through a press of frustrated office workers. Behind the police line, in the middle distance, the Cenotaph stood swathed in smoke from a nearby building that still curled spirals of flame from its upper floor windows.

'Any chance we could cut through?' Bryan asked the nearest police officer.

'No. We're waiting for the lads from bomb disposal.' The man chuckled, 'Unless you've got a screwdriver handy and you think you know the difference between a dud and a time-delay.'

'Thank you,' Bryan tipped his cap. 'Seems I forgot my toolbox.'

They doubled back to the river and dropped down the steps next to the impassive warrior queen onto Victoria Embankment. Fire tenders lined the road and their hoses snaked across the walkway, looped over the wall and disappeared into the cold, grey water of the Thames. Here and there a collapsed wall had flung a few errant bricks across the road, but the generous width of the riverside promenade meant it remained largely unobstructed. Stepping over the leaky hoses, the three airmen made their way past the worst of the destruction.

At the northern edge of the bomb strikes they found Charing Cross tube station open. They cut through the station and up the hill to The Strand. Ducking up a side road they stumbled on a small café on the edge of Covent Garden.

Bryan led the way into the eatery. The salty smell of fried bacon hung in the warm air, pricking saliva into the mouths of the hungry men.

'Do you have any bacon left?' Bryan asked.

'A little.' The man behind the counter winked.

'Then we'll have three bacon sandwiches and three mugs of tea, please.' Bryan placed some coins next to the till and joined the other two at a table by the window.

'Everything's carrying on as normal.' Moss gestured at the people passing by outside, seemingly unconcerned and unhurried, 'How can that be?'

'I don't know,' Carson shrugged. 'Safety in numbers, perhaps?'

'More likely denial,' Bryan said sadly. 'Ponder on it too much and you end up like a rabbit in the headlights.'

The café owner brought over the sandwiches and teas.

'Not meaning to pry,' Moss opened his sandwich to sprinkle in some pepper, 'but is that what's happening with your girlfriend?'

Bryan pursed his lips, 'She wants me to transfer to a training unit. Somewhere that's safe.'

'You should do it,' Moss spoke around a mouthful of breakfast. 'With your experience, they'd take you at the drop of a hat.'

'Rubbish.' Carson grasped his sandwich in one hand and reached for his mug with the other. 'Now we're ironing out the tactical kinks, there's very little danger in what we do.' He swilled a mouthful of tea. 'If we do our job properly, the bandit need never know we're there until it's too late, and there's nothing on earth those cannons can't rip to shreds. I'm staying on night-fighters for the duration, my friends. It's a cushy number.'

'Do you have a girlfriend?' Moss asked him.

Carson shook his head as he crammed the last of his sandwich into his mouth.

***

They left the café and strolled along the road.

Bryan looked at his watch, 'Pubs open in a few minutes. I know a nice little drinker on the other side of the plaza.'

They cut through the backstreets, zig-zagging their way until Covent Garden Apple Market opened out in front of them, the main building hid coyly behind its piles of sandbagged protection.

Something climbed a sonic tone above the traffic hubbub seeping up from The Strand and the hairs on Bryan's neck raised in warning.

'Listen.' He stopped and raised his hand to quell the questions of his companions. 'Aircraft.'

The noise swelled and three Messerschmitt fighters barrelled over the roofline from the east at two hundred feet in a vee formation. Harsh against their pale blue undersides, the dark lumps of bombs nestled, one under the fuselage and smaller ones under each wing.

They flashed over the plaza and were lost to sight for a moment behind the buildings, before reappearing in a long climbing bank to starboard. Their bombloads, flying free, terminated their unseen trajectory in a series of muffled detonations away to the west. An occasional rifle report echoed from the stonework as sentries around the plaza loosed off pot-shots at the raiders. Unperturbed, the German fighters completed their turn and throttled up for the southwards dash for home.

***

Bryan sat on a stool in The Lamb and Flag, swinging his shoe against the bar and staring into the depths of his pint.

'What's the point of bombing Leicester Square? How does that advance their war effort?' Moss furrowed his brow. 'Why risk three pilots to knock in a theatre's windows?'

'Why creep up and murder civilians?' Carson scratched his head. 'That's a better question.'

'That, gentlemen' – Bryan straightened his back and flexed his shoulders – 'is the nature of our enemy. The intentional murder of civilians seems not to trouble him.' He swilled down the remains of his ale and signalled the barman for another round. 'I'd like to think none of us would do such a thing. But I suppose there's only so much turning of the other cheek that any nation can stand.'

Moss shook his head, 'But we'd never *purposely* target civilians?'

Bryan put down his empty tankard and picked up a full one, 'I fear there may not be any other way to win this war.'

'Explain.' Carson cheeks were reddened with alcohol.

'The last time around we beat the German Army on the field,' Bryan took another swig of ale, 'but we let them march home beating their drums and waving their flags. That gave the civilian population the wrong message about how matters had come to an end. So, the whole bloody country sat on its resentment and paranoia for nearly twenty years and, hey presto, National Socialism and Great War Two, or whatever they end up calling it.

'Winston above all others understands this. He knows it's only the thick skin of the British public that stands between him and a Nazi noose. He'll happily scythe his way through the ordinary German population if it gets him Hitler's head in the long run.'

'Crikey,' Moss whispered. 'Do you think?'

'Yes,' Bryan nodded gently, 'I think.'

'Tosh.' Carson's voiced was greased with the edge of a slur, 'Let's find a different pub, this one has become too depressing.'

They drained their beers and spilled out onto the pavement, the cold air gripping their bladders as they hurried north up Charing Cross Road. Moss, most in need of a toilet, scouted ahead at a crooked lope. He stopped to peer in at a pub window and the other two caught up with him.

'This one looks nice and rough,' he said. 'The blackboard says they do pies.'

They bundled into the warm smoke-filled pub. Moss scurried to the toilet and Carson went to the bar. Bryan noticed a public telephone in the snug and reached into his pocket in search of change.

He dialled the number he now knew by heart.

'Hello?' Alice's voice.

'Hello, Alice. It's Bryan here. Is she in?'

'She's at the hairdresser. Are you drunk?'

'Not quite yet. I was calling to see if she is alright.'

'She's quieter than normal, busy with work. Yes, I think she's alright.'

Bryan paused, thrown by the flat calm brevity of the answer. 'That's good.' His voice dropped a tone, 'I worry about her... you know.'

'You should listen to her, Bryan. Do yourself a favour. Look, I'm sorry, I have some milk on the hob. Bye.'

The dropped line buzzed with indifference into his ear. He replaced the handset and walked to the bar.

Chapter 14

Tuesday, 3 December 1940

'Contact!'

Tommy's shout was an instinctive reaction to the blip slewing across the pulsing green screen.

'Damn! Lost it. Pull her into a starboard turn, Flight. See if we can pick him up again.'

'Turning starboard.' Bryan's voice rolled as smoothly as the tilt of the fuselage.

Tommy stared at the upper half of his display, willing the blip to swing back into view. The turn continued as Tommy agonized, then the fuzzy dot slid across the screen, departing from the other side.

'Turn to port,' he blurted. 'Not so steep. Increase revs.'

'Roger.'

The fuselage wallowed in the opposite direction and the engine noise climbed a quarter of a tone. Tommy waited, his jaw muscle flickering with tension. The blip reappeared at the top of the trace, traversing more slowly this time.

'Hold this course. He's dead ahead at extreme range. A touch more throttle, please.'

Once more the engine note rose, like a choir of baritones ascending a scale, and Tommy watched the blip begin its slow descent of the screen.

'He's flying straight and level, Flight. We've got him cold.' Tommy studied the second screen, 'He's a few hundred feet below us by my reckoning.'

Bryan leant forward against his straps and squinted into the void ahead and below. High above, a cloud drifted aside and the wan light of the quarter-moon softened the darkness.

'I can see him,' Bryan said. 'He's reflecting the moonlight. Not sure what it is, though. I'm losing altitude to get below him. Take a look, Scott. Tell me what you think.'

Tommy swiveled his seat and stared out over the cockpit. He caught the faint glimmer of reflection and pieced together the aircraft's shape in his mind's eye.

'It's definitely not a Heinkel, Flight.' Tommy squinted harder as they dropped below their prey.

Putting the target between them and the bisected moon unfolded a harder edge to its silhouette.

'Could be a Junkers,' Tommy mused. 'But it seems too fat in the fuselage and its nose is too stubby.'

'So, what are you calling?'

'Gosh… I think it's a Beaufighter.'

'So do I.' Bryan switched from intercom to radio transmission: 'Blackbird C-Charlie to Night-warden Control. Can you confirm our contact as hostile?'

'No!' The controller's relief scuttled his radio protocol. 'We've been tracking both of you for five minutes. That's Blackbird G-George. Disengage, repeat, disengage.'

The black shape suspended above them flashed on its navigation lights and rocked violently from side to side.

'Ah, my good friend Carson,' Bryan chuckled to himself. 'Thank you, Night-warden. Disengaging now.' Bryan pushed the throttles forward and peeled away.

Wednesday, 4 December 1940

'Carson!' Bryan called across the field at the stocky figure stomping head-down towards the mess. Carson detoured towards him.

'Come with me.' Bryan started across the field.

Carson trotted to catch up, 'Where to?'

'Stores.' Bryan lit a cigarette and leered a grin at his companion. 'I got a visual on you last night.'

'I know! You scared the bloody life out of me. What sort of game do you think you're playing?'

Bryan smiled at him, 'You all look the same on Scott's screen. You're just lucky we like to confirm exactly what we're shooting at before we blow it out of the sky.'

Carson's pallor whitened.

'Anyway,' Bryan continued, 'the point is, we approached from slightly above and you reflected the moonlight like a bloody glitterball. Something needs to be done.'

'So why are we going to the stores?'

'To order some paint, obviously.'

They arrived at the Quartermaster's hut and went to the counter. Rows of shelves and racking filled the space behind the opening and someone moved amongst them, rearranging boxes.

'Hello,' Bryan called, 'service?'

A man in a brown warehouse coat emerged.

'How can I help?'

'Matt black paint, please.'

'How much?'

Bryan turned to Carson, 'What do you think? About three gallons per aircraft?'

Carson stared blankly back at him.

'Yes,' Bryan readdressed the storeman, 'I reckon thirty-six gallons should do it. Let's make it forty to be safe.'

A long moment of silence stretched into the space between them.

'Would you like me to call the Military Police?'

'You can call the King if you like, as long as I get my paint.'

***

Squadron Leader Lawson regarded Bryan standing to attention before his desk and sighed.

'Stand easy, Hale. In fact, sit down.'

'Thank you, sir.' Bryan seated himself and sat straight-backed.

'What were you planning to do with forty gallons of black paint?'

'Paint the aircraft, sir.'

Lawson's raised eyebrows asked his silent question.

'I had occasion to be flying above another Beaufighter last night. It was reflecting the moonlight enough to be visible, if you happened to be looking for it.'

'I see.'

'Our standard attack position is below and behind our target, sir. And now they know we're about, there'll be a ventral gunner whose main concern will be searching for us. It would make things more difficult for him if our aircraft were painted black.'

'I take your point, Hale, but there are ways of going about things, you know.'

'Yes, sir.'

Lawson scribbled something on his desk pad.

'Leave it with me. Dismissed.'

Friday, 6 December 1940

The windows in the operations hut rattled in the gusts and the stove in the corner belched an occasional halo of woodsmoke from the edges of its ill-fitting door. Bryan and Tommy sat near each other, sucking on cigarettes and listening to the soughing wind.

'How's the family?'

'Really well, as far as I can tell,' Tommy smiled. 'Robert's coming up for two months old already. Lizzy's a good girl, she's learning the ropes quite quickly.'

Bryan frowned, 'As far as you can tell?'

'It takes a while for our letters to get where they're going, and sometimes they cross in the post.' Tommy crushed his cigarette butt under the heel of his flying boot. 'If I get a letter that's a bit mopey and send a reply to chivvy her along, by the time she gets it she's cheered herself up and thinks I'm being maudlin.' Tommy chuckled to himself, 'It's like having a conversation with echoes.'

'When are you next going to visit her?'

'I don't know, Flight. But it ought to be soon, I need to take her the pay I've saved up.'

Bryan surveyed the flying rota, 'We're on first patrol tomorrow night. What do you say we go up early Sunday morning in the Humber?'

'I'm game if you are. Shall I meet you at The George again?'

'No, bugger that. I'll pick you up outside the sergeants' mess.'

The adjutant opened the door and entered, holding his cap on against the swirling breeze.

'Good evening gents.' He smiled around the gathered crews, 'Met Office has forecast strengthening winds for the rest of the night. Hang about here, please, in case they're wrong.'

Chairs scraped as card schools coalesced.

'By the way Hale, sector command has authorised your black paint. It seems our recent kills have made them take us seriously.'

Sunday, 8 December 1940

Tommy clambered into the Humber's passenger seat. It was still dark, but he pulled down his cap and hunched his neck lower into his greatcoat to be unrecognizable to any casual observers.

Bryan glanced across as he pulled away.

'Are you alright?'

'It looks a bit strange,' Tommy eyed the guard's hut warily as they drove past on the way out of the station, 'what with you being an officer.'

'Ha!' Bryan snorted, 'If nothing else, this war ought to change some of that.'

'I don't know if it will.' Tommy sighed in relief as the station receded behind them. 'No-one else in the sergeants' mess remotely likes their pilot.'

'Well, the RAF isn't a social club.' Bryan took out his cigarettes and offered one to Tommy. 'Somebody's got to do what somebody else tells them, or else nothing would get done.'

Tommy chuckled, 'Let's not forget that on patrol it's the operator telling the pilot what to do.'

Bryan smiled. 'I started this war in Blenheims. I'm quite certain my crew absolutely loathed me.'

Tommy sucked on his cigarette and gazed out at the dawn's glimmering disc nibbling away at the black bar of the horizon.

'I sometimes think about my old crew. I wonder how it ended for them. Sometimes I feel a bit guilty I wasn't there to help them out.'

He wound down the window and flicked his cigarette through the gap. The slipstream tore a cascade of sparks from its burning end as it spun away into the void like a stricken aircraft.

***

The sun rolled up its shallow trajectory, dribbling its callow illumination across London's grey visage. The Humber reached the city's outskirts and entered the bustle of Sunday drivers and half-empty buses. Military trucks growled along on thick tires, delivering ordnance to anti-aircraft batteries, the attendant soldiers sat astride the crates of shells in the back like implacable milkmen delivering provisions from hell.

Along the pavements and walkways, couples moved together. Some walked arm-in-arm, others with hands thrust in their pockets against the cold. All wore their Sunday best on this weekly pilgrimage to church. They went to beg for forgiveness, pray for redemption and hope for deliverance, while somewhere, not too far away across the water, engines were oiled and bomb loads assembled.

'It's always nice to get back to London,' Tommy breezed, 'always good to come home to Peckham. Where do you call home, Flight?'

'I was born in Hampstead, if that's what you mean. I'm not sure I'd call any particular place *home*.' The word left his lips like a bad taste.

'What? Not even at Christmas?'

'Probably especially at Christmas.'

'That's a shame.'

***

Bryan pulled up outside Tommy's house.

'You'll come in for a cuppa?'

Bryan climbed out and hung back while Tommy opened the door and surprised his wife. Judging they'd finished their greetings, Bryan followed him in and closed the door.

'Hello, Mr Hale.' Lizzy's eyes shone with the pleasure of the moment. 'Come through, it's lovely to see you again.'

Bryan went into the kitchen, ducked under a washing line of drying nappies and sat at the table.

'You'll stay for lunch?' Lizzy's open, smiling face made it impossible to refuse.

'Only if it's no trouble.' Bryan felt a pang of admiration for this woman. She lived in difficult circumstances during uncertain times, yet she clearly loved both her life and her husband to the fullest capacity of her heart. He sat in silence and listened to them speak, catching the tone and inflection rather than the meaning of the words, the undercurrent of simple trust and contentment they shared.

An hour later they tucked into vegetable stew with wheat crackers. After the meal, Lizzy found her wedding album and sat with Bryan, going through the photos while Tommy rolled up his sleeves and washed the pots and plates.

Bryan flipped an album page to reveal a group of four photos. The bride and groom standing in front of a weathered church door, beaming with irrepressible happiness, were dead centre of each composition. The only change between exposures was the surrounding press of relatives; aunts and uncles, nieces and nephews, photographed in tribal gatherings according to bloodline.

'Everyone looks very happy,' he ventured. 'When was it?'

'Sixteenth of February, 1939.' Lizzy sighed, 'Before we knew what we had coming.' She flipped forward a couple of pages to photos of the reception.

She rested a finger on one of the pictures. 'This is my friend, Daisy, and her boyfriend, Lionel.'

Bryan tilted the book slightly to defeat the reflections on the glossy prints. In the photograph, Daisy's big, bright eyes echoed the smile that danced on her lips. She held Lionel's hand across the trestle table. Lionel gazed at Daisy rather than the camera, but his lips mirrored her smile. His forage cap lay neatly folded under the epaulette of his infantry blouson and his hair was neatly slicked back with hair oil.

'Lionel went missing on the retreat to Dunkirk,' Lizzy's voice caught in her throat, 'and Daisy got killed during one of the first raids on London in September. She was sitting pretty in a proper deep air raid shelter. But they say the bomb went down the ventilation shaft. One-in-a-million chance, they said…'

Bryan looked up into her glistening eyes. 'It's very dangerous, living here so close to the docks. Is there nowhere else you can move to?'

Lizzy shook her head, dabbing at her cheek with a handkerchief, 'No, Mister Hale. All my family are hereabouts. I put my faith in God and carry on. He'll protect me and little Robert. I believe He will.'

Tommy turned from the kitchen sink, wiping his hands on a tea towel. He regarded his wife with a mixture of love and sadness.

'Who wants tea?' he asked.

***

Jenny snuggled against his chest, breathing deeply with steady contentment, her ivory skin reflecting the insipid moonlight that filtered through the open bedroom curtains. Bryan's insides still buzzed from their love-making. He swallowed against the swelling emotions in his breast, like a channel swimmer standing irresolute in the face of the rise and fall of cold, grey waves crashing onto raucous shingle, searching for the will to wade through their violence to begin his journey. He grasped for his courage.

'I've decided to apply for a transfer.'

Jenny's shoulders tensed a fraction under his arm, but her head remained still.

'Why?'

'I thought you wanted me to.'

'I do.' She tilted her head up to regard him, 'The question is; why have *you* decided to do it?'

Bryan stroked her hair away from her cheek. 'There can't be a future where I don't end up losing something.' His eyes wandered her upturned face, skipping between the dark shadows of her irises and the fine line of her nose. 'And maybe I can stand losing anything except you.'

'Maybe?'

Distant flashes glittered the horizon to the east and long fingers of light unfurled from amidst them to probe the clouds for the invisible assailants.

Bryan sighed, 'The docks again.'

'Shush.' Jenny shifted her weight and swung herself onto his body, sitting astride his hips. She leant down to kiss him and her dark hair fell around his face, blotting out the distant glow of cascading violence and cocooning him in the warm fug of desire.

***

Beneath the table, Lizzy tore two pieces of cotton wool from the roll and twisted them carefully into her baby's ears. Robert cried fitfully in her arms and she hummed a low, rambling tune to quieten him and bolster her own nerve. She could see the outline of Tommy's legs in the dark as he stood by the kitchen window, watching the raid plastering garish light across the Surrey Docks. The occasional detonation of high explosives punctuated the ever-increasing glow of developing fires.

'I think it's mostly incendiaries.' He surveyed the sky with a professional eye, 'There's enough moonlight to keep their bomb aimers on target. I don't suspect anything will drift this far.'

Lizzy placed the snoozing baby into his cot and wriggled out from under the table. She stood next to her husband and put her arm around his waist, gazing out to the north-east where the distant flames coloured the cloud base orange.

'It's the second Sunday of Advent, Tommy.' She pulled him closer. 'What's to become of us when the fires of Hell burn on our doorstep in the season of goodwill?'

PART 3

VESPERUM

Chapter 15

Tuesday, 10 December 1940

Bryan sat in the corridor twiddling his thumbs. He considered the two separate worlds in which he now lived: His new world, London, with its streets, its people, and Jenny, with her warm bed and warmer skin, tugged at his heart night and day. His old world, the sky, with its infinite expanse, its sudden danger, its noise, fear and fire, had its talons firmly embedded in his soul. He was content in both, but could no longer travel between them so freely. He chewed his bottom lip and waited.

The door opened and the orderly leaned out, 'Flight Lieutenant Hale. The squadron leader will see you now.'

Bryan stood, straightening reluctant joints, and walked through the orderly's office. He knocked on the squadron leader's door and entered.

Lawson stood leaning on his desk, supporting his bulk on splayed arms as he regarded a folder of documents opened on his blotter.

'Ah, Hale,' he looked up and smiled, 'come in, take a seat.'

Bryan approached the desk and sat down.

'Actually, I'm glad to have this opportunity to speak with you.' Lawson sank back into his chair. 'I heard you had some misgivings about flying up and down on standing patrol while raids were clearly in progress elsewhere.'

'Erm, yes,' Bryan muttered, 'it was only an observation. My operator has family in London…'

'No, it's a perfectly reasonable point.' Lawson stabbed at the documents on his desk with a finger, 'Which is why you'll be interested in this little lot.'

Bryan leaned forward and squinted at the upside-down document stamped Top Secret in red ink.

'They've come up with what looks like a simple solution,' the older man continued, 'they're taking a homing beacon, exactly like the one that guides you back to the aerodrome, and setting it up in open countryside, down near the coast. We get several Beaus airborne and they circle the beacon at different altitudes. That way, control knows where everyone is. Then, when a target presents itself, control vectors a fighter onto it. Once the customer has been served, the fighter returns to the beacon and circles, waiting for its next turn to be vectored. A line of these beacons will be established, meaning we can concentrate forces on an incursion where it's happening rather than hanging about waiting for it to fly past.' Lawson beamed at Bryan, 'What do you think?'

Bryan nodded, 'A bit like a taxi rank, queueing for business. It could work out quite nicely.'

'Exactly, Hale. Crews like yours are the best weapon we have against the night raids and we need to get better at putting you into the right place to do your job.' Lawson leant back in his chair, 'What with this 'taxi rank' idea coming into operation before Christmas and the latest upgrades to the AI boxes, I'm expecting great things from you in the coming months.'

Silence descended on the desk and the men regarded each other across it.

'What was it you wanted?' the older man asked.

Bryan shook his head, 'I'm sorry?'

'*You* asked to see *me*, Hale.' Lawson raised one eyebrow, 'What was it you wanted?'

'Oh, yes,' Bryan stammered, 'nothing really…'

'Nothing?'

'Erm… except to thank you for your intervention on the black paint. I appreciate it could've gone a lot harder for me.'

'Don't mention it,' Lawson's eyebrow stayed cocked, 'we're all in this together, after all.'

Bryan nodded.

'Well, if there's nothing else?'

Bryan lurched to his feet, saluted and made for the door. He hurried out through the orderly's office, down the corridor and out into the chill December breeze. Releasing a lungful of breath he didn't know he'd been holding, he stood and regarded the flint-grey sky. The faint sound of rigger's banter interspersed with the clink of tools drifted across the field and a raucous laugh leaked from the mess bar where off-rota pilots had started drinking early. Bryan sucked the cold air through his nose and the undercurrent of aviation fuel tingled on his raw sinuses.

'*You have to promise me you'll live… or get on and die.*'

Bryan thrust his hands into his pockets and headed off to the crew room to check over his flying kit.

***

Bryan and Tommy walked out through the creeping dusk towards the dispersed Beaufighters. The hunched, predatory aura of the aircraft was made more sinister by the black, night-time disguise that blurred their edges against the retreating daylight.

'Are you alright, Flight?' Tommy offered a cigarette, his brow creased with concern.

Bryan accepted the smoke, 'Yes, Scott. I'm fine. A little worn down perhaps. Trying to keep too many promises.'

'How do you mean? Promises to who?' Tommy held up a burning match in his cupped hand.

Bryan's cigarette glowed and he regarded his operator with momentary dispassion.

'For a start, your wife believes you're safe because you fly with me.'

They stopped a short distance from C-Charlie to finish their cigarettes.

Tommy chuckled to himself, 'Well if they get me, it's likely you'll buy it too, so at least you won't have to explain yourself.' Tommy sucked hard on the last half-inch of his cigarette, its end illuminating his face with an orange glow. 'Every war has its veterans,' he patted the breast pocket where he kept the locks of his family's hair. 'We just need to stay lucky. Speaking of which… I've applied for leave, three days over Christmas. They'll let me go if you're happy to sign it off.'

Bryan dropped his cigarette butt onto the grass and crushed it out with the heel of his flying boot.

'Of course.' He cuffed the other man on the shoulder. 'Now, let's get up there and stay alive.'

***

The Beaufighter's metal skin thrummed in satisfied union with the double roar of Hercules engines as Bryan climbed steadily eastwards away from base. At three thousand feet the aircraft broke through the cloud into a clear, dark sky rimed with silver moonlight.

'Night-warden Control to Blackbird C-Charlie, turn due south and listen out.'

The fuselage tipped as the fighter lounged into a starboard bank, then levelled out, slightly nose-up as Bryan continued the climb towards the coast.

Tommy gazed at the vault of stars sparkling from heaven to horizon, their exuberance intersected by the night-fighter's black wing. Only the blue and red roundel mitigated its dark density, staring blindly upwards like the dead eye of an alien creature.

As they crossed the coastline, the cloud cover ended in an abrupt line, like the cleaving edge of a wide glacier edging into the sea above the luminous chalk-white cliffs stretching west from Beachy Head. Tommy watched the intermittent lines of breaking waves recede into the haze as the Beaufighter ran out into the channel.

'Night-warden Control to Blackbird C-Charlie, orbit. I repeat, orbit. We have picked up a bandit coming in at angels twelve. Listen out.'

'Understood,' Bryan's voice resonated with the quiet patience of the skulking hunter. 'Orbiting. Listening out.'

The engines' growl took on a more guttural tone as he pulled the nose up and around, spiralling to greater height to lay in wait for their prey.

Night-warden fed Bryan with vectors while Tommy settled down to watch the AI display. Glancing at his compass he noted their controller was shuffling them over to one side, allowing the intruder to pass. Then came the vector that straightened them onto a course back towards the English coast. One more course correction was followed by a moment's tense silence.

Then: 'Blackbird C-Charlie, flash, repeat, flash. Good luck.'

Tommy's gut knotted and he pressed his forehead closer into the visor, scanning the mute green screens for a sign.

'Nothing yet.'

Bryan made no reply. The aircraft hummed in exhilaration as it sliced through the night air into blind blackness.

Tommy squinted and sweated. There… a bulge gathering in the ground returns. He waited and watched until it strengthened into a blip.

'Contact. Range five thousand yards. Slightly off to port. Well below us.'

The blip started its journey down the trace, veering to the left-hand side of Tommy's screen.

'Check step to port.'

The fighter swung to port for a moment and then regained its previous heading, side-stepping to the left behind the quarry. The blip centred again and resumed its slow progress down the screen.

'Range three thousand yards. We need to lose some height before we get much closer.'

Diving to lose altitude added too much speed and risked overshooting the target. Instead, Bryan throttled back slightly and lowered the undercarriage to increase drag. The whine of the landing gear ended in a *'clunk'* as the wheels locked into place. Tommy's stomach fluttered as the craft sank. The range decreased at a comfortable rate.

'Level out now. Range is still over two thousand yards. Increase speed again.'

The undercarriage clattered back into their housings and the engines purred up a notch as Bryan squeezed open the throttle.

'Range one thousand yards. Throttle back a touch. Target is dead ahead and high.'

The blip continued its progress down the trace.

'Range seven hundred yards. Dead ahead. Fifteen degrees above.'

The blip crept closer to minimum range and Tommy fought the urge to turn away from the screens and search the sky for the enemy himself.

'Range four hundred.'

Bryan remained silent.

'Range three hundred. Still ahead. Thirty degrees above.'

The engines droned on.

'Range two hundred.'

A small tremor ran through the aircraft; a twitch of gloved hand on control column; 'I can see it.' Bryan's voice was tinged with relief. 'You can take a look.'

Tommy dropped the cover over the AI visor and gazed up into the darkness to where a darker shadow was stamped onto the night.

Bryan settled in directly underneath the enemy and crept to within one hundred yards. The blacker smudge of sky acquired an outline that became a recognisable shape.

'Heinkel 111.' It was more a statement than a question.

'Without a doubt, Flight.'

'Alright. Attacking now.'

Bryan began a measured ascent. The enemy aircraft dropped slowly, like a holed vessel settling in the water, until it sank almost below Tommy's line of sight. He held his breath as Bryan jiggled the target into the centre of his gunsight.

The cannon breeches in the floor flashed with violence and the clatter and thud of their fire shook the fuselage. Acrid smoke drifted up around Tommy, stinging his nostrils. He didn't notice this, nor the sudden silence as the firing ceased. He simply gawped at the bomber flying on straight and level, seemingly unconcerned about their attack.

'The guns have stopped.' Bryan's voice, terse with tension, brought him round. He unlatched his harness and jumped from his seat, stamping on the magazines with his heel.

'Still plenty of ammo in the drums, Flight.'

'Alright, let's try again.'

Tommy climbed back to his perch and looked ahead at the bomber, still ploughing sedately through the night.

The cacophony reprised and Tommy watched the concentrated smattering of white sparkles dancing over the target's starboard engine as it flew on unperturbed. Then silence fell again.

Tommy jumped down to the cannon breeches and bent to examine them.

'Shit!' Bryan's exclamation came as the Beaufighter lurched over into an evasive turn, knocking Tommy off his feet. 'They're firing back.'

Tommy grabbed out for handholds and hauled himself up to peer through the dome. Red balls of tracer floated towards him, curved and flicked over the wing like angry insects bursting from a disturbed nest. Bryan peeled away to the left and the return fire followed their trajectory, whipping past but never hitting the airframe.

The firing quelled. Bryan levelled out and banked onto a parallel course to the Heinkel, still visible in the moonlight.

'We've lost air pressure to the breeches, Flight.' Tommy was surprised by the ragged edge in his own breathing. 'It's not something I can fix.'

'Alright, Scott. Never mind.'

The two men kept a watch on the Heinkel. It slowed down and tipped into a shallow descent as it wallowed in a wide bank to head home across the channel. Grim visions intruded on Tommy's imagination; scenes of death and maiming, panic, fear and the dread of cold channel water. None of this could be fathomed from the serene, dark fuselage that they shadowed.

'At least they haven't bombed anyone,' Tommy's voice sounded distant to his own ears.

'It might be as well for them to get home. Unloading that crew might put the fear of God into the others.' Bryan banked away from the retreating intruder, 'Give me a bearing for home.'

Wednesday, 11 December 1940

Jenny ran her thumb down the fat wedge of papers squatting in her in tray and sighed. She stood and walked to the window, stretching her legs and letting the blood return to her numbing buttocks. Her gaze drifted along the street where pedestrians hurried by in the brisk winter air. Her eye was drawn to a man carrying a Christmas tree over his shoulder. Green fronds poked out at the top of its sack wrapping, bobbing stiffly with the man's purposeful gait. The brightness of the winter sunshine attested to cloudless skies. Last year such weather might've gladdened her heart. Today, once the sun had set, such clear skies would become the bombers' friend, colluding with the near-full moon to illuminate their targets.

Jenny fought the urge to look at the clock as she returned to her desk and the pile of documents she'd processed during the morning. She hefted the papers onto her forearm and walked to the bank of filing cabinets that stretched across one wall of the large office. A thin tang of perfume mixed with talcum powder hung in the air above the dozen or so women working in the space. The muffled clatter of a typewriter underpinned the soft murmur of a conversation. The sharp ring of a telephone sliced through both.

Jenny laid her burden on a table and squinted at the hand-scrawled label on the first folder; *November 1940 – Domestic dwellings damaged beyond repair – East London.* Jenny paused, the thick wad of documents weighed heavy in her hand, a mute testament to the disaster that had befallen that part of the city. She pulled out a filing drawer and tucked the folder in front of a similarly fat file containing October's figures.

'Jennifer.'

She turned to the sound of her supervisor's voice. The woman was accompanied by a stranger. A man dressed in a tailored suit of brown tweed flecked with green. Under the jacket he wore a mustard moleskin waistcoat from which hung the silver loop of a watch chain, and a red silk tie nestled in the collar of his white cotton shirt. A shock of thick black hair sat atop his quietly handsome face, his aquiline nose emphasised by the bars of thick, ebony eyebrows that slanted over dark brown eyes.

'This is James Bartlett, a new arrival in the Housing and Architecture department.'

James held out his hand and Jenny shook it.

'He's working on a project that will need a fair bit of archive research. As you're the best archivist we have, I've assigned you to do the work.'

Jenny opened her mouth to ask a question, but the supervisor was already hurrying away to complete an interrupted mission elsewhere.

'I'm still finding my feet,' James spoke into the gap she'd left, 'setting up my desk and learning who does what. So, it might be a while before I have any work that needs your expertise.'

Jenny felt an unbidden blush creeping up her cheeks, 'What's the nature of the project?'

'Infrastructure mostly. I'm an architect.' He smiled, 'Why don't I come to see you early next week, after I've got my bearings? We can spend a day going through the document index and I can choose what I'd like you to dig up.'

Jenny smiled and nodded.

'Good. I look forward to it.'

Jenny watched his back as he wove between the desks and left the room.

***

The haze of cigarette smoke corralled under the wooden roof of the operations hut rippled in the draught from an ill-fitting window. The crews sat beneath it, most lighting their next cigarette with the dog-end of the last, waiting for the word to go.

The squadron leader shuffled through the meteorological report before dropping the papers onto the table and straightening his back to speak.

'Gentlemen.' Murmured conversations amongst the aircrews atrophied to silence. 'The clear skies over the Channel have given way to a build-up of cloud. Cumulus and cumulonimbus can be expected along the coastal regions, with the possibility of electric storms. On top of that there's a bombers' moon, so we can reasonably count on a lot of custom coming through the shop tonight. Bear in mind, the stronger moonlight will make it more likely you'll be spotted. So, once you get a contact, think carefully about the best angle of approach. Good luck and good hunting.'

The crews surged to their feet, retrieving helmets and gloves before shuffling to the door.

'Bloody full moon,' Bryan muttered. 'I can really do without getting shot at again.'

Tommy followed him out into the refreshing cool of the evening air.

'He never got anywhere near us last night.' Tommy held his arm out straight and swept it in a slow arc. 'He needed to add a couple more degrees of deflection, then we might've been in a spot of bother.'

Bryan gave him a sidelong look, 'That's nice to know.'

Tommy tapped the left side of his chest, where his single-winged air gunner badge still adorned the tunic underneath the flying suit. 'Just my professional opinion.'

They walked out across the grass and the hunkering profiles of the night-fighters in dispersal loomed out of the gloaming.

'Look at them,' Tommy breathed in admiration. 'They want to go hunting.'

***

Blackbird C-Charlie was the last in line to take-off and Bryan sat tapping his fingers on his knees, waiting for the call to taxi. Faint scuffles intruded from the fuselage as Tommy checked the spare ammo drums were secure in their stowage. Bryan's eyes flicked over the oil gauges; temperatures climbing slowly. He tweaked the throttles back a notch, listening to the Beaufighters ahead of him get clearance from the controller, interspersed with already airborne night-fighters being vectored onto contacts.

'Night-warden Control to Blackbird C-Charlie. Clear to take off.'

'At last,' Bryan muttered to himself, released the brakes and eased the throttles forward. He heard more scraping behind him as Tommy clambered into his seat and strapped himself in.

'Operator to pilot. All shipshape back here.'

The Beaufighter raced across the grass and eased itself into the winter air. Bryan retracted the undercarriage and flicked off the navigation lights. He tipped the aircraft into a starboard bank and pulled the nose over the horizontal to climb away from the airfield on a course towards the coast. The turbulence in the clouds rocked and buffeted the fuselage until they slipped out through the top of the weather into clear, ebony skies. Towering groups of cumulus, rent apart by dizzying gorges, jostled like moonlit icebergs in the turgid, swirling current of the night. On occasion, the deepest bowels of these ethereal monoliths illuminated with the foetal flashes of the storms they incubated.

'Night-warden Control to Blackbird C-Charlie, we may have a customer for you. Make angels ten and listen out.'

Bryan dropped into a ragged orbit, skirting the edges of the fomenting clouds to camouflage the fighter's silhouette over the darkened landscape across which they marched.

'Night-warden to Blackbird C-Charlie. Vector two-seven-zero. Bandit is outgoing. He should be crossing your nose from starboard to port. Flash.'

Tommy bent closer to the cathode ray tubes and watched the static coalesce on the right edge of the screen. It writhed for a moment, then gave birth to a solid blip that edged its way across the green glow.

Tommy flicked on the intercom, 'I've got contact, Flight. Range two thousand yards. Start a shallow turn to port.'

The fuselage tilted to the left.

'Thank you, Night-warden, we have contact.' Bryan's voice gave way to silence, ruffled only by the sound of his breathing amplified by his oxygen mask.

Tommy watched the blip drift towards the centre of his screen. 'Straighten up, Flight. Speed is good. He's jinking a bit.'

The German aircraft was heading south, flying in a series of uneven curves, snaking its way towards the coast. The Beaufighter's straight vector cut off the corners and the range closed steadily.

'Six hundred yards' – Tommy glanced between the two screens – 'altitude good.'

The engines thrummed their sonorous song through the padded visor into his forehead, the noise underpinned by Bryan's slow and steady breathing in his ears.

'Three hundred yards, slow down a touch.'

'I see him, Scott. You can take a look now.'

Tommy wound down the brightness on the AI and swivelled his seat to face forward. Peering ahead through the plexiglass dome he caught the black bulk of a Heinkel 111 suspended in the night above them. To each side the billowing cloud-mountains ascended to form a moonlit valley. The German wound his way between these cliffs to avoid the turbulence within them. Tommy was struck with the absurd certainty that the enemy pilot was humming with pleasure at the surreal beauty of the scene around him.

Strengthening flashes of lightning, like the cameras of jostling newshounds, flared the scene into stark relief. Tommy felt his jaw tighten; the black-painted Beaufighter sat naked and vulnerable, as visible to the German gunners as they were to him.

Bryan closed the gap and Tommy followed the bomber's silhouette as it swung closer, teeth gritted against the expectation of flashing tracer.

Mirroring the Heinkel's languid weaving between the cloudbanks, Bryan settled in directly below it. 'Everything alright, Scott?' Bryan's voice betrayed his own suppressed tension.

'Sweet as a nut, Flight.'

'Right, attacking now.'

Tommy watched the bomber sinking towards Bryan's sights. The lightning flashes reflected on the Perspex casing of the raider's ventral gun position, barely eighty yards ahead.

'He's asleep,' Tommy muttered to himself. 'He *must* be asleep.'

Silver-blue exhaust flames fluttered delicately along its engine cowlings as the German bomber settled in front of C-Charlie. The Beaufighter made a slight twitch to the right as Bryan centred the gunsight. Then the cannons in the floor erupted into thudding cacophony.

The sky ahead immediately blossomed into bright orange flame that engulfed the night-fighter as it ploughed through the explosion. The Beaufighter heaved upwards with Bryan's instinctive attempt to avoid disaster. A large, soft bundle bumped off the observation dome, cartwheeling backwards into space, and shards of metal clattered along the fuselage, like nuts and bolts strewn against a corrugated-iron shed. Then the night-fighter broke through to darkness.

Tommy blinked against the coloured blobs that mired his vision and pulled his gasping breath back under control. The engines' roar continued smooth and untroubled.

'Are we still in one piece?' Tommy's voice rang brittle in ears still clanging from the cannons' noise.

'Yes.' Bryan sounded dazed. 'I think we got away with it.'

Tommy glanced at the AI displays. A blip fell away on the right side of the screen. He craned his neck out to scan the starboard quarter, catching his breath at what he saw.

The wrecked Heinkel dropped through the night, its one intact wing propelling its dive into a languid spin, drawing a spiral of burning petrol that traced its progress seaward. The severed wing followed, spewing occasional coughs of flame and reflecting flashes of moonlight as it spun downwards into the storm-wracked clouds.

'Blackbird C-Charlie to Night-warden Control.' Bryan's voice had regained an enforced steely edge. 'Have dealt with your customer, do you have any more waiting?'

'Good work, C-Charlie. No, they've all gone home. Thank you and goodnight.'

The Beaufighter swung around to a northerly course and started to shed altitude. Tommy loosened his harness a notch and gazed up at the stars as cordite fumes cloyed in his throat.

Chapter 16

Monday, 16 December 1940

Jenny trotted up the steps, showed her pass to the guard on the door and entered the warm fug of the ministry's foyer. Untangling her scarf from her neck she hurried across the parqueted floor to catch an open lift. She closed her eyes for the few precious seconds it took the lift to tick up to her floor. Dragged from her reverie by the opening doors, she emerged into the corridor and clacked towards the records office. Her supervisor approached, pushing a file trolley in the other direction, and raised enquiring eyebrows.

'Bus detour,' Jenny blurted as they passed. 'Road blocked. Sorry.'

Dashing into the large open-plan workspace, Jenny at once slowed her rush; her eyes fell on James sitting in a chair by her desk, legs crossed, engrossed in a newspaper. She peeled off her overcoat as she crossed the room.

'Mr Bartlett, I'm so sorry I'm late.' She draped her coat across the back of her chair, 'There was a road blockage from last night's raid. The bus had to take a huge detour. I hope you haven't been waiting long.'

James lifted his head and smiled.

'Think nothing of it.' He folded his paper and shoved it into his jacket pocket, 'It's always good to catch up with the news.'

Jenny sat down and faced him across her desk. Her scramble through the heated building in her winter coat had left her cheeks glowing with warmth. A bead of sweat formed at the nape of her neck and trickled down between her shoulder blades. She straightened her back against its tickling passage and felt it dissipate below her waistband. Her lower back prickled gently with the heat and she tensed her buttocks to unstick her skin from the fabric of her underwear.

'Where shall we start?' she asked.

James pulled a notepad from a briefcase by his feet and flipped the pages.

'I'm primarily interested in the areas of London that have suffered the largest concentration of destruction from the bombing, areas where most buildings are beyond repair.'

Jenny picked up a pen and started notes of her own.

'Residential or industrial?'

'Either… both. It doesn't matter as long as whatever stood there before has been flattened. I need detailed street maps indicating property use and land registration where possible.'

Jenny glanced up as she scribbled, 'What about dock facilities?'

'Include them, but mark them as such. I imagine they're being repaired ad hoc, no matter what the damage, so they may not be relevant.'

She nodded, 'Churches?'

'Identify them, along with the extent of damage if known.'

Jenny glanced up again, 'Monuments?'

'Ditto.'

Jenny scratched this last note without looking down, preferring to watch the other's dark eyes flitting over his papers as he ticked off his points.

'Now, once we've got that organised, I'll need charts of the corresponding infrastructure; everything underlying these areas. Sewerage, water supply, gas and electricity supplies, to street level only.' He smiled briskly, 'How long do you think you need?'

'It's a big job,' Jenny glanced at her in tray, 'and it's getting bigger.'

'You're right, let's do it in chunks. Start at The Tower and map east. Do the north of the river first, then the south. Let me know when you've got the first batch sorted.'

He held Jenny's gaze for a moment before he rose from his chair and left.

Jenny glanced from her notes to her in tray and back again.

'Tea first.' she murmured to herself.

Thursday, 19 December 1940

'Blackbird C-Charlie to Night-warden. We're still stooging around. Have you forgotten about us?'

'Hello C-Charlie. Sorry, nothing doing at the moment. No trade.'

Tommy amused himself by following the other Beaufighters in the taxi rank as they drifted across his screens, checking their altitude differed enough to pose no threat of collision. He glanced up through the Perspex dome into the deep, clear night. There were no clouds and little turbulence. The moon, not yet full, reflected sufficient light to navigate by the glinting waterways, yet left adequate gloom to obscure a slinking raider.

Tommy shivered against the metallic chill in the fuselage. He wound down the brightness on the tubes and let his eyelids droop.

The rasp of a voice on the radio jerked Tommy back to consciousness; '…return to base. Thank you and goodnight.'

He turned up the brightness and watched the aerodrome's homing beacon swing onto the screen.

***

'Where the bloody hell were they?' Bryan made a wide gesture at the crystal black sky, 'The conditions are perfect.'

Tommy clumped through the rough grass next to him on his slightly shorter legs.

'According to *The Daily Mirror*, bomber command hit Mannheim on Monday. They were aiming for factories, but by all accounts they made a merry mess of the town centre. Maybe that was enough to make the Germans see sense. Perhaps they've given up bombing as a bad job.'

Bryan slung him a sideways glance.

'Why would they?' his voice carried the tension of his frustration. 'Their losses are miniscule. It's more likely they've run out of bombs and are waiting for a delivery.'

They trudged without speaking for a few moments and Bryan's irritation dissipated.

'Would you like a lift home at Christmas?'

'That's very kind, Flight. Are you going to see your girlfriend?'

'No. I'm going to visit my parents.'

'But, I thought…'

'Whatever other faults she may have, my mother still makes a halfway decent Yorkshire pudding.'

Friday, 20 December 1940

Jenny picked up the telephone and dialled an extension.

'Hello, Mr Bartlett? It's Jennifer from archives. I have the first batch of documents ready for you.'

The handset clattered back into its cradle and Jenny waited. She found herself watching the door, a slow buzz of expectation settling in her bowels. Moments later James entered the archive office and threaded his way across to her desk.

Jenny rose and smiled, 'This way. I've laid the plans out in the meeting room.'

He followed her to a room sectioned from the main office by half-glazed walls. His step quickened when he caught sight of the plans and he pulled a pair of tortoiseshell glasses from his top pocket.

'I've labelled each map with its London postal sub-district.' She fished a sheet of paper from amongst the maps, 'These are the colour codes for the different types of building. Solid colour indicates undamaged or repairable, cross-hatched indicates severely damaged or destroyed. There's a corresponding plan of services for each area. I'm sorry to say they are not the same scale, but I've marked the boundary of each map onto the service plan so they can be cross referenced. It goes without saying, this is only as accurate as the reports I've received. Who knows what will change tonight?'

James nodded, 'We can be sure it won't be getting better, though.'

Jenny stepped back, clasped her hands in front of her and watched him shuffle and pore through the charts and diagrams. The moments ticked by.

'Is it what you expected?'

'Yes.' James straightened up and removed his spectacles. 'It's really good work. Thank you so much for your efforts.'

Jenny beamed a smile, 'May I ask how the maps will be used?'

James pulled up a chair next to the meeting room table and sat down.

'How's your history?'

Jenny pulled up a chair opposite him. 'Test me.'

'1666?'

'The Great Fire of London.'

'That's correct. As you know, great swathes of shops and houses were razed to the ground.' James folded his specs and tucked them back into his top pocket. 'When Sir Christopher Wren saw the extent of the damage, he realised a great opportunity existed for him to recast the city of London in a more European style. He drew up plans for squares and plazas with roads radiating out from them like sunbeams from the sun, new streets and thoroughfares lined with new shops and houses, new apartments with domed roofs and balconies.

'He drew up exquisitely detailed plans for a New London and presented them to parliament. But while he was busy at his drawing board, and later, while the politicians ground away in their committees, the people who had owned the buildings came back. They swept away the ashes, uncovered the foundations of their shops and homes and started to rebuild everything exactly the way it used to be.'

Jenny frowned, 'That seems perfectly natural.'

'Maybe so, but simply ending up with what you had before seems like a lost opportunity to me. Surely it's better to build something new with passion rather than restore what your ancestors accepted as good enough?' James tapped the pile of papers, 'So this time around we've decided to get on with the planning before the fires go out.'

'But don't we need to beat the Germans first?'

James regarded her, a shadow of amusement flitting across his features. 'It will need rebuilding, whoever wins.'

**

Jenny folded a silk blouse and draped it into her suitcase.

'When are you leaving?' Alice leant against the door frame watching her.

'Tomorrow, probably lunchtime.' She leafed through more hangers, choosing another blouse to pack. 'I feel like a bit of a traitor, having a full week holiday when there's so much work on.'

'We can't stop being human, Jen. We can't let them take everything away from us. Here, I got you a little gift.' Alice brought a small brown paper package from behind her back and held it out. 'It's homemade, nothing much. Open it now.'

Jenny pulled at the string bow and peeled back the paper. The package contained a knitted figure of a man, about six inches tall.

'It's a voodoo doll.' Alice beamed with pleasure at her cleverness. 'You can pretend it's that nasty salesman from Highgate and stick pins in it when you're angry. Or it could be Bryan and you can stick pins in it when he doesn't do what's expected of him.'

Jenny turned the figure over in her hands. It wore a blue tunic and sported a flash of blond hair.

'Alice… you've made it *look* like Bryan.'

'Or,' Alice ignored her comment, took a step forward and laid a palm on Jenny's shoulder, 'you could put it in your bottom drawer and save it until you meet someone else, just in case he's not quite so perfect as you hope he is.' She pressed a card of pins into Jenny's free hand. 'Happy Christmas.'

Saturday, 21 December 1940

Jenny crunched over the gravel, through the gates of Du Cane Court and onto the pavement. She hefted her small suitcase in her hand and headed north towards Clapham South. Passing under the railway bridge she glanced across to the tube station entrance. A couple of vans stood parked next to the pavement. In one, a workman poured tea from a thermos. He caught her eye and winked over the hand-rolled cigarette dangling from his lips.

Jenny smiled and walked on, the beneficence of Christmas already infecting her heart. Her step faltered as she passed the fresh tarmac that traced the circular ghost of the bomb crater and she glanced up at the scaffolded frontage of buildings in which there could be no seasonal cheer.

'Where are you off to, young lady?' An old gentleman with grey hair squeaked his bicycle to a halt next to her and dismounted. 'Can I be of any help?'

Jenny had intended to take the bus to Clapham South, but she allowed the prospect of pleasant company to sway her: 'I'm going as far as the next tube stop. Yes, that would be very kind of you.'

The man hoisted the suitcase onto his crossbar and began pushing his bike along next to the pavement, the case wedged in place under his armpit.

'Are you off to spend Christmas with your sweetheart?'

'I don't know,' Jenny smiled at the man's easy geniality, 'I suppose I'll see if he's there when I arrive.'

'I hope for his sake he makes it. This will be a Christmas we'll need to remember for a long time.'

***

Jenny climbed the steps, emerged through the red brick maw of Hampstead station and stood blinking on the pavement. An otherworldliness hung in the ether that even a bombing war had failed to ruffle. The piles of sandbags either side of the entrance looked brand new, practically starched. The air, although tinged with the petrol fumes of revving cabbies, held no bitter undertones of burnt wood and brick dust. It was the first time in weeks she'd seen a street that nursed no broken windows.

'Jenny!'

She turned at the boom of the familiar voice, 'Hello, Daddy.'

Her father grabbed her suitcase and kissed her cheek in one swooping movement. 'Come on, my love. I'm parked in the next road at a bus stop. Can't afford to hang about.'

He bustled off the way he'd come and Jenny trotted after, a broad grin creasing her face. They dodged around the corner and he redoubled his speed at the sight of a double-decker bus crawling through the traffic towards them.

'Quickly!' He dropped the suitcase into the boot and they clambered into the car. 'Now, come on old girl, don't let me down.'

The car coughed into life at the first turn of the key and they pulled away, the driver's cry of victory drowned out by the blaring horn of the bus looming behind them.

Jenny's father glanced in the rearview mirror and tutted: 'I don't know, Jen. Why is everyone so impatient these days?'

'It's his job to be on time, Dad.' She squeezed his hand where it rested on the gear stick.

'Even so, young lady, there is such a thing as common courtesy.'

Jenny smiled again and gave up the argument. She relaxed into the seat and surrendered to the warm glow of coming home.

It was a short drive from the station along well-appointed streets to the Freeman home. The detached house stood behind a tall garden wall. In between the wall and the front porch there was space for a circular rockery around which the car crunched on deep shingle.

'Welcome home, Jen,' her father said and climbed out to retrieve the case.

Jenny clambered out and pushed her way through the front door. The rich scent of Christmas baking filled the hallway and she hurried through to the kitchen to find her mother testing a cake with a metal skewer, her eyes squinting at her creation from a visage reddened by the kitchen's heat.

'A couple more minutes, I think.' She picked up the baking tin and approached the cooker, 'Fruit cake. Your favourite.' She slid the tin back into the oven and turned to regard her daughter. 'Terrible job getting the cherries.'

'Hello, Mother.' Jenny crossed the room and melted into the woman's embrace, 'It's good to be home.'

'Sit down, my love.' She took a speculative glance at her watch, 'Too early I fear, it'll have to be tea.'

Jenny heard the clump of her father climbing the stairs, taking her case to her old bedroom. The room they kept the way she'd left it, just in case. Glancing around the kitchen she was hard-pressed to spot anything that hadn't been there forever. It could've been the night all those years ago when her mother sat her at this same kitchen table, filled the same dark brown teapot from the same whistling kettle and broke the news about Richard.

Her mother placed the tea tray on the table between them, 'So,' she said from beneath arched eyebrows, 'any news?'

Jenny picked up the pot and poured. 'None that I can tell *you*.'

The older woman glanced up sharply, gauging the humour behind the words, 'So, you're still single.'

'I'm not ready to give up my job yet, Mummy. There's too much important work to be done and I don't want to be stuck in a kitchen while someone else does it.'

'The time is running away from you, Jennifer. Good Lord, you'll be twenty-nine next August. Don't leave it too late, my darling. That would break my heart.'

Jenny reached across and squeezed her mother's hand, 'I'll know the right man when he comes along, Mummy. After all, I can't have your grandchildren with just anybody.'

The older woman smiled and stood up, 'Come on. Bring your tea, let's go and look at the Christmas tree.'

Monday, 23 December 1940

The two women strolled down Hampstead Grove on their way towards the press of shops and cafes clustered around the tube station. The sky formed a blue, cloudless dome over their heads and the tepid, yellowing sunshine cast ever-longer shadows as it descended to its early rest.

'There have been a few bombs, of course,' Mrs Freeman said. 'But we stopped going to the shelter a long while ago. Out here we're more likely to get run over in the blackout than killed in an explosion.'

'The hit on Balham tube station was the closest thing to us.'

'I heard. Nasty business.'

Jenny refrained from elaborating and simply grunted agreement.

'It does rather prove,' her mother continued, 'that nowhere is truly safe.'

Hampstead Grove narrowed and the high walls on either side channelled the chill breeze. The downward slope hurried their feet along and Jenny felt a pang of anxiety, a stab of unbidden emotion: The road opened to a junction and they veered down towards Holly Hill. To their left, set back along a narrow alley, sat The Holly Tree public house. She hadn't been there since her last visit with Richard and ghosts of that time flocked around the door. Jenny pulled her eyes away and let the jumble in her heart subside.

The slope steepened and within two hundred yards disgorged the pair onto the main street opposite the station.

'Right, young lady.' Mrs Freeman caught her arm, 'Let's find you a Christmas present.'

***

Jenny's mother busied herself at the table with wrapping paper and ribbons, while her father occupied his habitual perch at his desk with a fountain pen in his hand, writing a letter or crafting a diary entry. Jenny scanned the newspaper on her lap: Three consecutive raids on Liverpool had inspired some young hack to dub it the *Christmas Blitz*. Apart from this flash of diabolical creativity, the article was written in a stark, factual style. Three shelters had taken direct hits, killing nearly two hundred people.

Jenny gazed at the number, trying to penetrate its meaning. Fifty families or more?

She pushed the paper away and it slid to the floor. Her eyes rested on the glass ornaments dangling from the tree, sparkling against the odds in the dimly-lit room.

'I had a chat with the postman, this morning.' Mr Freeman's head remained bowed over his papers as he spoke. 'Apparently there's some speculation about a truce over Christmas. A bit like 1914.'

Mrs Freeman finished wrapping a parcel and tucked it under the tree. 'Perhaps Hitler will see the light and move for peace in the new year.'

Her husband stood and stretched. 'It's gone too far for that, my love. I don't think 1941 can be a particularly happy new year for anyone.'

He opened a drawer in his desk and rummaged around, 'Who's for a game of cards?'

Chapter 17

Christmas Eve, 1940

It was approaching 9 o'clock in the morning when Bryan dropped Scott outside his house. Bryan waved to Lizzy when she opened the door for her husband and smiled with genuine pleasure at the kiss she blew back. Grinding the Humber into gear, he pulled a laborious three-point turn in the narrow road and started back the way he had come, his exhaust swathing great coils of condensation into the crisp winter air.

He headed north up Peckham Hill. The grimy terraced houses resembled an old man's dentures: some teeth missing, others broken. Along the pavements and on top of the rubble-heaps children played, wrapped in grubby overcoats and knitted balaclavas, each child a firecracker of barely-contained excitement ubiquitous amongst the innocent on this day of days.

Bryan steered west onto the Old Kent Road. Here shopkeepers and stallholders bustled about their business, eager to take a last few coins before their customers melted from the streets to shut themselves away in homes full of family. A pub stood with windows thrown open to clear the fug of the previous night and the landlord bent to sweeping his doorstep in readiness for a late afternoon rush of workmen bonding in seasonal camaraderie, and bosses treating the typing pool to a glass of sherry.

He continued west, through Elephant and Castle and on to Lambeth. Here the people moved along the streets with a certainty of purpose and a sense of belonging. It was Christmas and they were home; nothing could hurt them today.

Bryan slowed as he jostled with double-decker buses to cross Westminster Bridge. Parliament brooded behind its ramparts of bagged sand, and terse-featured guards, with their rifles slung, regarded last-minute shoppers with a tinge of envy.

Hard right onto the Embankment and the traffic loosened. Ahead, above the docks, a miasma of soot stained the horizon, rising from burnt-out timber yards that had smouldered for weeks. On the river, an RAF launch plied its way seaward, curving gracefully between the tugs labouring their loads in the opposite direction.

Striking north now, through Holborn, Russell Square and Bloomsbury. More women on the pavements here, some with packages, some arm in arm, all better dressed.

Through Camden to Belsize Park and a sudden flood of memories that had lain in wait for his return. Pubs he knew, shops he had frequented, the side road to St Christopher's, his old school. And finally, Hampstead.

Bryan hauled a left turn onto Church Row and there, towards the end of the road, stood the church of St John. The building sat squat amongst the elegant Georgian terraces, like a gothic power station supplanted from the age of steam. Its bleak brick tower supported a diminutive verdigris spire, a small afterthought to soften the gruff industrial façade with a hint of righteousness. Here, with all its oppressive inertia, stood his father's palace of dogma.

'God help me,' Bryan breathed.

He crawled the Humber along the road next to the wrought iron railings that stood in the shadow of the church walls. Stones, marking the graves of long-dead gentlemen traders and their families, slid by, inexorable. Directly behind the church stood a substantial house with a columned porch, thickly painted in years of white gloss. Bryan parked on the road outside.

It took only a few moments before a curtain moved to one side and his mother's face appeared at the window. Her querulous expression melted into wide-eyed surprise as Bryan climbed out of the car and pulled his kitbag off the back seat.

Bryan walked up the porch steps and the door opened before he reached it.

'Shhh…' his mother held a finger to her lips. 'Your father is working on his sermon for midnight mass. Mustn't be disturbed.'

'Hello, Mother,' Bryan bent and brushed a kiss onto the woman's cheek. 'Happy Christmas.'

'Shhh. Come through.'

Bryan set his bag down under the hat rack in the tiled hallway and followed his mother past his father's closed study and into the kitchen. She ushered him in and gently shut the door.

'Well, here's a surprise. Let me look at you,' a smile brightened her worn features. 'How long do we have you?'

'I'll be leaving on Boxing Day.'

She filled a kettle and set out three cups and saucers. 'I expect the turkey is big enough.' She broke off her tea-making and turned to regard him, her smile broadening as her surprise at his arrival dissipated. 'How are you, Bryan?'

'Never mind me, what about you? Still walking on eggshells around the old man, I see. Haven't you put in sufficient time to earn some privileges?'

'Now, now, don't be disrespectful. It's for better or worse, you know that. He has a calling to answer, and he puts his heart into it.'

Mrs Hale placed the tea cups on the table and arranged some oatmeal biscuits on a plate, overlapping them neatly into a circle. The kettle's hiss changed to a warble which escalated to a full-throated screech. She turned off the gas and filled the teapot.

'He'll be through in a moment,' she said, under her breath, inclining a nod to the kitchen door.

Bryan turned as the door opened. Reverend Hale stepped into the room and hesitated. He regarded Bryan with the air of an engineer evaluating an unexpected fault.

'Tea,' Mrs Hale announced, 'and look; Bryan's visiting us for Christmas.'

The tall man's neck swivelled against his dog collar from Bryan to his wife and back again. His features relaxed, as if a conundrum had been satisfactorily explained and he stepped forward with his hand outstretched. 'Good morning, Son.'

Bryan stood and received the handshake. 'Hello, Father.'

They all sat, and the tea was poured and sipped in silence. The Reverend picked up a biscuit and nibbled its edge.

'How is the sermon coming along?' Bryan asked.

'Very well, thank you.'

'It must be a difficult one to pitch, this year. What with London being crucified by air raids practically every night?'

The older man hesitated under his son's provocation for a moment, then decided to turn the other cheek; 'We can always rally to the flag of faith when all around seems lost to chaos.'

Bryan nodded sagely, 'A very fine concept for a sermon writer sitting in a vicarage drawing room. But how might it play to the bombed-out families of Coventry, or Liverpool, or the East End? Those people only believe in Hitler and the devils that work for him. I expect they'd like to know why God allows them such free rein.'

Mrs Hale cleared her throat, 'I need to make up a bed.'

The Reverend watched her go and took another bite of his biscuit. The kitchen door clicked closed and he leant towards Bryan, his expression locked into its habitually beneficent altruism despite his underlying rankle.

'God has allowed this war to happen in order to spur us on towards a solution; some way to bring about everlasting peace, to prevent such things from ever happening again.'

'Father,' Bryan looked the older man in the eye, 'outside our aerodrome there's an iron age hillfort. It was built for the same reason that takes me into the sky in a heavily armed aircraft searching for people to kill; self-defense. How can war be stopped when there's always someone ready to steal everything you've got?'

The Reverend leaned back in his chair and drained his tea, 'I thank God for your deliverance from the danger.'

'I assure you that's purely a matter of luck.'

'Well,' Bryan's father hauled his tall frame upright, 'I must go and finish my sermon.'

Bryan swivelled on his shiny wooden chair to watch his father walk towards the door.

'I suppose you know the Nazis believe God is on *their* side?'

***

The bar at The Flask public house embraced a throng of sweating customers, mostly married couples, intent on squeezing out whatever merriment might be available for the coins they possessed, while the log fire roared out its broiling heat to further ruddy their faces. Occasional hoots and cackles of laughter split the air as the crowd jostled under a turgid layer of tobacco smoke wallowing against the ceiling like an inverted moorland fog.

Bryan's dinner sat like a lump of chalk in his stomach. It had been eaten in silence, not because anyone held a grudge, but because that's the way it always was. He vaguely regretted goading his father, if only because his mother was likely to suffer the consequences of the resultant brooding. The man gave no credence to Bryan's opinions on anything, especially religion, so the sparring was ultimately a pointless sport. Perhaps his attendance at the church would oil the choppy waters.

Bryan wore his crumpled civilian suit and he'd long since pulled his tie loose. But even that, and the six pints of ale he'd swilled, failed to liberate him from his bleak mood.

'Cheer up, mate,' a man nudged him in the ribs with a bony elbow. 'It might never happen.'

Bryan shuffled sideways to let the man through to the bar.

'I'm almost certain it will,' he muttered to himself.

The large clock on the wall, a trophy from a French railway station, struck ten. The crowd whittled away, women calling farewells and Christmas wishes to neighbours across the room. Within twenty minutes Bryan was left with barely a dozen drinking companions, mostly hard-bitten older men whose eyes reflected their losses from a previous war.

Too bloated to drink any more ale, Bryan ordered a large port and brandy, partly to salve his indigestion, but mostly to dull the impending ordeal of his father's midnight mass. The deep, blood tingling warmth of the ruby-red liquid loosened the knots in his stomach and blunted the edge of his senses.

Draining the glass, he wriggled into his overcoat, waved his goodnight to the barman and pushed through the blackout curtains to the chill winter night and the short walk to St John's Church.

***

Bryan trudged up the path between the gravestones and through the church doors. A verger smiled in greeting and held the blackout drapes to one side. Bryan nodded his thanks and stepped through.

Sconces thronged with candles danced and flickered their light around the vast cream-white interior. The painted columns, marching in pairs down the body of the church, supported sweeping arches and balconies, both rimed with plaster decorations clothed in gold leaf that glinted in resonance with the guttering flames below. A thousand times he'd been inside this building, almost every time against his will or better judgement, yet in spite of himself, it never failed to move him with its simple, clean beauty.

Bryan bowed his head in habitual respect towards the high altar and slid onto the rearmost pew, closing his eyes and allowing the low, rambling organ melody and the hushed murmur of conversation to unfocus his mind. Footsteps shuffled past him up the aisle as the great, the good and the generally worried folk of Hampstead arrived to fill the sixty or more rows of seating that spanned the stone-clad floor, each seeking the solace and affirmation of congregating humanity.

Someone sat beside him.

Bryan raised his chin from his chest and flared his nostrils to gather the familiar scent, 'Happy Christmas, Sweetheart,' he murmured, his tone slightly blurred.

'Are you drunk?' Jenny whispered.

'Not half as much as I need to be.'

'Shhh... that's not very Godly.'

'I'm only here because it's the family business. What's your excuse?'

'Oh, I love midnight mass. It makes me feel all Christmassy.'

Bryan opened his eyes enough to squint at her. 'In that case, welcome to the pleasure dome. The show's about to begin.'

'Merry Christmas, Bryan.' She leant across, kissed his cheek and regarded him for a long moment. '*Yet, here we sit,*' the echo of the words made her smile.

The volume of the church organ swelled and the tune changed from contemplative meandering to processional vigour. The worshippers in front of them stood. Jenny elbowed Bryan and he hauled himself upright.

A choirboy passed at a slow march, carrying a polished brass cross on an ancient wooden stave. Reverend Hale followed at the head of the surpliced choir, each luminous member floating like disembodied goodness through the candlelight. The reverend peeled off at the front of the congregation, the others continued into the chancel and shuffled into the choirstalls.

The organ dropped into startling silence and the memory of its voice throbbed in ebbing waves of delicious reverberation. Bryan's father allowed the sound to shimmer away to nothing, then raised his head.

'Please remain standing. Our first hymn is Hark the Herald Angels Sing.'

'Oh,' Jenny exclaimed, 'my favourite.'

***

The last chord thundered into stillness and the congregation reseated themselves, straight-backed and attentive. Reverend Hale ascended a few narrow steps to the pulpit which was supported on a single stout column of oak, lending it the incongruous aspect of a polished wooden wine goblet. He arranged his notes while, behind him, the choirboys fidgeted and yawned.

'Good evening.' The cavernous body of the church reinforced the sonorous strength underpinning his voice. 'On this most glorious of nights I have chosen as the subject of my sermon' – he smiled mischievously at a small girl sitting between her parents on the front pew – 'a cat.'

His smile evaporated and he swept his gaze over the assembled heads, quietening persistent shufflers and drawing his congregation into his presence.

'This cat was lost. An emaciated stray in the City of London, dodging the dangers of the traffic and scavenging scraps to eat from the gutters and the bins. On one miserable afternoon she sought shelter from the rain in the house of God; St Augustine's on Watling Street, in the very shadow of St Paul's Cathedral.

'The verger of St Augustine's, a man with no love to spare for cats, discovered her and put her outside again. But the animal persevered and, after another two or three evictions, eluded her tormentor and passed the night in the dry, curled up on a kneeler.

'The next morning, overruling his verger's objections, Father Henry Ross, the rector of St Augustine's and the man who related this story to me, decided the cat would stay, and named her Faith. "After all," he reasoned with the verger, "she had the faith to try again after you had thrown her out three times."

'Faith settled in at the church, paying her keep by hunting mice and greeting parishioners attending service. But she must've maintained something of a private social life, because she was soon blessed by the birth of a single black and white kitten.

'One day, at the end of August, she began behaving in a strange manner; she sat in front of the basement door all day, nuzzling and clawing at it, begging anyone who passed to open it for her. Eventually Father Ross unlocked the door and Faith dragged her lone kitten, by the scruff of its neck, down the basement stairs.

'It was cold down there and the walls sometimes ran with damp, so Father Ross made several attempts to take the kitten back upstairs. But Faith returned him to the basement, insistent that this must be her family's new home.

'It was the 7th of September, I'm sure you will recall, when the diabolical evil of aerial bombardment made its first visit to our city. On that evening, Father Ross found himself away on church business. It was lucky for him that he was, because the church received several hits. The bombs smashed great holes in the roof, collapsed the floors and set fire to pews and pulpit.

'When the rector came back later that night, fire crews were damping down the smoking remnants of his church. Father Ross sidestepped the firemen and climbed down into the rubble, distraught that Faith and her kitten might lay in the basement beneath the tiles and broken joists of the ruined floor. In response to his calls came the sound of a *meow* amongst the wreckage.

'Pulling aside remnants of roof trusses and singed hymn books, Father Ross discovered Faith squeezed into a corner, dusty but unhurt, serenely nursing her kitten. The cat was, in the rector's own words, "Singing such a song of praise and thanksgiving as I had never heard."'

Reverend Hale paused to let his story settle, once again sweeping the congregation, this time his smile was one of satisfaction at his allegory.

'In these dangerous times we must take our own faith, our faith in God, our faith in the redemption that is Jesus, given to us on this day, and find a secure corner of our heart where we know we have the strength to preserve it and feed it. Each and every one of you must jealously protect your faith to ensure it will survive whatever this terrible war has yet to bring. So when, with God's grace, we once more find our way to peace, our faith will be there to support and guide us to the merciful path of the righteously victorious… Let us pray.'

***

The congregation drifted down the aisle, shaking hands and exchanging muted Christmas wishes. Bryan and Jenny sat shoulder to shoulder as they flowed past.

'I'd forgotten how beautiful this church is,' Jenny sighed. 'On the inside that is. The outside is as ugly as sin.'

'Careful. You're talking about the love of my father's life.'

'He looks well on it,' she beamed at Bryan. 'And such a lovely sermon about the brave little cat.'

Bryan shook his head and mirrored her smile, 'The Christmas spirit has certainly got you in its talons. What are your plans now?'

'Straight home. My mother prefers a mid-morning service and she'll expect me to go with her.'

'Then I shall walk you there.'

They stood and followed the stragglers towards the door. Behind them a verger fussed about, clearing up the hymn books and straightening the kneelers.

Outside, Reverend Hale stood surrounded by parishioners eager to deliver their personal festive greetings. Bryan slipped past with Jenny on his arm, glad to leave without having to engage with his father. He guided Jenny through the side gate and across to Holly Walk. The narrow lane sloped upwards, bounded on one side by the main parish graveyard where the massed stones stood starkly outlined in the austere moonlight.

Jenny shivered, pulled her collar closer around her neck and scanned the sky. 'Aren't the stars beautiful? That's one good thing about living on a hill in the blackout; it makes the stars stand out.' She squeezed Bryan's arm, 'We mustn't forget the beautiful things, Bryan. We mustn't forget the things that bring us joy.'

Bryan regarded the press of monuments in the cemetery and said nothing.

Jenny slowed her pace and stepped closer to the black railings. Close by, on the other side, a large statue surmounted a tomb, protected from the elements by a four-columned ciborium. The figure, weathered to verdigris, depicted a winged angel clasping a dying woman to his breast.

'She looks very young,' Jenny's voice trailed with sudden sadness. 'I wonder if everyone gets their own angel when their time comes.'

'I'm not sure there are enough angels to go around.'

They continued along the lane and the graveyard gave way to a stocky terrace of Georgian houses punctuated with the façade of a Catholic church. The strains of earnest singing seeped from the door.

'Maybe I should try having more faith in the future,' Jenny mused, 'maybe I should be a braver little cat.'

'Well, I reckon we'll have a better idea about our future come June.' The exertion of climbing the long slow incline gave Bryan's voice an edge of breathlessness. 'If the Germans invade, it will largely be up to the Navy to get in their way. If the Navy can't stop them, it will be down to each of us to decide how, or if, we fight on.'

'And if the Navy succeed?'

'Then you might be justified in having some faith in the future.' They turned the corner up a steeper alley. 'But it will probably be in a satellite state all but ruled by a Nazi Europe.'

The alley let them out onto Holly Hill and they walked north along Hampstead Grove.

'How does it get back to the way it used to be?' the weight of Jenny's question compressed her voice.

'I suppose there's a small chance we could make that happen. But everyone who is able will have to fight as hard as they can, for however long it takes to make the Americans wake up to the danger.'

They walked in silence for long moments.

'Which is why,' Bryan murmured with a sigh, 'I haven't put in for that transfer.'

He felt Jenny's arm stiffen for a second, then relax.

A few moments passed before she broke the silence, 'What are your plans for the rest of the day?'

'I'll have to do lunch at least, I suppose. Generally, once that's cleared away, the only option is to sit and watch my parents fossilise in front of a teapot.'

'Alright,' she squeezed his arm, 'why don't you call on me about mid-afternoon? We can take a stroll and try tracking down a pub that's open.'

They reached the Freeman's gate and Jenny hugged Bryan to her.

'No more talk of Nazis and invasion,' his overcoat muffled her words, 'not 'til after Christmas.'

She stood on tiptoe and kissed him lightly, then once again with a flare of passion, before turning on her heel and retreating up the drive.

Bryan lit a cigarette and walked back down the hill. The effect of the alcohol drained from his brain and a dull headache moved in to take its place. He gazed up at the black vault, momentarily peaceful, encrusted with the sparkling jewels of an indifferent universe.

Chapter 18

Christmas Day, 1940

Reverend Hale whipped the sharpening steel backwards and forwards on the blade, eyeing the roasted turkey like a sacrificial lamb on the sacred altar of his dining table. The noise set Bryan's teeth on edge and he clamped his jaw muscles tight to defeat the sensation.

'So, what is it you're doing these days?' the clergyman asked as he put down the steel and bent to carve the bird.

Bryan grimaced and ran his tongue over his teeth to resettled their jarred nerves. 'Night interception. It's supposed to be secret.'

'Is it working?'

'No, they hardly notice us.'

'So why are you doing it?'

'Because we have to do something, no matter how bloody useless it turns out to be.'

Mrs Hale placed a jug of gravy on the table between the bowls of vegetables and spooned sprouts and carrots onto the plates. 'No swearing at the table, Bryan.'

Silence settled on the room, interrupted only by the occasional scrape of the knife against the carving fork and the clink of serving spoon against china.

Bryan studied his mother's face; how she held her features in quiet serenity to accompany her air of a satisfied administrator surveying a situation safely under control. He had always supposed he hated her, but he had to concede in this moment it was unlikely he did. It was true that she had not so much brought him up, as managed his childhood from an emotionally safe distance. It was, at least, a project she'd completed, although with little enjoyment of the process or pride in the results. But it was enough of an effort to preclude his hatred.

The knife scraped again, this time more harshly, sending a twinge through Bryan's teeth. He switched his reverie to his father. His malign feelings towards this parent brooked no softening. Bryan knew the considerable intellect behind those flinty eyes and it should've engendered some questions, made some contribution to the theological debate. Instead, his father had made blind faith a career decision, and the more lucrative the trappings of his position, the blinder his faith had become.

'Shall I say grace?' The reverend asked no-one in particular and bowed his head.

Bryan followed suit and studied the food on his plate. There were no Yorkshire puddings.

***

The watery sunlight slanted through the bare branches as Bryan knocked on the Freeman's front door.

Jenny answered, 'Goodness, hello Bryan,' she said, then whispered, 'You're a surprise.'

'I've heard that before,' he muttered and followed her into the hallway.

'Wait here.'

Jenny ducked through a door and the murmur of conversation filtered back from the room:

'…old school friend…'

'…but we'd planned a card game…'

'… just for a short walk…'

'…when you come back, then, I suppose…'

Jenny emerged and pulled a coat from the rack, 'Quick, let's escape.'

The heavy door clunked shut behind them and Jenny scampered out of the gate. Bryan quickened his stride to catch her.

'You're a real dab hand at subterfuge.'

'Yes,' she said, 'I learnt it from a man at quite an early age.'

Bryan sensed the edge in her voice and dropped the subject, 'Shall we walk down the hill and see where that takes us?'

Jenny nodded and they strolled south, down the incline.

The sunlight softened to a mellow gold that danced off the auburn tones in Jenny's dark hair. Bryan stayed quiet, sensing his companion's contentment.

As they levelled out into Hampstead's main street, Jenny chose to break the silence: 'I've been thinking about things,' she said. 'Without all of this going on,' she gestured at the ether, 'it's almost certain we wouldn't have bumped into each other.'

'Almost certain.'

'And,' she continued, 'I would give anything for all this not to be happening; it would be my dearest wish that the war had never started. Even if it meant I'd never meet you.'

'You're not blaming me for the war, are you?'

Jenny stopped walking and turned to look into Bryan's face, 'I'm trying to explain why I don't love you.'

'I didn't ever think-'

'And it's alright not to love you,' she cut across his apology. 'Despite all we've said and done, it's *alright* not to love you. What we have is part of the war. And it's made the war bearable. Perhaps it could make the war survivable. Perhaps it doesn't matter.'

Jenny's eyes glistened in the last of the dying light and Bryan bent to kiss her upturned face, 'You don't believe I could make you happy?'

'I don't know. I only know you stop me from feeling unhappy, most of the time.' She reached under her coat, 'Here, take this.'

Bryan looked down at the small knitted figure, 'A doll?'

'It's you!' she laughed. 'See? It has messy hair.'

He smiled in spite of himself, infected by her sudden gaiety, 'Why are you giving it to me?'

'Because I don't need it. Come on, let's find a pub.'

Boxing Day, 1940

Gunmetal cold lay leaden across the city's morning sky as Bryan drove south, retracing his route across the river. The streets were all but deserted, people preferring their hearth to the icy grip of the London air. The roads carried only military vehicles interspersed with the occasional die-hard taxi driver.

Bryan pulled up outside Scott's house and tooted his horn. While he waited, he idly tapped the accelerator, making the engine growl like a frustrated cat.

The passenger door opened and Tommy bundled his kitbag onto the back seat.

'Morning, Flight. Would you like to-'

'No. We have to be away.'

Tommy let the door swing to and Bryan avoided looking in the mirror at the couples' farewell embrace. The Humber's engine growled a tone deeper.

The door opened again and Tommy clambered in. He put a small package wrapped in brown paper on top of the dashboard, 'Christmas cake. Lizzy made it herself and wanted you to have a slice.'

Bryan nodded his thanks and pulled away.

Tommy arched his back and yawned behind a cupped palm, 'The little blighter kept us awake most of the night. I reckon he's so used to the noise of air raids that he can't settle in the quiet.'

'As long as it didn't spoil your celebrations.'

'No fear of that. We had a wonderful time. Most of Lizzy's family came round for lunch and we sang carols all evening.'

Bryan nodded slowly.

Tommy cast a sidelong glance, 'How was your visit home?'

Bryan pursed his lips, 'About the same as ever. I'm almost glad to be going back to work.'

Friday, 27 December 1940

'Night-warden Control to Blackbird C-Charlie, we have trade preparing to cross the channel. Vector one-five-zero. Angels twelve.'

The Beaufighter banked smoothly onto the southerly bearing and Tommy glanced out of the dome over the dipped port wing. The early evening sky was hard and clear, glowing with the dying embers of daylight. Bournemouth slid by underneath and, in the middle distance, the chalk spires of The Needles hunched in the freezing mists like a coven of skeletal witches plotting dark deals with fate.

The minutes rolled past and the strange luminosity clung on, reflecting around the hard dome of the heavens, defying the fall of darkness. Tommy's gunner instincts took over: He dimmed the cathode ray tubes and looked ahead, quartering the sky with unfocussed eyes, searching for any hint of movement. He smiled as a tiny shape shimmered into being.

'I see him, Flight. Above us to port.'

The silhouette grew, a small, hard-edged, black hole in the ethereal sheen of twilight. As it grew, it acquired the unmistakable outline of a Heinkel.

Bryan hauled the fighter into a tight left bank and dropped into station a thousand feet below and behind the intruder, shadowing its north-easterly course towards London.

'This is ticklish,' he said. 'They can't fail to spot us.'

Tommy screwed his head about to check down-light. The sky behind them darkened into the slate haze of the sea and the water swallowed what light there was into its thick murk.

'We might get away with it, Flight.'

'Well, let's give him a little time.'

Bryan held their position and the two aircraft droned on in tandem towards the English coast. The white chalk boundary drew a line across the horizon, starkly visible against the gloom. Several miles before landfall, the Heinkel pulled into a long, slow turn to starboard.

'Looks like he's got the jitters.' Bryan banked to shadow his quarry's flightpath.

A strange swell of relief made Tommy's skin tingle. There was no need to risk a dangerous attack now, there was no imperative to kill anyone. This crew could go home.

The Heinkel wallowed through 180 degrees but didn't straighten up. The turn continued around the clock until it settled back onto its previous course.

'Well I'll be,' Bryan muttered. 'The poor sod was waiting for it to get darker.'

The last of the light shrank away, one or two stars blinked into life and the darkness they had played for closed over the German crew like a shroud.

'Enough,' Bryan said. 'It's time.'

The engines swelled a tone higher as he eased the throttle forward and climbed towards his target.

Tommy's throat constricted with dread and he displaced his fear by rechecking the air pressure gauge to the cannons and making sure the safeties were set to fire.

The Beaufighter climbed steadily. Tommy scanned the sky above and behind. Their backdrop still wasn't completely dark. If the ventral gunner was on the alert, he simply *had* to spot them.

'Attacking now,' Bryan's voice carried an edge of kindred tension.

'*Thank God,*' Tommy muttered to himself.

The cannons leapt into life, pounding like demon blacksmiths hammering in the devil's own forge, belching clouds of smoke and cordite around Tommy's boots. Looking ahead through the dome Tommy saw explosive strikes peppering their adversary's tail and, as the Beaufighter drifted to the right, these walked down the side of the fuselage and into the starboard wing root. The Heinkel cocked into a gentle dive as the ammunition ran out and the cannons shuddered into silence.

Tommy jumped down onto the catwalk, hauled the empty drums out and swung them into the racks. He lowered the new drums into the guns, muscles tightening against their weight and sweat prickling on his forehead from the heat of the breeches.

'Reloaded. Ready to fire,' Tommy scrambled away from the cannon mechanisms and regained his seat.

'I've lost him. He dived below the horizon. Shame he's not on fire.' Bryan tilted the Beaufighter into a shallow bank to ameliorate any evasive action the bomber might be taking. 'Can you pick him up again, Scott?'

Tommy cursed under his breath and turned up the cathode ray tubes. He blinked against the sudden, smarting brightness and squinted at the screens. A small blip travelled off the extreme right of his screen.

'He's heading due west. I think he's still diving. The contact isn't steady.'

Bryan threw the night-fighter onto a westerly heading and pushed the nose down to give chase. Tommy sat helpless in front of two screens that filled with increasing interference as their altitude dropped, until each became a scrambled mess of ground returns.

Tommy gave up, 'We're too low. I'll never find him now.'

'No matter. Take a look.'

Tommy craned his neck forward. A line of incendiary strikes stitched their way across the landscape a couple of miles ahead, perforating the darkness with angry yellow flashes. Moments later a gush of red and orange flame plumed at their extreme end as the Heinkel ploughed into the earth and exploded.

Sunday, 29 December 1940

'Come on, Alice,' Jenny chided, 'they have a piano player up there on a Sunday. I'll pay, belated Christmas present.'

Alice looked up from her prone position on her bed. 'What about the warning? What if there's an air raid?'

'Nothing's dropped within a mile of here for weeks.' Jenny tugged at the other's foot, 'I believe we're through the worst of it. I really do.'

Alice closed her magazine, 'Still infected with Christmas cheer, I see.'

'It's my New Year's resolution. I'm going to be more optimistic. Come on, it's only upstairs. We don't even have to go out into the cold.'

***

Alice pushed the potatoes around the plate searching for any sign of chicken in her casserole.

'So, I take it you had a lovely Christmas at your parents?'

Jenny smiled, 'It's always a joy to go home. I saw Bryan, too.'

Alice measured her tone, 'How is our knight of the sky?'

Jenny shrugged, 'Same as ever. Married to the war.'

'I don't know why you bother–'

'Because I like him. Anyway, it is what it is.'

'You deserve better. Especially after your salesman…'

Jenny shook her head, 'I can't carry that load forever. I understand that now. I need to set it down and move on.'

'Don't sell yourself short, that's all I'm saying.'

Jenny grinned at her friend, 'Don't worry, I know my price tag. Now, I wonder if they still have any coffee…'

***

Jenny paid the bill and they walked back down the dimly-lit corridors and opened their flat door.

'Did you leave a candle burning?' Jenny frowned.

At the other end of the hallway, a flickering light danced and shimmied against the walls.

'I haven't been in there.' Alice kicked off her shoes and headed for her bedroom.

Jenny walked to the living room and tottered to a standstill.

The light came from outside. The opened blackouts framed a skyline ablaze. Swirls of orange flame writhed into the air from the dense, huddle of buildings in The City, their silhouettes cut with sharp edges against the hellish glow of the conflagration.

'Alice?' Jenny croaked, 'Alice, come here.'

Her friend padded into the room and a gasp escaped her lips.

'They're back.' Jenny's voice wavered, 'It was too good to be true.'

Alice came to stand at her friend's shoulder and the two women gazed through the glass with the fascinated dread of children in a reptile house.

'London's burning,' Jenny said. 'I wonder if Faith will survive this one.'

Tuesday, 31 December 1940

'This feels a bit strange,' Tommy said, 'going hunting on New Year's Eve. I'd normally be supping a few brown ales down the local.'

The darkness thickened over their heads as they trudged out to their Beaufighter. Silhouettes of airmen in ones and twos floated along the barely discernible junction of field and sky, their breath curling away behind them like fleeing spirits.

'How did you used to celebrate Old Year's Night, Flight?'

'I didn't; it always struck me as a bit pointless.'

'How is it pointless?'

'All you get is a hangover and a different number on your gravestone.'

Tommy barked a wry laugh, 'Let's not tempt fate. I'm aiming for the biggest number I can get.'

They reached their fighter, climbed in and launched into the habitual routine to ready themselves and the aircraft for flight and combat. Like factory workers arriving on shift, they started up the systems specifically developed to destroy human life at freezing altitudes in the dark. Catastrophic injury, fire and explosive destruction were the intended outcomes of the tools contained in this sleek, black raven of death.

Tommy whistled while he worked.

**

Bryan was still climbing to patrol altitude through thick cloud cover when control directed them to a contact. Tommy picked up the trace on the AI and control signed off.

'It's well above us, Flight, and travelling fast.'

'Thank you, Scott. I'll climb in steps.'

Bryan levelled out to increase airspeed, then nudged the nose up for a minute before levelling out to recover speed before the next climb.

Tommy glanced out through the dome at nothing. The muffle of water vapour remained impervious to the penetration of moonlight.

'Range is reducing nicely, Flight. Keep up this rhythm.'

The minutes ticked by and the blanket of cloud covering the dome remained stubbornly opaque. The blip on the screen drifted towards minimum range.

'Range three-fifty, twenty degrees above. Throttle back.'

The engine note softened a shade and the blip drifted on.

'Range three hundred yards.'

Tommy squinted hard at the screens; the edges of the trace blurred as it settled onto the fringe of background interference.

'Range two seventy-five, now thirty degrees above. If we get any closer I shall lose him.'

'I'm still flying blind in ten-tenths. We'll hold position and see if it clears.'

Time stretched on and Tommy's eyes tingled with the effort of separating the blip from the clutter.

'He can't be flying in this soup on purpose. I'll drop back and climb a bit more.'

Tommy blinked in relief as the blip disentangled itself from the grass and the Beaufighter surged into a climb.

'It's clearing…'

The aircraft continued to rise.

'Ah, there he is. He's sitting right on top.'

Tommy looked forward. The Beaufighter, still semi-submerged, cut through the cloud like a torpedo. The seemingly disembodied propellers carved two furrows that lapped closed behind the speeding plane. Four hundred yards away a Heinkel skimmed the rolling sea of cloud, its propellers occasionally clipping the waves of vapour and throwing back twisting spirals of mist.

'Right,' Bryan said, 'let's get closer.'

The Beaufighter sank back into the roiling cloud like a wily orca and Tommy turned back to his screens.

'Range three hundred… two-fifty… two-twenty… losing contact.'

Tommy felt the night-fighter rise through the lightening mist and the wan moonlight penetrated the dome as he fought again to discern the close-range contact in the swirl of interference.

Bryan pulled the nose up another degree to settle the target in the gunsight and squeezed off a long burst of cannon fire. Pieces of debris spun back past the cockpit as the shells struck home, on and around the raider's starboard engine.

The Heinkel dived into the clouds like a wounded whale and Bryan dived into the blinding depths to give chase.

'Can you hold the contact, Scott?'

'I think so.' The blip became more distinct as the bomber increased speed and pulled away from them in the dive.

The Beaufighter broke through cloud base. Directly ahead the Heinkel continued diving, the right propeller milling aimlessly and smoke streaming from the engine. Bryan fired another long burst.

The enemy's dive steepened and the Beaufighter bumped and juddered through the turbulent air, engines howling like justice in pursuit of the guilty.

Two quick bursts of cannon fire stripped more pieces off the German machine that spiralled back in the bomber's slipstream and flashed past like aerial flotsam.

The dive steepened further and the Beaufighter's fuselage quaked and rattled under the stress.

'That's it,' physical strain stretched Bryan's voice, 'the controls are getting solid.'

The engines coughed, barking out orange flames from their exhausts as Bryan throttled right back and curved gently into level flight.

Tommy craned his neck to where he guessed their quarry might be, and thousands of feet below, the Heinkel's dive terminated in a sickly flash of orange and turquoise flame. Tommy looked on as the blossoming ball of flame dissipated and diminished to a sullen tangerine glow. He glanced at his watch, 'It'll be midnight in five minutes.'

'Mmmm…' Bryan murmured, 'no different number for those chaps.'

PART 4

NOCTIS

Chapter 19

Wednesday, 8 January 1941

Jenny sat at her desk, poring over scribbled damage reports. Her in tray overflowed with documents, all to be correlated to an executive summary which was, of course, required urgently by some shadowy committee operating elsewhere in the building. The staccato clack of typing nibbled at her concentration, an unrelenting sonic backdrop punctuated by the *whizz-clunk* of carriage returns. Her fingers stung with a dozen tiny paper cuts and her head throbbed with the effort of focussing in the face of this gentle, insidious bedlam.

'*Pssst.*'

She looked up to see Alice standing by her side, a folder under her arm.

'I was going to stay in town for a couple of drinks after work, if you fancy it?'

Jenny screwed up her nose, 'Not sure we should. It's the middle of the week, after all.'

'Come on,' Alice nudged Jenny's shoulder with her hip, 'you need to let your hair down.'

'Ok,' Jenny smiled. 'One or two can't hurt.'

'That's my girl. See you out the front at five.'

Alice strode off and Jenny bent to her task once more. The unrelenting clatter of typewriters marked out the time as the columns of casualty and destruction lengthened under her pen nib.

***

Jenny skipped down the front steps to where her friend waited on the dark-shrouded pavement. They linked arms and set off into the gloom.

'Let's head up to Liverpool Street,' Alice said. 'It's still quite lively up there.'

'Isn't that dangerous?'

'Isn't everywhere dangerous?' Alice sighed. 'But I have heard someone say the Germans are losing an awful lot of bombers to the big guns and they'll be giving up on bombing London any time now.'

'I hadn't heard that,' Jenny said, 'and if it were true, where are all these bombers crashing and why aren't there pictures of them in all the newspapers?'

'Oh, shush. I'll buy the first round.'

They walked along the unlit roads, now becoming busier as the capital's working day ground to an end. Gossiping about office politics and complaining about their workload filled the time it took to arrive at a pub that Jenny instantly recognised.

'Isn't this where we went with those sailors?' she asked.

'What if it is?' Alice grinned, 'Maybe you'll get lucky again.'

They pushed their way through the door and into the smoky interior. Jenny found a free table tucked away at the back of the pub while her friend went to the bar to buy drinks. Jenny looked around at the groups of customers scattered through the room. Most were workmen, drinking alone or in tight groups of three or four, squeezing in a couple of pints before going home to their wives and their evening meal. In amongst them stood servicemen in the process of arriving or leaving the city from the railway station across the road, exactly as Bryan had done three months before. There were men from all the services but, with the image of Bryan lingering in her mind, her eyes rested on a young man in RAF uniform talking with animated enthusiasm to a girl who nodded as she listened, but gazed over the airman's shoulder with glazed distraction.

'Here,' Alice put two gins and tonic on the table, 'I got doubles. These should sort us out.' She followed Jenny's eyes around the room, 'Seen anything you fancy?'

'Alice, please!' Jenny admonished. 'That's not the way it works.'

'It seemed to work that way the night you first met Bryan.'

Jenny inhaled a sharp breath to reply, but the words died in her throat. The clamouring conversations in the bar subsided into silence as another noise insinuated from the cold darkness outside. Moaning through the register and sliding into a flat, dead wail, the air raid sirens delivered their foreboding like the howling of mournful wraiths haunting the bomb-shattered wreckage of their family's hearth.

No-one moved for a long, leaden moment, standing transfixed by the hateful, grinding dirge of the warning. The light-hearted laughter in a dozen throats was strangled by a return to the baleful realities of London life. Faces sagged and heads dropped. Somewhere a man cursed under his breath and a few conversations restarted in lower, deferential tones. With the slow, deliberate movements of mourners in a church, many in the crowd finished their drinks, pulled on their coats and shuffled towards the door.

The blast sucked all of the sound from the air. Shattered glass fired through shredded blackouts, scything into the heads and faces of those nearest the windows with spinning shards of vitreous daggers. Jenny felt a sharp impact on the back of her head and saw a flash of red erupt from Alice's cheek before the lights failed and darkness dropped like oblivion.

The muffling compression of the air gave way to a billowing gust of turbulent winter breeze sucked in through the shattered pub frontage. Noise cascaded back into the room. Screams and cries filtered through Jenny's pressure-damped hearing, made distant and other-worldly by the high-pitched ringing that filled her skull. She reached out and grabbed for Alice, feeling her friend's hand grip her arm in reply. They sat clutching each other over their toppled drinks, impaled on their panic and disabled by terror.

Outside, a terrible whoosh, like the breath of an enraged dragon, ended in a deafening explosion followed by another and then another, as a second stick of bombs marched their circus of annihilation down the street.

Both women slid from their chairs, instinctively hunting for cover, pressing their soft flesh close to the hard, cold tiles on the floor. As they dropped, shrapnel buzzed across the space above their heads, searing calescent paths through the dust-laden darkness.

Then it was over. The shock of the new silence suppressed all movement; everything lay transfixed under its hushed weight.

Jenny felt her hair growing heavy and stiff with congealing blood. Next to her head, a ragged rasp of breathing reassured her that Alice was alive. Fighting against muscles cramped with shock, she lifted her face off the cold tiles. A thin trail of blood trickled from her nose onto her lips.

'Alice?' she whispered.

Alice began sobbing soundlessly into the floor.

The clanging of ambulance bells broke the spell and a resurgent wave of voices swelled through the room. Someone, badly injured, returned to consciousness and wailed against their agony. Another called out for a friend, repeating the name in frantic cadence.

More bells jangled into stillness outside and torch beams probed through the gloom. Men with satchels and white helmets followed the wands of light, kneeling beside prone bodies, bending heads to examine their faces.

'Alice,' Jenny persisted, 'can you get up? We need to get out of here.'

Alice coughed and spat, the dust grimed spittle dribbling down her chin. She nodded.

Jenny bunched herself onto her knees and forced her legs to lift her upright. She bent to help Alice to her feet and they fell into each other's embrace.

'I'm sorry, Jenny. We never should have come.'

Jenny hugged her friend, mute with the relief of survival.

A beam of light played over their faces and a medic loomed behind the torch, 'Are you ladies hurt?'

Jenny squinted into the painful brightness, 'Cuts and scratches, I think.'

The light dazzled her for a second longer as the man evaluated the pair. 'If you're alright to walk, make your way outside, someone will look you over out there.'

The torch moved on. Jenny saw it linger over the airman's prone body. A large slick of blood pooled under the man's head. Too large. The girl knelt next to his body, stifling her sobs with one hand, resting the other on his chest and gazing into his glazing eyes.

'Let's go,' Jenny turned away from the scene and grabbed Alice's hand. 'Follow me.'

The two women stepped gingerly into the darkness, skirting the pools of torchlight illuminating medics at work on motionless bodies, slipping and skidding on shards of glass and pools of beer. A warden spotted their progress and came to help, lighting their way to the exit, now standing door-less.

The fresh air washed over them and Jenny blinked against the dry mask of dust coating her face. Another warden met them on the pavement.

'If you don't need an ambulance, you ought to go to a shelter. Nearest one is that way,' he pointed along the road. 'Hurry, ladies. They haven't finished with us yet tonight.'

Jenny looked into Alice's dazed face, 'Come on, Alice. Stay close.'

The two women picked their way through the wreckage on the pavement, dodging stretcher-bearers labouring with their loads. Jenny glanced back into the ragged pub frontage. Through the tattered blackouts, silhouettes shuffled in the gloom, some crying, some staring in blank confusion and others moving with the careful stiffness of the calamitously wounded.

Emerging through the semi-circle of attending ambulances, she took in the wider view. Twenty yards from the pub, in the middle of the road, a crater breathed a black line of cloying, tar-scented smoke that corkscrewed into the night. Thirty yards further down the road another bomb had gouged a similar hole, gripping a passing double-decker bus and rearing it onto its end in the blast. With the driver's cab pointing skywards, the vehicle sagged, bent and broken, against the buildings. Panels on its side had peeled away like the jagged petals of a death-rose, and from the centre of this awful bloom lolled a naked corpse, unclad by explosive force, incongruously soft and pallid in the chaos.

Jenny held on tight to Alice and dragged her along, hugging the wall as they moved away from the destruction. The low growl of engines reverberated menace between the buildings and the heavy crashing rhythm of another bombload stitched its way through the city a few hundred yards away. Jenny gasped back a surge of panic and squeezed tighter onto Alice's hand, quickening their pace to escape a danger that couldn't be outrun.

The blue uniform of a caped policeman resolved from the blankness of the night. 'Straight down here, Miss. There's still some room in this one.'

He gestured them through a doorway and down a flight of concrete steps. At the bottom, the steps dog-legged into the cellar of an office block, lit by the flickering of a dozen candles. In between the racks full of boxes, huddled a hundred or more people, each head swivelling to regard the new arrivals. Jenny looked from face to face and tears welled into her eyes, tracing lines through the grime on her cheeks.

A middle-aged lady holding a candle emerged from between the racking and took Jenny's hand. 'Come this way, love.'

She guided Jenny across the room and Jenny dragged Alice behind her. They moved towards a bench set against the back wall. A man, stretched out to sleep on the bench, stood up as they approached, smiled reassurance at Jenny, caught up his blankets in a bundle and moved elsewhere in the shelter.

'Sit down, girls,' the lady purred. 'I'll be back in a minute.'

The light from the woman's candle receded as she moved away. The shadows closed around Jenny, and with them a creeping wave of fear crawled over her. Her skin shivered in spasms and her legs cramped with the need to run.

'Here we are.' The woman's voice startled Jenny back to lucidity. 'Take this for me,' the woman thrust the candle holder into Jenny's hand and placed a basin of water on the bench next to her. 'This is Doctor Allen,' she gestured at the old man by her side, 'he's going to check the cut on your friend's face.'

The doctor leaned forward and gently prised Jenny's fingers away from Alice's hand. He spoke to Alice in low tones and she replied, cracked emotion underpinning her monosyllabic answers.

'I'm going to clean you up,' the woman said, lifting Jenny's chin with her finger, 'you look a bit of a fright.'

The woman soaked a handkerchief in the water and dabbed at the blood on Jenny's top lip. Jenny concentrated on the woman's gentle movements and the sanctuary implicit in her soft brown voice. The tension in her muscles ebbed and she anchored her gaze into the woman's eyes.

'Whatever happened to the pair of you?'

'We went for a drink after work,' Jenny voice wavered, unnaturally high. 'We should be able to do that, shouldn't we?'

The turgid rumble of a nearby bomb strike vibrated the walls and a pulse of air stirred the dust at the bottom of the stairwell.

'The bomb hit outside the pub,' hot tears pushed their way out of Jenny's eyes. 'It was full of people. There was a bus…' She stammered at the memory. 'The warning was late.'

'Shush,' the woman's hands worked to wipe away the tears and filth from Jenny's cheeks, 'you're safe now.'

Thursday, 9 January 1941

Jenny woke with a start and winced at the stab of pain that clamped her neck muscles. She sat on numb buttocks at the end of the bench, leaning awkwardly against its hard, wooden back. Alice lay outstretched with her head resting in Jenny's lap, soft snoring vibrated her lips.

'Good morning, my dear.' It was the woman who'd helped them. 'The all-clear went a couple of hours ago, but I didn't have the heart to wake you.'

Jenny rubbed her eyes and blinked against the grit she dislodged from her eyebrows.

'What time is it?' she fumbled for her watch, 'we have to be at work.'

'I think they'll understand if you don't make it today,' the woman's cheeks crinkled above a weary smile. 'Where is it you live?'

'Balham.' Jenny's voice wobbled, like that of a child pretending to be brave.

The woman chewed her lower lip, 'I hear they hit Bank station quite badly, so I bet the tube line is closed.'

'I'm sure we can find a bus stop.' Jenny shook Alice's shoulder, but her friend snored on.

'Wait a minute,' the woman reached out to restrain her hand. 'That poor girl's in no state to catch a bus. Let me see if I can find you a taxi.'

***

The hot water sloshed into the bathtub, sending whorls of steam to condense against the cold, white ceiling. Jenny sat on the toilet lid, surveying her ruined clothes in disconsolation. The blood on the back of her head had solidly congealed, matting her long hair into a misshapen lump. She dared not touch it until it was her turn to bathe.

Alice peeled off her clothes and pulled the dressing from her cheek. A grimace of pain creased her face and brought glistening tears to her eyes. She turned off the taps and stepped into the water, sinking down and submerging her head for a long moment. She emerged slowly, like a hydra, her face still gaunt but her expression now steely, the cut in her cheek like a livid stripe of determination.

'I can't do this anymore, Jenny,' she murmured. 'I love this city, but I'm not prepared to get blown to pieces to fulfil Churchill's noble bloody prophesies. I'm going back to live with my parents. At least when the Germans arrive in the countryside, they'll arrive on foot and we'll have a chance to surrender.'

'When?'

'Today. I'm getting out of this rat trap today.'

'What about your job?'

'I'll send them a resignation letter.'

'What about me?'

'I don't know, Jenny. I really don't know.'

***

Jenny sat and watched the soap bubbles dry into a grimy tidemark around the edge of the bath while the sounds of packing drifted down the hallway from Alice's room. Tears prickled the backs of her eyes, but did not fall. Her face, still dry with dust, set itself into a grim mask. Her gaze, gradually unfocusing, sought to penetrate the dull shine of white enamel until the edges of her vision darkened with the effort.

'I'll come back on Sunday with my dad to pick up the rest of my things.'

Jenny let her eyelids close and felt her straining pupils relax into the crimson darkness.

'Jenny?'

Jenny opened her eyes.

'Yes, I heard,' she didn't look at her friend standing in the doorway, 'keep your key until it's all sorted.'

'You should clean yourself up, Jen. You know what I always say: If you look like shit…'

Jenny smiled in spite of herself and finished the sentence: '…you'll feel like shit.'

'I have to dash. The train connections are terrible and I want to be out of town before the warnings sound.'

Jenny finally looked into her friend's face and the teardrops fledged, 'I'll miss you.'

'Don't be silly. I'll see you on Sunday.'

Alice blew a kiss and ducked into the hallway to grab her coat and valise. The flat door clicked shut behind her.

Jenny stood, wiped the grime from the bathtub with a flannel and set the taps running. She undressed, examining each piece of clothing for damage. All could be salvaged, except her blouse and jacket, both heavily stained with blood. She stood naked, shivering while the bath filled, studiously avoiding her own reflection in the bathroom mirror.

Sinking into the bath, she gasped as the hot water tingled its way up her legs and torso. She shut off the taps with her toes and slid her buttocks down the slippery enamel until her hair submerged. The heat stung her wounded scalp, but she clenched her teeth against the pain and allowed the water to soften the dried blood.

Staring at the ceiling, she pictured the airman's girlfriend.

***

Jenny awoke with a jolt and stared in confusion at the jangling telephone. She blinked the sleep from her eyes and squinted around the unlit room. It was dark outside. *What time is it?*

She dragged herself off the sofa and picked up the handset, carefully exploring the back of her head with the other hand.

'Hello? Miss Freeman? It's the hall porter. I have a gentleman here to see you.'

'Oh, alright. Send him up.'

Jenny straightened her dressing gown and retied the sash. She pulled the blackouts closed and flicked the light switches on.

A knock sounded at the flat door and she hurried down the hallway to answer it.

'Hello, Br-'

Jenny blinked in surprise, 'Mr Bartlett.'

'I'm so sorry, Jenny, but we were worried about you. Someone said they'd seen you and your friend heading towards Liverpool Street. And then the big raid happened, and you didn't turn up for work…' He smiled in apology. 'The personnel department let me have your address and I thought I'd drop by to make sure you were alright.'

'No, don't apologise, please. That's very kind of you. Would you like a cup of tea?'

Chapter 20

Saturday, 11 January 1941

'Night-warden to all Blackbird aircraft, our tables are clear. Time to come home. Thank you, gentlemen.'

The Beaufighter's engines throttled back like a sigh of relief. Bryan dropped the port wing to scribe a wide circle over the channel waters and pull the nose into a northerly course.

Tommy glanced at the unfired cannons and turned to survey the sky. The darkness was complete in its confounding opacity. Thick, high clouds insulated the globe from the penetration of moonlight, and Blackbird C-Charlie had groped blindly for two hours like an aerial miner in the sense-sapping tunnel between the caliginous channel waters and the implacable dome of the night. As the English coastline slipped by beneath them, he called a bearing for home and wound down the brightness on the instrument.

Bryan pulled the nose into an upwards incline to buy enough altitude to approach the aerodrome well above any other aircraft in its landing circuit. Ahead, in the middle distance, the flare path's dull glow flicked into life, drawing scratchy lines of parallel light across the murk.

'Blackbird C-Charlie to Tower,' Bryan's voice had the weariness induced from a long uneventful night-flight, 'what is my approach, please?'

Tommy caught a flash in the corner of his eye, extremely low on the starboard quarter. 'Tracers!' the word blurted out as a feral cry laced with fear.

Tomato-coloured lights whipped a viciously short distance across the darkness before crashing to an explosive halt. Where they hit, their dull ruddy hue was suddenly swamped with a swathe of burning petrol that scored a coruscating arc to its catastrophic end in a plume of angry orange flame splashing across the ground.

'Shit!' Bryan's voice stretched taut with shock. 'Who's shooting at who?'

Instinctively he pushed the throttles forward, cursing under his breath as the exhausts belched a fleeting flash of flame.

'I'm going higher. Hold on, Scott.'

Bryan pulled into a climbing bank, keeping the airfield on the inside of his turn. Tommy scanned the space beneath the dipped wing.

'Somebody's on their approach with landing lights on,' he said. 'Surely the tower should call him off.'

The distant wingtip lights continued their descent like a pair of fireflies in close formation. Tommy held his breath in denial of the inevitable.

A second deadly cavalcade of tracer erupted, sweeping explosive splashes into the space bracketed between the landing lights. The lights dropped with a sickening lurch, birthing a second angry flower of burning fuel that bloomed into an unfurling spiral across the field.

'Damn it,' Bryan spat, 'that has to be a German fighter. Can you pick him up, Scott?'

Scott glanced at the garbled mess on the screens. 'Not possible, Flight. He's too low. If he's got any sense, he'll probably stay low.'

The Beaufighter lurched into a turn. Scott's compass ticked round and steadied as the aircraft levelled out. Bryan was heading south, weaving slightly as he searched the void below him. Scott waited, gritting his teeth against the tickle of fear that ran from the small of his back to the nape of his neck.

'Flight?' Tommy could no longer bite his tongue. 'There's nothing to say he's on his way home. He could be anywhere, and he's almost certainly got some ammunition left.'

'Shit!'

Tommy's stomach fluttered as Bryan instinctively pulled the Beaufighter into a shallow climb.

'Alright, Scott,' an undercurrent of fear chipped at Bryan's voice, 'keep an eye on the screens.'

Bryan banked into a shallow, climbing spiral that drifted back in a northerly direction, gaining height to extend the range of Tommy's detection.

'Blackbird C-Charlie to Night-warden Control. I am in a high orbit awaiting instruction.'

The open radio channel crackled in embarrassed silence for long moments.

'Hello C-Charlie. We have debris on the runway here, unsafe for landing. Please divert to Boscombe Down.'

Bryan levelled out onto a westerly course.

'Unsafe for bloody landing…' he muttered to himself.

Sunday, 12 January 1941

With muscles still aching from a night of restless sleep on a makeshift cot, Bryan hedge-hopped the dozen miles cross-country back to Middle Wallop as soon as daylight allowed. Scanning the sky above the aerodrome for errant air traffic, he buzzed the field to check the state of the landing strip.

A large black scar marred the grass on the runway's edge where burning fuel had crisped the winter grass. An impact furrow ran from its centre, away at an angle towards the perimeter. Trucks stood next to this earthen gash and men raised their faces as the Beaufighter roared overhead.

'Blackbird C-Charlie to Tower, requesting permission to land.'

Bryan banked into the circuit, dropped the gear, and planted a three-point landing. He taxied onto the hardstanding and swung around with a vicious burst of revs on the starboard engine. The fighter settled facing out across the field, like a roosting owl awaiting sunset.

Bryan shut down the engines and waited for the propellers to windmill to rest. He heard the *clank* of the rear hatch hitting the ground and the *clunk* of it closing as Tommy exited the craft. Moments later he dropped through the cockpit hatch onto the concrete and pulled off his flying helmet.

'I'll try to find out what went on,' he called over his shoulder as he started off towards the office block.

A subdued tension sat over the field. Ground crews moved methodically at their tasks but the usual sound of banter and laughter was absent.

Bryan pushed through the doors at the station office and approached the orderly's desk.

'Is he in?' Bryan cut an incongruous figure, dressed in full flying kit, his hair plastered flat.

'Wait a moment,' the man picked up the handset and made a hushed call.

Bryan paced up and down, a rankle of choler filling the gap in his demeanour carved by last night's fear.

'Please go right in.'

Bryan strode into the adjutant's office.

'Sir, I…'

The words died in his throat when he saw the other's drawn features and ashen pallor. The man sat with the broken disposition of a grieving uncle.

Bryan softened his tone, 'We saw the wreckage as we flew in. What happened?'

Campbell pushed a half-finished, handwritten letter away across his blotter and lifted solemn eyes to regard Bryan.

'We think it was a Messerschmitt 110. Whatever it was, it caught us stone cold. He joined the landing circuit and simply waited for his chance.'

Bryan lowered himself into a chair, 'Who bought it?'

'Carson in G-George and Moss in M-Mother, with their operators, of course. None of them stood a chance.'

Bryan's head sank into his hands, 'So what do we do now? They know where we live and they know what time we get home from work.'

The older man shook his head, 'There's nothing that can be done, not immediately, beyond posting observers on the ground to listen out for engine noise. The intruder came in far too low for RDF detection. And even if we detect them, we can't use Bofors guns in the dark.'

Bryan pursed his lips, 'So, we simply carry on and hope for the best?'

Campbell nodded, 'Unfortunately, that's all we can do.'

'Have the bodies been retrieved?'

'Yes. All four are in the mortuary.'

'May I go to see them?'

The adjutant's eyes regarded him with milky sadness, 'I don't think that would be a good idea.'

***

Bryan trailed out of the office block and walked back to his aircraft at the perimeter. Tommy sat on the concrete, leaning against the port tyre, tossing stones at a propeller blade. Each hit rewarded him with a metallic '*ting*'.

Bryan lit a cigarette and dropped the packet and matches next to his operator's leg. Tommy retrieved a smoke and struck a match.

'It was Carson and Moss,' Bryan's eyes settled on one of the distant trucks they had overflown. Several men bustled around the vehicle, heaving bits of wreckage onto the flatbed, 'and their operators, of course.'

Tommy looked up at his pilot, 'Desmond and Donald were their names,' he said. 'I was close to making them my friends.'

Bryan sucked in a lungful of tobacco smoke, 'Having friends is dangerous.'

Chapter 21

Friday, 24 January 1941

The Stygian sky arched above them with an opaque vacancy untroubled by the rayless new moon. Its impervious blankness lacked dimension and its impalpable solidity mocked the senses. The Beaufighter sped through this alien vault, while at once appearing suspended and still in its empyrean expanse.

'Night-warden Control to Blackbird C-Charlie, return to base.'

Tommy glanced out of the dome, his jaw knotted with frustration, 'What's happened to our luck, Flight? Not a sniff in ages.'

'Who knows?' Bryan said with wooden weariness as he pulled the aircraft onto a northerly vector. 'Give me a bearing for home, I'm tired.'

Tommy ducked his head back to the screens. Suddenly a blip burst through the clutter and rushed down the trace.

'Contact… Head on… Port about… Hard, hard!'

Tommy clenched his stomach muscles against the wrench of inertia as Bryan stood the big night-fighter on its port wingtip. His face compressed into the visor and the green glow darkened around the edge of his vision with the creeping onset of blackout. The blip slid over to the right, slowed and then receded, creeping back towards the centre. As the fighter came out of the turn and levelled out, the pressure eased.

'Bang on, Flight,' Tommy enthused, 'we've got him cold. Our luck has changed.'

'Where is he?'

'Two thousand yards. Dead ahead.'

Bryan stared out into the flat blackness, willing a shape to coalesce, while he performed the adjustments in course and power called through from Tommy.

'We're very close,' Tommy's voice stretched with tension. 'Approaching minimum range. I'm beginning to lose the contact.'

Bryan gritted his teeth. '*Where are you?*' he breathed to himself.

The fabric of the night rippled with a gentle anomaly. Bryan squinted, searching for a way to decode the teasing inconsistency that plucked at the edge of his vision. A shape suggested itself, shimmering in and out of his perception.

'I think I see something. It's fat enough to be a Heinkel.'

Tommy screwed his head around, the darker patch swam in his vision, gaining and losing the familiar shape of an enemy bomber.

'I don't know. Something doesn't look right.'

The ghostly smudge shimmered and morphed like a mirage. As the Beaufighter closed, the shape grew larger and flirted with solidity. In a terrifying rush, the black phantom coalesced and its tail reared out of the night.

'We're above it!' Tommy's shout tore from his throat.

With an ugly jolt, the night-fighter bucked over and past the bomber's fin. Noise thundered around Tommy as the fuselage floor blossomed with a frenzy of explosive flowers formed from dust and metal. The air by his head ripped with vicious suddenness and holes clanged into the metal skin above his face. A giant assailant punched him hard in the kidneys with a red-hot fist, jerking him against his straps and knocking all the wind from his body. His head tilted for a moment, listening with awful detachment to the receding rattle of the Heinkel's dorsal gunner.

His empty lungs burned like acid and he forced his spasming muscles to suck in some air. His head jerked back with the effort and the icy blast from the holed dome dragged tears into his eyes. Incongruous warmth spread across his buttocks and down the backs of his legs. His head lolled forward and he stared without comprehending at the dark liquid dripping from his boots. Somewhere far away a voice shouted and he bent his will to make out the words…

'Scott! Scott!' Bryan's voice cut through the fog. 'For Christ's sake, man. Are you there?'

Tommy heaved in another breath and coughed against the foul taste of bile in his throat.

'I've been hit,' his voice sounded disconnected in his own head. 'My back hurts like hell.'

'Alright. Hang on. I'll get you back. Can you give me a heading for home?'

Tommy squinted at the screens and leant forward. Pain jolted like lightning strikes up and down his spine. He straightened, pushing against his backrest.'

'No. I don't think I can.'

Tommy's vision grew indistinct, a veil of softness blurred the details and beckoned him towards the warm cocoon of slumber. Bryan's voice calling control for an emergency bearing drifted to fuzzy irrelevance and then slipped into silence.

***

The Beaufighter clunked onto the grass between the flarepath lights and Bryan eased on the brakes as hard as he dared, slewing the aircraft off the runway onto the rougher grass. As he pulled at his harness buckle, he caught sight of trucks approaching, their muted headlights squinting their way through the night. Bryan pulled off his flying gloves and jabbed on the cabin lights. Twisting out of his seat, he swung through the armoured door and stopped dead.

Tommy slumped in his chair like a sleeping drunk. The bumpy landing had rocked his head backwards and his open eyes were raised skywards, gazing without depth through the shattered dome.

Bryan stepped forward, his feet sliding thickly in the slick, oily puddle that settled beneath the operator's chair.

'Scott?'

He leaned forward and unbuckled the lap strap, then reached around Tommy's back to hoist him from his perch. Something hot and flaccid slipped over his hands and hit the metal floor with a wet slap.

'Scott?'

Tommy's head slumped forward in a slow, stiff motion, coming to rest with a gentle bump on Bryan's shoulder.

The access hatch dropped open and a medic scrambled up the short ladder.

'Sir. Let me get to him.'

The man reached between them and grabbed Tommy's shoulders, pushing his torso upright into the chair. Tommy's head swung back and his face caught the weak glow of the cabin light.

Bryan looked into milk-glazed orbits that no longer reflected the world.

'Pilot,' another medic called from the hatch, 'this way, please. Come out this way.'

Bryan latched onto this new, vibrant face and meekly obeyed, climbing down into the sudden freshness of the freezing, still air.

'Come and sit in the ambulance where I can get a proper look at you.'

'What about Scott?'

'He'll go in the other ambulance, sir. Don't you worry.'

Bryan nodded once and then gave way to the quaking, trembling shudders of shock.

Saturday, 25 January 1941

'Hale. Wake up.'

Bryan's eyelids fluttered open to the strident, bright blankness of a whitewashed room. The heavy scent of iodine prickled his nostrils.

'Hale?'

Bryan forced his eyes into focus and the adjutant's face appeared, haloed in the glare.

'They gave you something to help you sleep,' Campbell leaned over him. 'Apart from that, you're all in one piece. How do you feel?'

Bryan hoisted himself onto his elbow and wiped the sleep from his eyes, 'Scott's dead, isn't he?'

Campbell nodded, 'Blood loss.' He sat down on the chair next to the bed. 'He'd died before you reached the ground.'

Bryan exhaled a long sigh and closed his eyes to shut off the hurt.

'Has his wife been told?' he asked quietly.

'I'll telephone sector headquarters this morning. They'll arrange a telegram, probably later today or tomorrow.'

'No!' Bryan looked into the other man's face, 'I want to tell her. I've met her. She's been kind to me.'

'I'm not sure the medical officer would agree to it. You've had quite a shake up, it's unlikely to be good for you.'

'I did it for my best friend. I want to do it for Scott.'

The adjutant frowned in thought for moment, then stood and left the room. He returned a few minutes later.

'Alright,' he said, 'as long as you have a quiet night, they'll discharge you first thing in the morning. Bear in mind, I'll want you back on the flying rota for Friday. We'll have a replacement operator assigned by the time you get back.'

Bryan nodded wearily, sank back onto his pillow and stared into the virtuous serenity of the white ceiling.

Sunday, 26 January 1941

Bryan pulled up the collar of his greatcoat against the morning chill as he trudged behind the adjutant across the courtyard to the operators' barracks.

Two sergeants leaving the building averted their eyes to the ground and nodded in salute as they hurried away.

Bryan and the adjutant pushed through the door and paused inside the now-unoccupied building. Glancing down the rows of beds it was easy to spot which had been Tommy's by the suitcase that sat at its foot. The two men approached the bunk.

A few loose items sat on top of the suitcase. Bryan picked up the lock of hair tied in red ribbon and twirled it around in his fingers.

'These few bits were on his person,' the adjutant explained.

Bryan tucked the lock of hair into his tunic's inside pocket and put the wallet and identity disc into his greatcoat pocket.

'And we found this,' the adjutant held out an envelope, 'under his pillow.'

Bryan took the letter. On the front, in scrupulous handwriting, it read; *To Elizabeth and Robert*.

He picked up the suitcase and both men walked out of the barracks.

'Good luck,' the adjutant said. 'Come straight back. I want you rested up before you get back in the saddle.'

'Yes. Thank you.' Bryan walked towards his Humber parked outside the officers' mess. Behind him, a Beaufighter on flight test opened it throttles and bumped along the grass runway, the ragged roar of its engines singing a song that lay somewhere between despair and defiance.

***

The implacable nature of creeping inevitability was the enemy of every man on active service. It crawled into the head like a malicious insect and gnawed away at courage, capability and reason. Bryan had tacitly acknowledged this mathematical reality would haunt his life. But now, on the quiet, sullen drive to London, it sat close on his shoulder and whispered doubt into his ear; '*Promise me you'll live, or get on and die…*'.

He drove steadily, his brain empty and aching like the exhausted muscles of a failed athlete. He had no need to plan what to say: Arriving without Tommy would be enough. He lit a cigarette and watched it vibrate to the chronic trembling that dogged his hands. The tobacco rasped its harsh flavour across the back of his throat. Wisps of smoke curled up his face and stung his eyes, dragging a tear over his eyelid and down his cheek. He let it run.

The London streets rolled past the windows as he steered mechanically along the familiar route. The further east he travelled, the more a slinking dread nibbled at his guts. Lizzy Scott had trusted God to keep her husband safe. But no faith could account for the clumsy flying error that had laid them bare atop the enemy's gun muzzles; no prayer could deflect the fragments of disembowelling metal tearing through soft, mortal flesh. Bryan pictured Lizzy humming with contentment, her babe in her arms, enjoying her last few minutes of serenity before his knock at her door stole away her future.

Bryan passed the railway station and turned left onto Tommy's road. He followed the gently curving thoroughfare, his apprehension bubbling like boiled porridge. Tommy's house stood at the end, on a right-angle corner, his front windows facing directly down Bryan's approach. The curve of the road unfurled before him. Tommy's house was not there.

The Humber shuddered into a stall. Bryan got out and, on unsteady legs, walked the last twenty-five yards.

Scott's house, and its neighbour in the terrace, lay demolished. The next along still stood, but without most of its connecting wall. The shattered remains of broken contents flapped in desultory harmony with the breeze that penetrated the crippled building.

Large piles of rubble bore the only testament to the erstwhile presence of two family homes, and these, with the detached civic efficiency of a city in crisis, had been shovelled and swept into enforced neatness. Bryan stood and stared.

'Are you alright, sir?'

Bryan spun round at the sound of the voice. A postman regarded him with a concerned smile.

'When did this happen?'

'Late on Friday night.'

'Where is Mrs Scott?'

'They think she was in the outside privy when it took a direct hit.' The postman looked away, chewing the inside of his cheek, 'They only collected a few bits and pieces… but who else could it have been?'

'What about the baby?'

'They dug it out the next morning.'

'*It* was a boy,' Bryan said, 'Robert.'

'They found him under a table,' the postman continued. 'Would you believe it? They took him to a hospital somewhere. I couldn't say where. Are you family?'

'No. I flew with her husband. I came to tell her that he'd been killed.' He turned back to the fetid rubble, 'But it seems she already knew.' Bryan stared at the ruins with unfocussed eyes, his shoulders sagging under the weight of atrocity.

The postman coughed apologetically and sauntered away. A train chuffed along the line on its southerly journey, slowing as it passed above the bombsite as if testing the viaduct, like a child tests the ice. Bryan glanced up at the faces pressed to the carriage windows, then swung back to the postman's retreating back, fighting an irrational outrage, a surge of helpless anger at these people for just carrying on.

A chill possessed his skin. Loss and loneliness, fear and doubt jumbled in his chest.

'Jenny,' he breathed and stumbled back to the car. 'Jenny…'

Bryan hauled his car around, cursing the narrowness of the road, swearing and grinding the gears, rage and malice boiling in his guts. Finally facing in the right direction, a pain stabbing across his chest forced him to stop. He knocked the gearstick into neutral and pulled on the handbrake. The pounding of his heart pushed fluttering panic up his throat and his pulsing blood throbbed behind his ears. He sucked in sharp, violent lungfuls of air and his hands twitched and shook in front of his face with mounting extravagance.

He squeezed his eyes shut and gritted his teeth, willing his body to come back under his control. The banging in his chest peaked and slowed. When it no longer thumped like a trapped animal against his ribs, he opened his eyes, pulled off his driving gloves and fumbled for his cigarettes with fingers that creaked on the edge of cramping.

The nicotine coursed into his veins, smoothing away the tension in his arms and neck. He sucked hungrily at the smoke and its creeping solace buzzed across his forehead. He crushed the long, glowing end of the cigarette into the ashtray and watched the dying fumes curl up and across the stained roof of the vehicle.

The panic and anger ebbed away, leaving a persistent desire to go to Jenny, to hold her face in his hands and feel her living warmth. He put the Humber into gear and pulled away.

Chapter 22

Bryan drove down Balham's high street, bumping onto the new black tarmac covering the spot where the German bomb had blasted its hellish crater. It sat like a vast scab over a healing wound, a veil drawn over the memories of horror.

An engine at the station belched steam into the frigid air and the breeze curled it into ethereal fingers that reached down to catch him in their insubstantial grasp as he slipped by under the bridge. Du Cane Court loomed like a tor against the bruised January sky brooding over the rooftops of south London. Bryan pulled into the courtyard and parked against a wall.

Acutely conscious he would be barging into Jenny's day, he wavered for a moment. Maybe he should leave, take the burden in his chest and exorcise it with booze and killing. But the tight knot of human need that wrapped his heart in horsehair resolved him to switch off the engine. Breathing deeply and steadily to dismiss the close-by memory of panic, he groped in the glove compartment for his comb, seeking the reassurance of a mundane action to restore some oblique normality.

He tilted his rearview mirror down to study his face. Behind his head, a familiar shape, a cherished movement caught his eye. The hand holding the comb dropped into his lap as he focussed on Jenny, walking arm in arm with a man. She was explaining something, her face animated by a glowing smile. The man, dressed in civilian clothes, nodded and laughed. Bryan tilted the mirror to follow their progress until they passed into his normal field of view, walking towards the building's grand entrance. He waited for them to stop and say their farewells. He waited for her friend to turn on his heel and stride away, intent on arriving at another place that he needed and wanted to be.

They walked on. The man reached out to push the door.

Bryan bundled out of his car, 'Jenny!'

The couple turned. Bryan registered the flash of shock on Jenny's face and the confusion on her companion's. She said a few words to the man. He asked a question and she shook her head in reply.

Jenny walked back towards Bryan while her friend opened the door and vanished inside. Bryan bit down of the well of rage that brought hot acid into his throat and watched her approach. Her hips moved differently. It wasn't caution, it wasn't disdain, but neither was it desire.

She stopped, out of reach, and looked into his face, 'Hello, Bryan.'

'Jenny?' He glanced at the door, the only way he could form the question he daren't ask.

She dropped her gaze for a moment, 'I'm sorry.'

Bryan swayed fractionally backwards on his heels, the power of the implications moving him like the shockwave of a distant detonation. 'Who is he?'

Her eyes returned to Bryan's face, searching his features and gauging his strength. 'His name is James. He's an architect. I met him at work, at The Ministry.'

Bryan's mouth felt hollow and dry, 'An architect?'

'We're working on plans to rebuild the bombsites. He said he was going to help make London the most beautiful city in the world. I fell in love with that idea.' She paused and scanned his face anew, 'He's the kind of man I believe I could marry.'

'What about me?'

'James is part of the peace,' a sad smile crept across her face, 'whenever that might come. You'll always be part of the war.'

Bryan raised his eyes over Jenny's head and glowered at the building where the architect sat waiting for her.

'I'm sorry,' she whispered and turned on her heel.

Bryan listened to her retreating footsteps as hot tears stole his vision.

Monday, 27 January 1941

Anthony Francis dropped the folded sack onto the frost-glittered grass next to his wife's grave and knelt down. Drops of water dotted the top of the gravestone where the low shafts of early sun melted the rime, each watery bead embroidered the light with refracted rainbows that shimmered away across the hard granite. He lit his pipe and bent to trimming the fresh holly and fir cuttings he'd brought to place in the flower urn; it was the best decoration this spartan season could provide. As he worked, the rattle of a car engine grew louder, finally choking to silence on the road outside the graveyard.

The wrought iron gates creaked open and Mr Francis turned to hail the new arrival. His call of greeting died in his breast; a spectre in an RAF greatcoat, head bowed and hands thrust into its pockets walked slowly up the path. It stopped at his son's grave, faced the stone and stood stiff and silent.

Mr Francis regained his feet, put his pipe in his pocket and walked cautiously towards the apparition. As he approached, the ethereal quality of the uniformed man melted away leaving a familiar figure, unkempt and slumped in the demeanour of defeat.

'Bryan?'

The figure raised his head, 'Hello, Mr Francis.' Bryan's voice was vulnerable without weakness, human without emotion.

'What's happened?'

'I've killed my operator.'

Wednesday, 29 January 1941

The blue RAF staff car rattled along the country road. The sombre brown of the flat, naked fields stretched away behind the threadbare, winter hedgerows. Rabbits flashed for cover up the verges and incurious wood pigeons tilted their heads at the engine's grumbling. Eventually the agricultural tableau revealed the chill and turbulent North Sea bounding its edge; a band of dark grey scoring a hostile line across the distant horizon, holding up a sky broiling with the threat of winter storms.

Three men travelled in the vehicle. Muffled in thick blue greatcoats, their breath condensing in the air around their heads. The driver, hunched over the wheel with a map open on the passenger seat, cursed under his breath at the long ridges of stone-filled mud fused onto the tarmac by the incessant passage of begrimed farm vehicles. Behind him, two men sat on the backseat, each regarding the bleak Anglian landscape sliding past their windows through eyes ringed with dark lines of fatigue.

The road dived through a line of trees and past the elegant solidity of a parkland gatehouse, squat and solid behind its green-painted railings. Emerging from the tree line, the car crested a rise and the twisting road revealed the first outlying houses of Wells-On-Sea.

Skirting the landward side of the town, the car cruised past the small railway terminus and laboured up the hill towards the town centre. Outside the station, men with nothing better to do marked its passing with lazy suspicion. At the top of the incline, dominating the travellers' route into town, stood The Railway Hotel, a three-storey Georgian edifice, its plain brick façade reflecting dependable utility under the belligerent tin-coloured sky.

'There it is,' one of the men in the backseat pointed to the Humber parked in the yard. 'Pull in here.'

The driver slid in next to the black car and the two other men got out to peer through its windows.

'It's definitely Hale's,' the older man said and moved to ring the doorbell. Almost immediately the manageress opened the door.

'I saw you pull in. You know, I thought something wasn't right. You'll find him in the bar.'

The two men entered the lobby and ducked through a door to the small hotel bar.

Bryan perched on a barstool, slumped and ruffled like a sickly owl, his disconsolate gaze lost in the half-drunk pint pot of amber ale in front of him. He looked up at the new arrivals and greeted their intrusion with a flat, expressionless acceptance, as if the world had lost its ability to surprise.

'Hello, Madge,' he drawled, a heavy slur fudged his diction. 'Nice of you to visit. Sit down.' He slapped the bar and cast around for service.

'Of course, you realise you're AWOL,' the adjutant said, pulling up a barstool.

'I know. Isn't it wonderful?' Bryan drained his pint and tapped the empty glass repeatedly on the bar. 'In any event it's probably better than being dead.'

The manageress scuttled into the room, her face drawn with disquiet. She caught the adjutant's eye and he nodded once. She picked up the empty glass and pulled another pint, her cheeks quivering slightly with the stress of the increasingly peculiar situation. She pushed the pint across the bar and looked to the officer for direction.

'We'd both like some tea, if that's possible,' he indicated the orderly standing quietly behind him, 'it's been a long drive.'

The manageress hurried to the kitchen and Stiles turned squarely to the shabby figure at the bar.

'So, what's it about, Bryan? I believed you were made of sterner stuff than this.' The adjutant's voice held no accusation, only regret.

Bryan looked up and a sudden lucidity tightened his features, 'I could cope when all I had to do was fly and fight. You *know* that, Madge. I was *good* at that.' He scooped his greasy fringe away from his forehead and squinted back into his pint. 'Even when some kraut just about had my bollocks on a trowel, I could do something about it. But those poor bastards in London, under the bombers… They have to sit and wait for it to drop on their heads. And it goes on and on, night after night while they pray for it to stop.'

'I could've carried on, the way it used to be, but they stopped playing fair. They turned it into cold-blooded murder.' Bryan gazed again into the older man's eyes for a long moment. 'I had to come away, Madge, I needed to work it out. I needed to square my place in this unholy mess so I might be able to carry on.' A ragged edge caught Bryan's voice, 'But I'm alone.'

He fumbled for a cigarette. Lighting up, he watched the burning match wobble in his trembling fingertips. As the flame progressed towards his skin, he dropped the twisted charcoal shard into the ashtray to gutter and die.

'There's no-one left to be my benchmark… Andrew, George, Alan… all gone…' his voice trailed off to silence and he shook his head. 'But even that is alright, in a way. Each of them only had themselves to look after, they were responsible for their own mistakes.'

The manageress brought in the tea tray and placed it on a table against the wall. Bryan averted his face to hide his growing distress. The adjutant waited for the woman to leave and leant forward, placing a hand on Bryan's arm.

'I'm here to help you.'

Bryan regarded the hand resting on his tunic, his face pale and pinched with anguish, 'Do you know what's happened to me?' he looked up, his eyes searching the other's face.

Stiles nodded, 'Mr Francis tracked Bluebird Squadron down and spoke to me on the telephone. Of course, he didn't realise you'd transferred. So, I called the adjutant at Blackbird Squadron, he was kind enough-'

'I've failed everyone,' Bryan cut across the officer's velvet discourse. 'Scott got killed because of a bloody stupid mistake. I practically dangled him in front of their guns. His wife trusted me, Madge. She fed me in her kitchen… in Peckham of all places… corned beef hash… So, I needed to get to her before they sent their bloody awful telegram. I had to explain to her what happened… how he died… try to apologise… anything to soften the blow. But I couldn't even do that, because when I got there, I found the Germans had already murdered her.'

Stiles moved his hand to squeeze Bryan's shoulder and steady his increasing animation, 'You can't carry the can for all of this. It's a bloody war. It's not your fault.'

'And then Jenny… She wanted me to step down from combat flying. But I didn't do it. Even for her, I didn't do it. Now Scott is dead and I've lost her to an architect.' Tears sprang to Bryan's eyes and trickled unheeded down his cheeks, 'A bloody architect.'

The adjutant moved the pint of beer away along the bar and put his arm around shoulders that shuddered gently in rhythm with Bryan's sobs.

'You need to go and get your things, Bryan. You're coming with us.'

Bryan scrubbed away his tears with the heel of his hand, 'What do you mean?'

'The transfer papers are already on their way to Middle Wallop.' Stiles smiled at his broken friend, 'You're coming home to Bluebird Squadron.'

Chapter 23

Thursday, 1 May 1941

The medical officer picked up the sheaf of documents from his desk and slotted them back into their folder. He crossed his small office, pausing by the coat rack to look through the window. Outside, the strengthening spring sunshine cut sharp shadows through the limpid Scottish air. He decided to leave his coat on its hook and, carrying the papers under his arm, he stepped down the corridor and through the entrance of the station sickbay.

The faint breeze still held enough chill to tighten the skin on his cheeks and he quickened his pace against it. The medical facility stood on the opposite side of the field to the hangars and administration buildings, so the MO strode around the perimeter track past Spitfires draped in tarpaulins that still glittered with clusters of dew-drops. He hurried past open hangar doors where men worked on stripped Merlins amidst the pervasive odour of ancient engine oil, overlaid now with the sharp tang of recently spilled aviation fuel. Reaching the administration office, he mounted the wooden steps, nodded to the orderly manning the front desk and approached the adjutant's door. He knocked once and entered.

'Good morning, sir,' the MO laid the documents on the desk. Visible in red ink on the cover were the words: *Bryan Hale (Flight Lieutenant) – Operational Tiredness.*

'Good morning.' Harry Stiles glanced at the folder and then up at the medic, 'How is he progressing?'

The younger man pulled off his cap and sat down, 'I'm ready to sign him off. I think he should resume active duty as soon as possible.'

'So, he's well?'

The medical officer looked down at his shoes for a moment. 'No, sir. He's not well. But he's as well as I can make him.'

The adjutant pointed to the folder, 'It says 'Operational Tiredness'. How can you suggest he returns to operations if he's not fully recovered?'

'He still carries a considerable weight of guilt on his shoulders,' the younger man said. 'We've worked out some of his demons and he's made real efforts to forgive himself for what's happened. But I sense he needs the absolution of action. I believe, unless he gets back into real combat flying, he'll make no more progress. He's like an eagle in a cage. If we don't let him out to hunt, he'll lose his will to carry on.'

The adjutant scratched his chin, 'And you think it's safe for him to resume ops?'

The medical officer smiled, 'He won't be a danger to anyone but himself and the enemy. But I think that's always been the case.'

'Well, Bluebird Squadron will likely be stuck in Scotland until the autumn, at least. They want ample numbers of interceptors up here in case the Germans come after the Navy prior to invasion.'

The medic shook his head, 'Constant standing patrols with no action will not help him. That's just putting him in a different cage. He needs to be in the front line.'

The adjutant sighed, 'There is something… I was hoping to keep it under my hat.'

The younger man raised an enquiring eyebrow.

'They're looking for volunteers for operations in the Med and North Africa. Hale's pre-war service in Egypt and his combat record since Dunkirk make him a perfect candidate.' Stiles looked up, his face scored with concern, 'I consider Bryan to be my friend. Is this really the best thing for him?'

The medical officer nodded slowly, 'If you choose to keep him safe, you'll have to watch him go mad.'

The adjutant pulled on his cap, squared it on his head and stood up.

'Right then,' he said, 'Let's go and tell him.'

I hope you have enjoyed Blackbirds and will consider leaving an honest review on Amazon.

Visit my website at **www.melvynfickling.com** and sign up for the Bluebirds Newsletter for updates on the next books in the series.

Like my Facebook Page at **Facebook.com/MelvynFicklingAuthor** for day-to-day news about my writing.

Follow me on Twitter **@MelvynFickling**

Glossary of Terms

Adjutant - Administrative assistant to a senior officer
Airframe - Structural skeleton of an aircraft
Aileron - Movable surface usually near the trailing edge of a wing, controls the roll of the aircraft
AI - Air Interception, early onboard radar equipment
Andersen Shelter - DIY bomb shelter supplied by the government
Angels - Code word for altitude, angels ten means 10,000 feet
ARP - Air Raid Precautions
AWOL - Absent without leave
Bandits - RAF slang for enemy aircraft
Beehive - Fictional codename for the sector control room at Kenley
Bf 109 - German single-seat Fighter - Messerschmitt 109
Biplane - Aircraft with two sets of wings, one above the other
Blast Pen - Three-walled construction designed to protect aeroplanes from bomb damage
Blenheim - British twin-engine light bomber aircraft
Boffin - Slang for scientist
Bofors gun - 40mm anti-aircraft autocannon
Bogey - Unidentified aircraft suspected of being hostile
Bought it, Buy it - To get killed in action
Bounce - RAF slang for attacking from above
Brylcreem - Styling cream for hair
Brylcreem Boys - Semi-affectionate slang for RAF fighter pilots
Bumf - Slang for toilet paper
Buster - Running a fighter engine on full boost - not recommended for long periods due to likelihood of damage and/or fire
Canopy - Also known as Hood; covering for a cockpit
Check step - A lateral movement in an aerial chase
Chocks - Triangular lumps of wood used to wedge against aircraft wheels to prevent movement on the ground
Chop (The) - To get killed in combat
Cowling - Curved panel covering the engine of an aircraft
Crate - RAF slang for aeroplane
Cupola - Gun turret

Dispersal - Area where planes are scattered widely to reduce potential damage if attacked
Dorsal - Machine gun position on upper side or back of a bomber
Elevator - Movable surface on the tail, controls pitch of the aircraft
Flaps - Movable surface on an aircraft, usually near the trailing edge of a wing, increases lift and decreases speed
Flap - RAF slang for emergency
Flash - Coded command to turn on Airborne Interception
Flight - A fighting unit usually consisting of six aircraft
Fuselage - Main body of an aeroplane
Gen - RAF slang for intelligence, information
GP - General Practitioner (English Doctor)
Hampden - British twin-engine light bomber aircraft
He 111 or Heinkel 111 - German twin-engine bomber
Heavies - RAF slang for heavy (four-engine) bombers
Hood - Also known as Canopy; covering for a cockpit
Hurricane - Single-seat British fighter, slightly poorer performance than the Spitfire
Incendiary - Type of bomb designed to start fire
Jerry - Slang for German
Jink - To fly erratically to put off an attacker's aim
Ju 88 or Junkers 88 - German twin-engine bomber
Kite - RAF slang for aeroplane
Kraut - Slang for German
Madge - Affectionate nickname for Bluebird's adjutant, Harry Stiles
Me 109 or Messerschmitt 109 - German single-seat fighter
Med - Mediterranean
Met - Abbreviation for Meteorological Office (Weather forecast)
Milk-run - A low risk mission
Milk train - Earliest departing train
MO - Medical officer
Monoplane - Fixed-wing aircraft with a single main wing plane
Night-warden - Fictional codename for Night-fighter Controller
Ops - Operations, active service
Orbit - To fly in a circle
o'clock - Used to locate the enemy in relation to line of flight, 12 o'clock is straight ahead, 6 o'clock is directly behind

Orderly - Officer in charge of administration of a unit or establishment for a day at a time
Pea-souper - Slang for very heavy fog
Peepers - Slang for eyes
Plots - Air Interception (radar) contacts
Port - Lefthand side of an aircraft, a port turn is to the left
Prop-wash - Blast of air caused by a propeller
Revs - Revolutions of an engine
RAF - Royal Air Force
RDF - Radio Direction Finding – later known as Radar
RFC - Royal Flying Corps, precursor to the RAF
Rigger - Member of ground maintenance crew
Rigmarole - Official procedure
Roger - Affirmative response to radioed instructions
Roundel - Concentric red white and blue circles used as identification for British planes
Rudder - Movable surface on an aircraft, usually on the tail, controls yaw of the aircraft
Scramble - To take off, generally in a hurry
Section - Fighting unit of aircraft usually consisting of two or three aircraft, normally codenamed with a colour
Sector - Geographical area with dedicated RAF administration services
Shilling - A British coin
Slip-stream - Flow of air around an airborne aircraft
Spitfire - Single-seat British fighter, slightly better performance than the Hurricane
Squadron - Fighting unit of aircraft usually consisting of twelve aircraft with six in reserve and 24 pilots
Staffel - German word meaning Squadron
Starboard - Righthand side of an aircraft, a starboard turn is to the right
Stick - Control column
Stick (of bombs) - A 'gaggle' of bombs dropped from the same aircraft
Stooge - To fly around without an apparent aim
Tailplane - Also known as a horizontal stabiliser, a small lifting surface located on the tail
Tally-ho - Huntsman's cry to the hounds on sighting a fox, adopted by fighter pilots and used on sighting enemy aeroplanes

Ten-tenths - Solid cloud with zero visibility
Tracer - Ordnance that glows in flight to show path of bullet-stream
Undercarriage - Wheels of an aircraft, can be fixed or retractable
UXB - Un-exploded bomb
Vector - Code word for heading
Ventral - Machine gun position on the underside of a bomber
Vic - Arrowhead formation of aircraft
WC - Water closet, archaic term for toilet
Wellington - British twin-engine, long range medium bomber
Windy - RAF slang for cowardly
Yaw - Twist or oscillate about a vertical axis

Author's notes

This is a historical novel based on real events. It is not a history of those events or of the people who found themselves entangled in those events.

AW Fagan was the name of the intelligence officer at Kenley during the Battle of Britain. His name is used here as tribute to all the supporting players who never featured in combat reports or citations. The Fagan who serves Bluebird Squadron is wholly fictionalised and any similarity to persons living or dead is coincidental. All other characters in this novel are fictional and any similarity to persons living or dead is coincidental.

Locations are real, although the details of real locations have been fictionalised in a sympathetic manner.

The backdrop of actual events against which the novel is set is well documented elsewhere. I have kept as close as possible to the actual timeline, but some events may have been shifted slightly to accommodate plot requirements. In particular, the development of Air Interception equipment and techniques has been compressed into a shorter timescale than was actually the case.

The Balham bomb is well-documented in contemporary photographs, and readers will note that I make no mention of the double-decker bus that ended up in the crater. I chose to make this omission for two reasons: Firstly, I could find no concrete information on what happened to the driver and any passengers who were on the bus, and I was reluctant to invent these details. Second, I wanted to preserve the dramatic impact of the bomb-damaged bus at the Liverpool Street incident that occurs later in the text. It is also worth noting that the nature of the fate of those killed in the tunnel at Balham is based on the rumour promulgated at the time. No disrespect is implied or intended to the people who were involved in any of these events.

On a technical note, the Bristol Beaufighter carried six machine guns in its wings to compliment the cannons located in its fuselage. I have ignored these smaller guns in my narrative, preferring to allow the cannons to be my *dramatis personae* in night engagements.

Sources

The Secret History of The Blitz - Joshua Levine

The Blitz, The British Under Attack - Juliet Gardiner

The Night Blitz 1940-1941 – John Ray

A History of Du Cane Court - Gregory Vincent

Battle of Britain, The Forgotten Months - John Foreman

Night Fighter - C F Rawnsley and Robert Wright

Diary of a Night Fighter Pilot 1939-1945 – Douglas Haig Greaves

Night Fighter Navigator – Dennis Gosling DFC

Instruments of Darkness – Alfred Price

The Bluebirds Trilogy continues with Falcons.

Bryan Hale is a damaged man. The stresses of combat flying in England's summer skies during the Battle of Britain, and night-fighting in the icy darkness of The Blitz, together with the loss of friends and a broken heart, have left him broken and grounded.

Fortress Malta, and the unrelenting Nazi siege that aims to grind it away, will be the furnace that forges him anew...

Join the Bluebirds Newsletter at www.melvynfickling.com to be in the front of the queue on publication day.

Printed in Great Britain
by Amazon